TAR
THE MAGIC PENCIL

Story & Art by **Sango Morimoto**

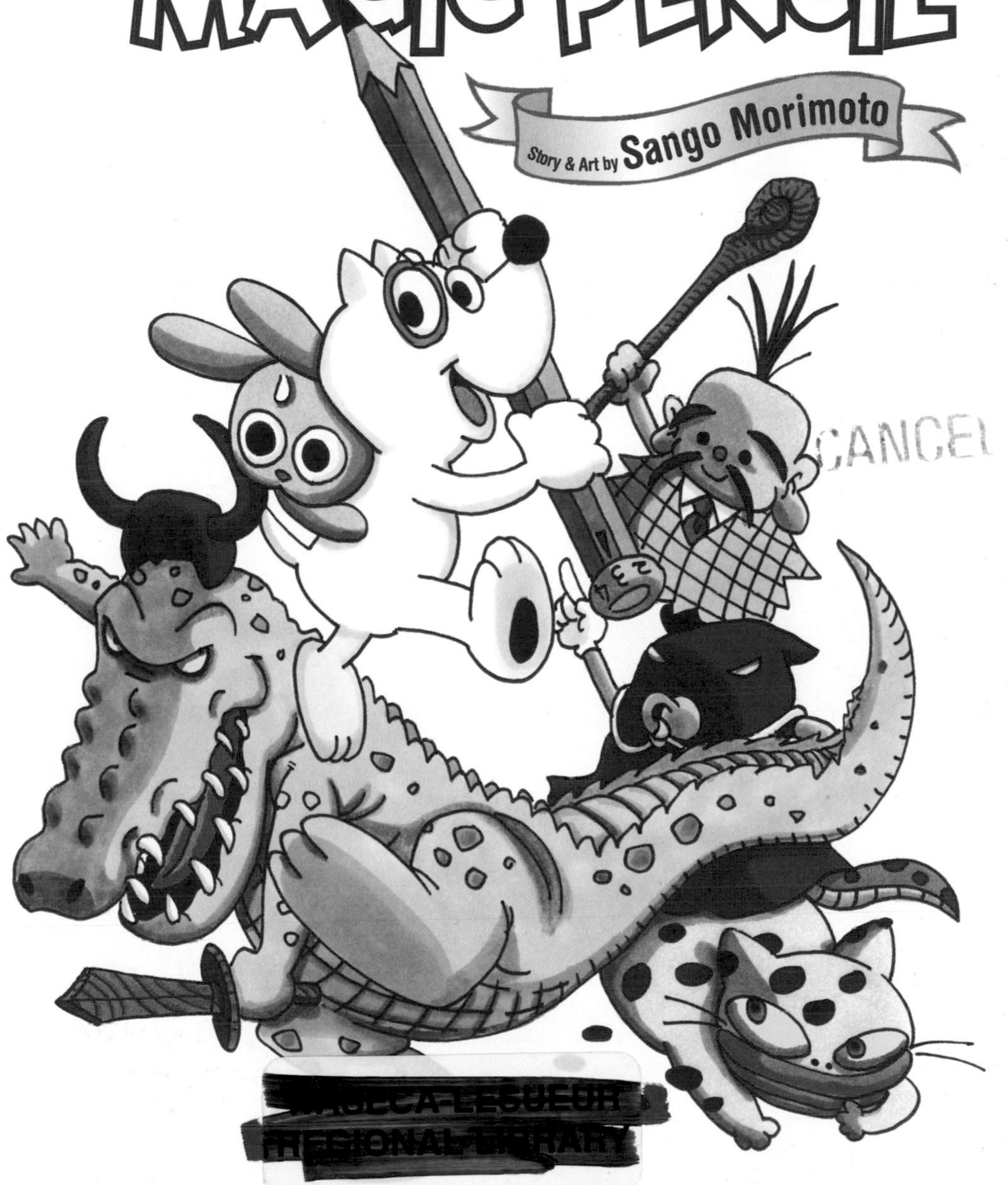

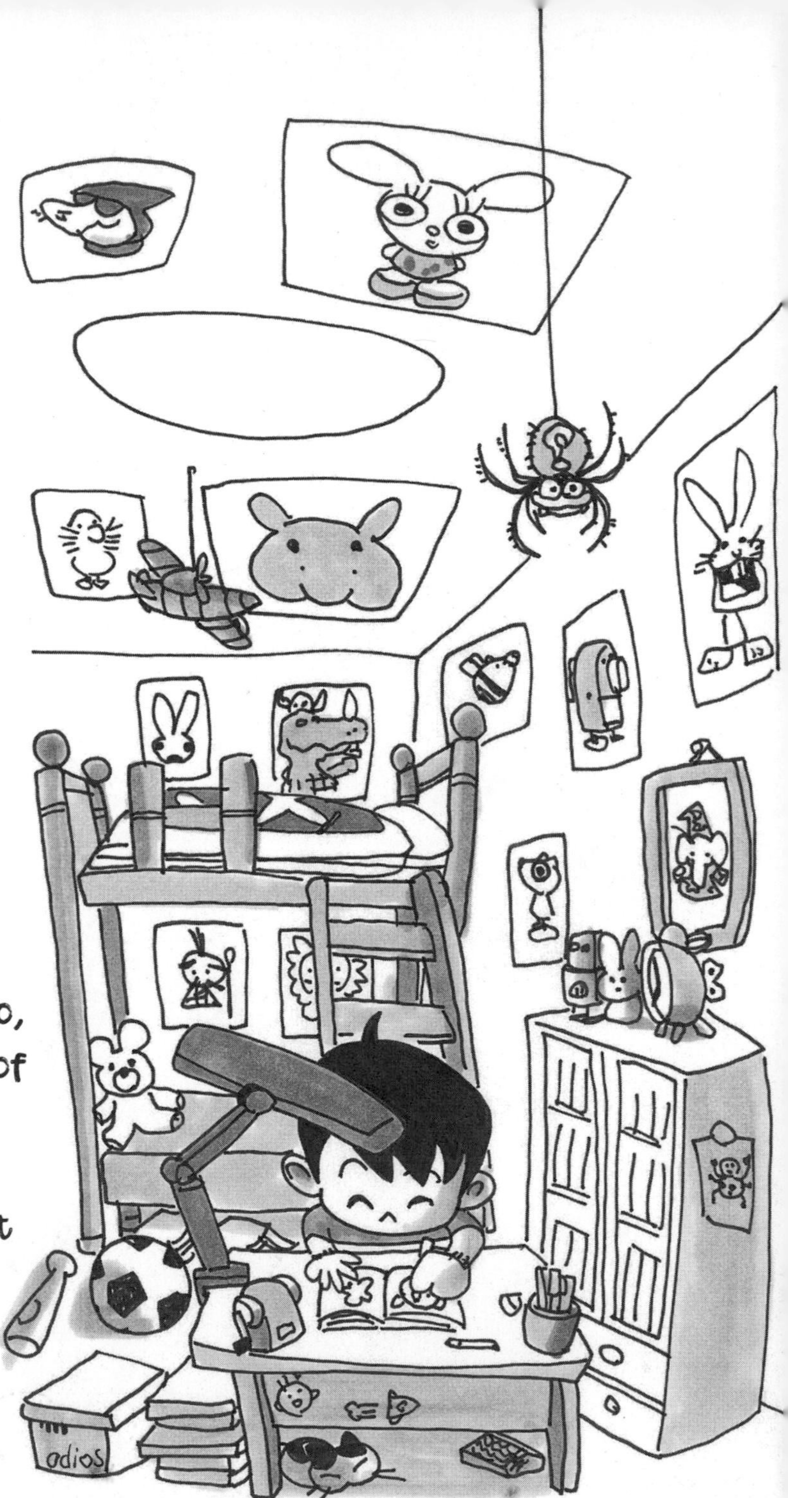
adios

This is Taro, the Prince of Comics. At least that's what his friends call him.

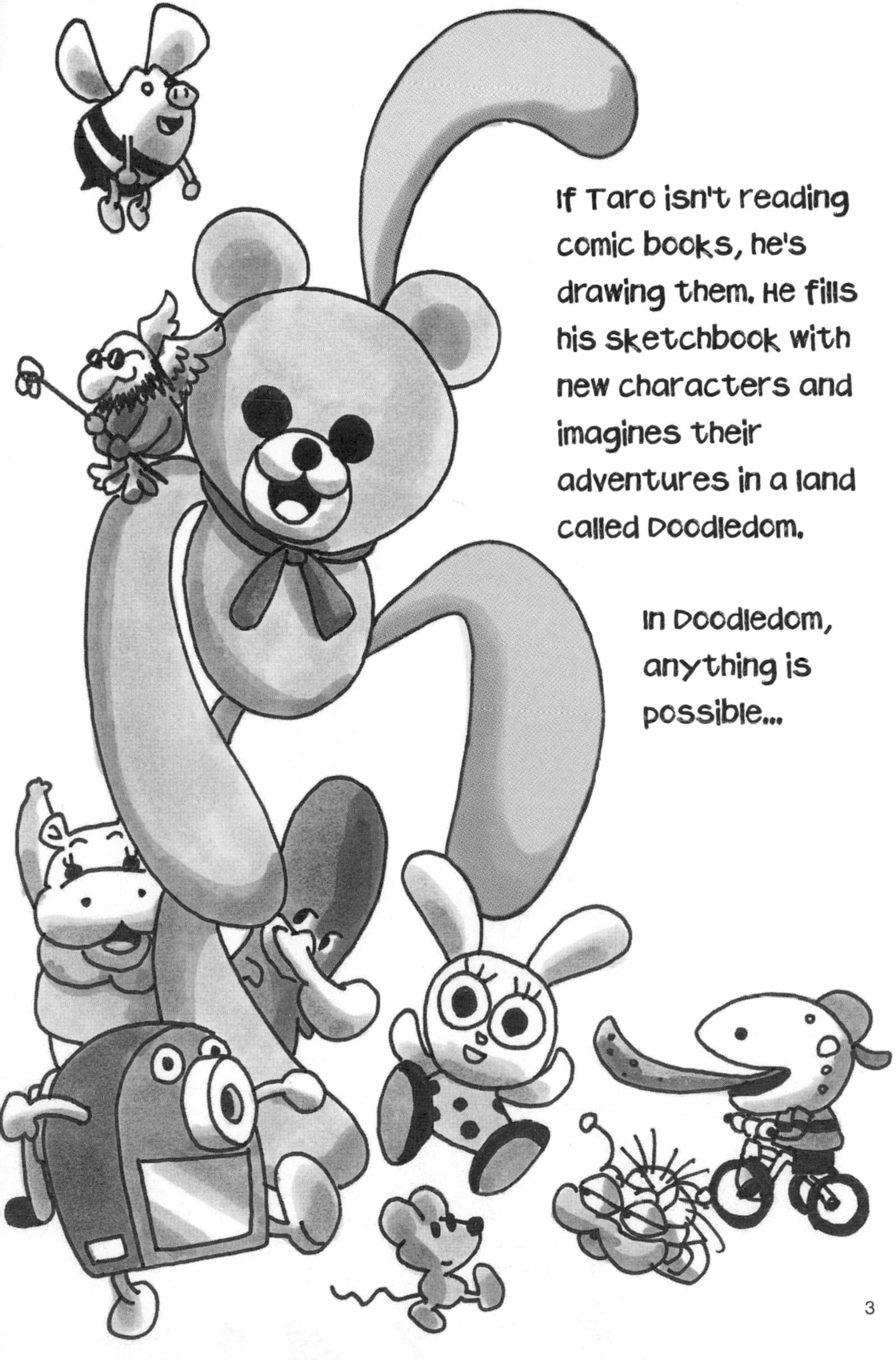

If Taro isn't reading comic books, he's drawing them. He fills his sketchbook with new characters and imagines their adventures in a land called Doodledom.

In Doodledom, anything is possible...

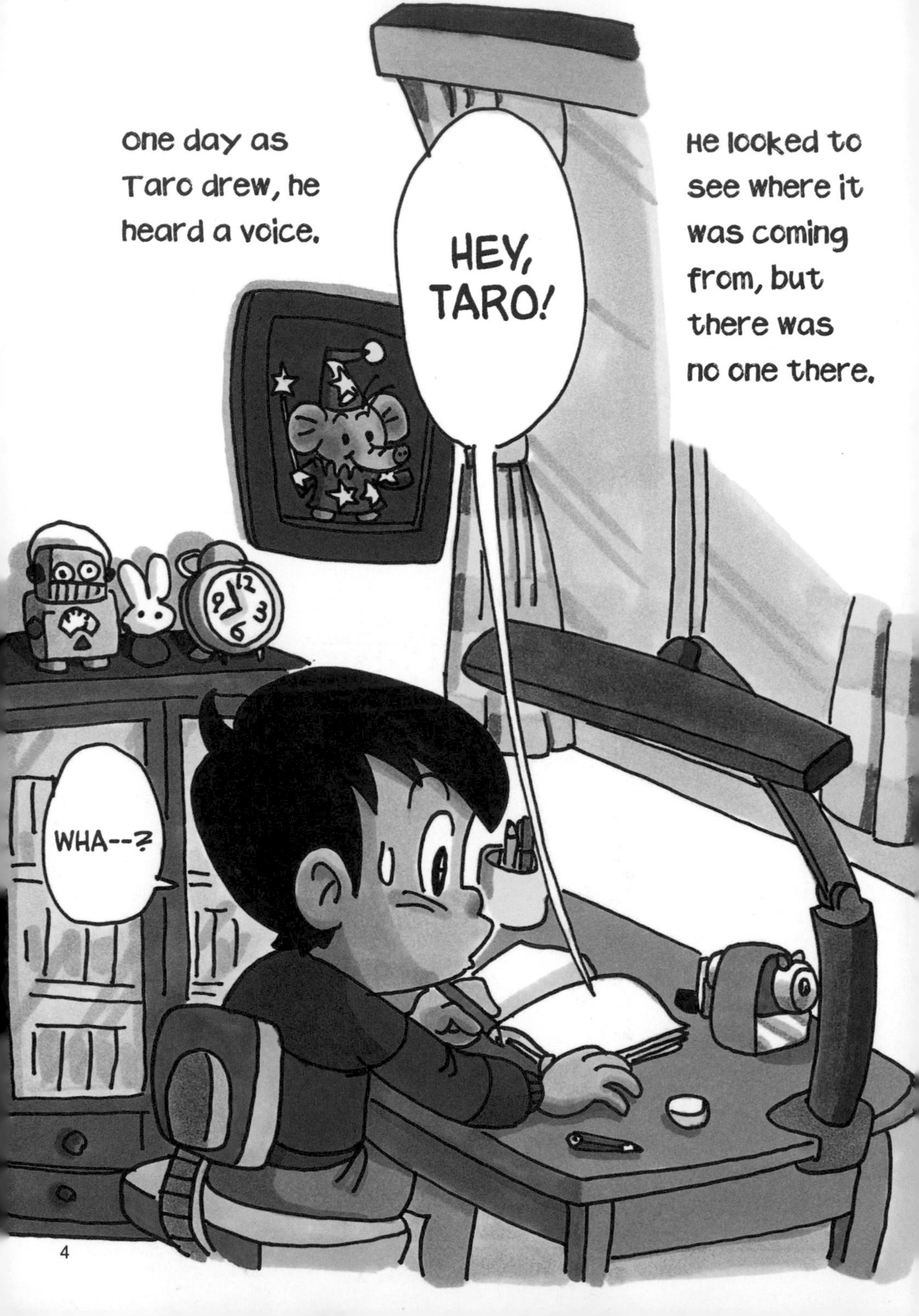
One day as Taro drew, he heard a voice.
HEY, TARO!
WHA--?
He looked to see where it was coming from, but there was no one there.

Could the voice be coming from inside Taro's sketchbook? It didn't seem possible, and yet...

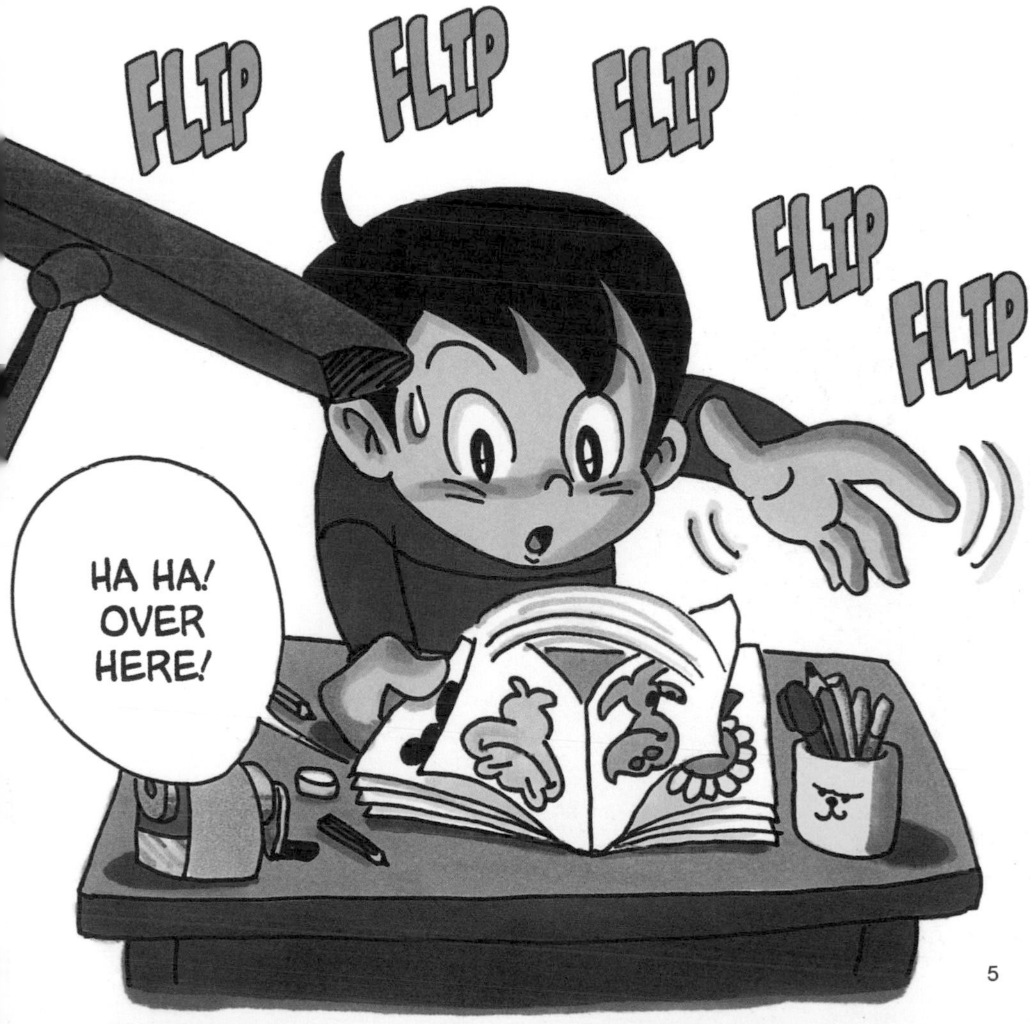
FLIP
FLIP
FLIP
FLIP
FLIP
HA HA! OVER HERE!

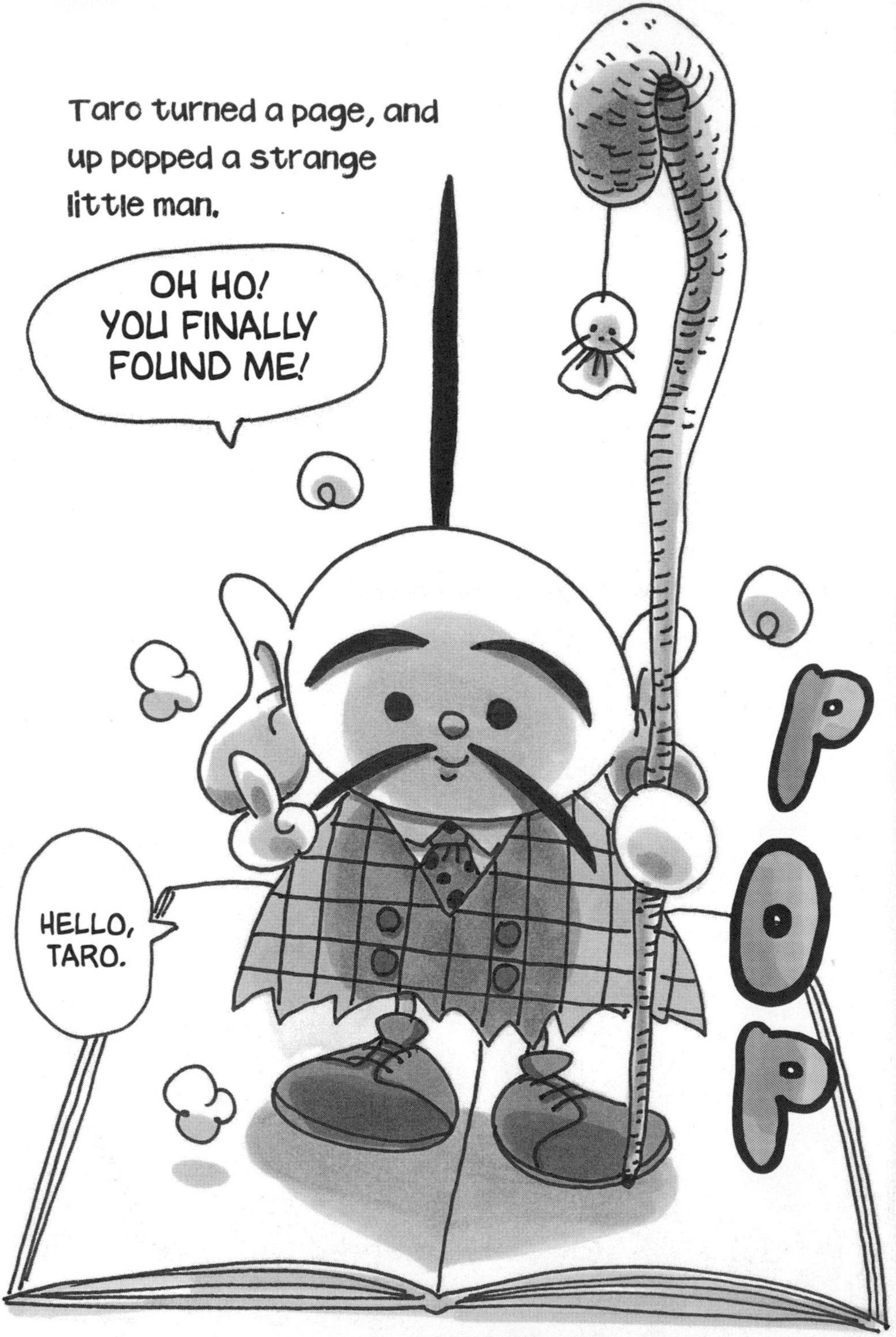
Taro turned a page, and up popped a strange little man.
OH HO! YOU FINALLY FOUND ME!
POP
HELLO, TARO.

It was the Wise Magician, the very first character Taro had ever drawn. Because he was the first, the magician knew all there was to know about Doodledom.

Taro had always imagined that the magician was the only character who could travel between Doodledom and the real world.

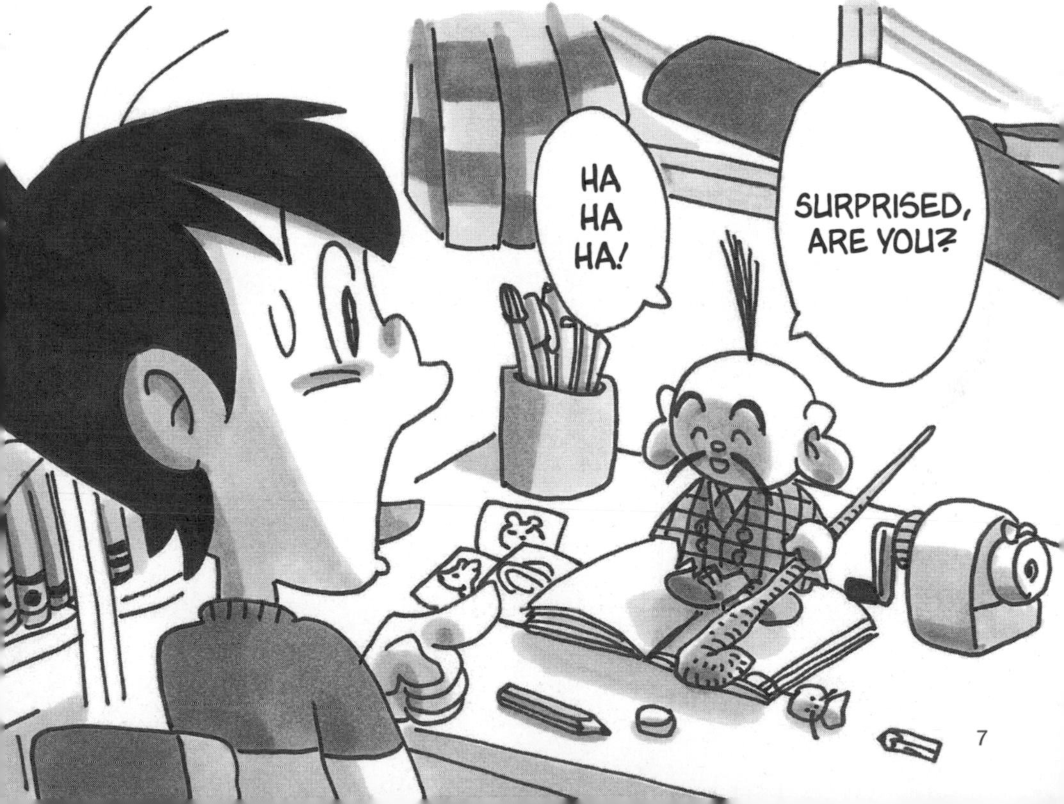
SURPRISED, ARE YOU?
HA HA HA!

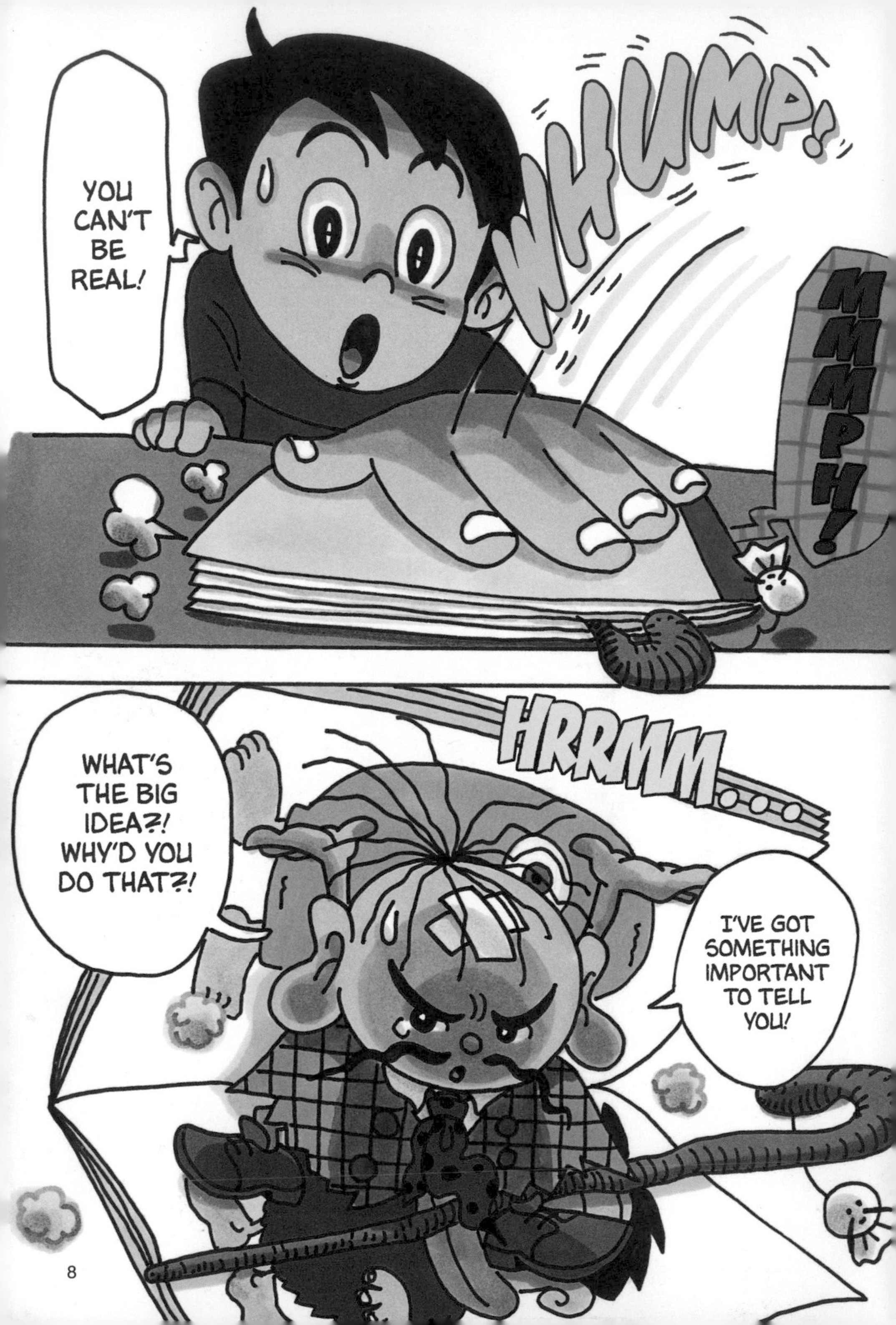
YOU CAN'T BE REAL!
WHUMP!
MMMPH!
HRRMM....
WHAT'S THE BIG IDEA?! WHY'D YOU DO THAT?!
I'VE GOT SOMETHING IMPORTANT TO TELL YOU!

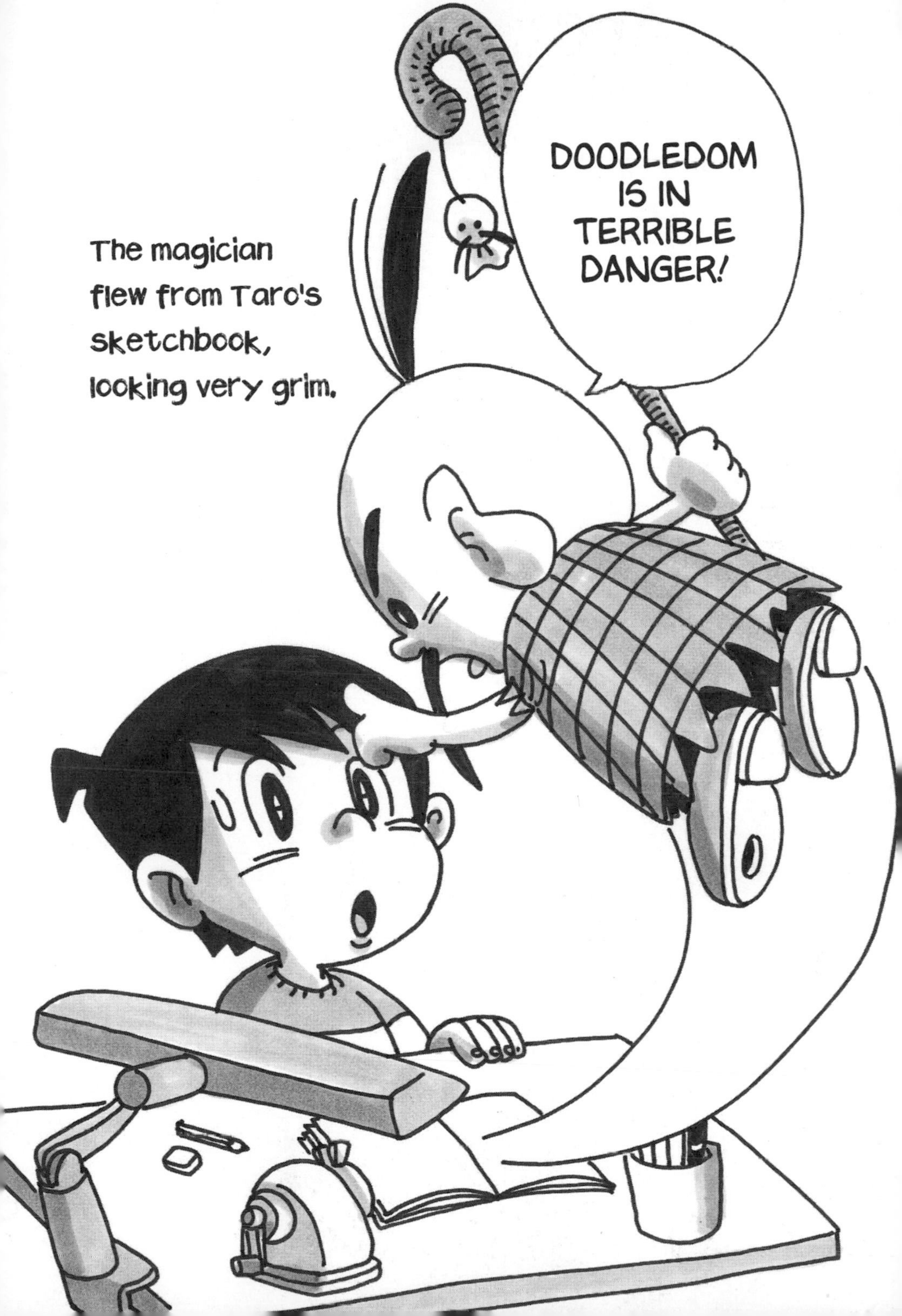
The magician flew from Taro's sketchbook, looking very grim.
DOODLEDOM IS IN TERRIBLE DANGER!

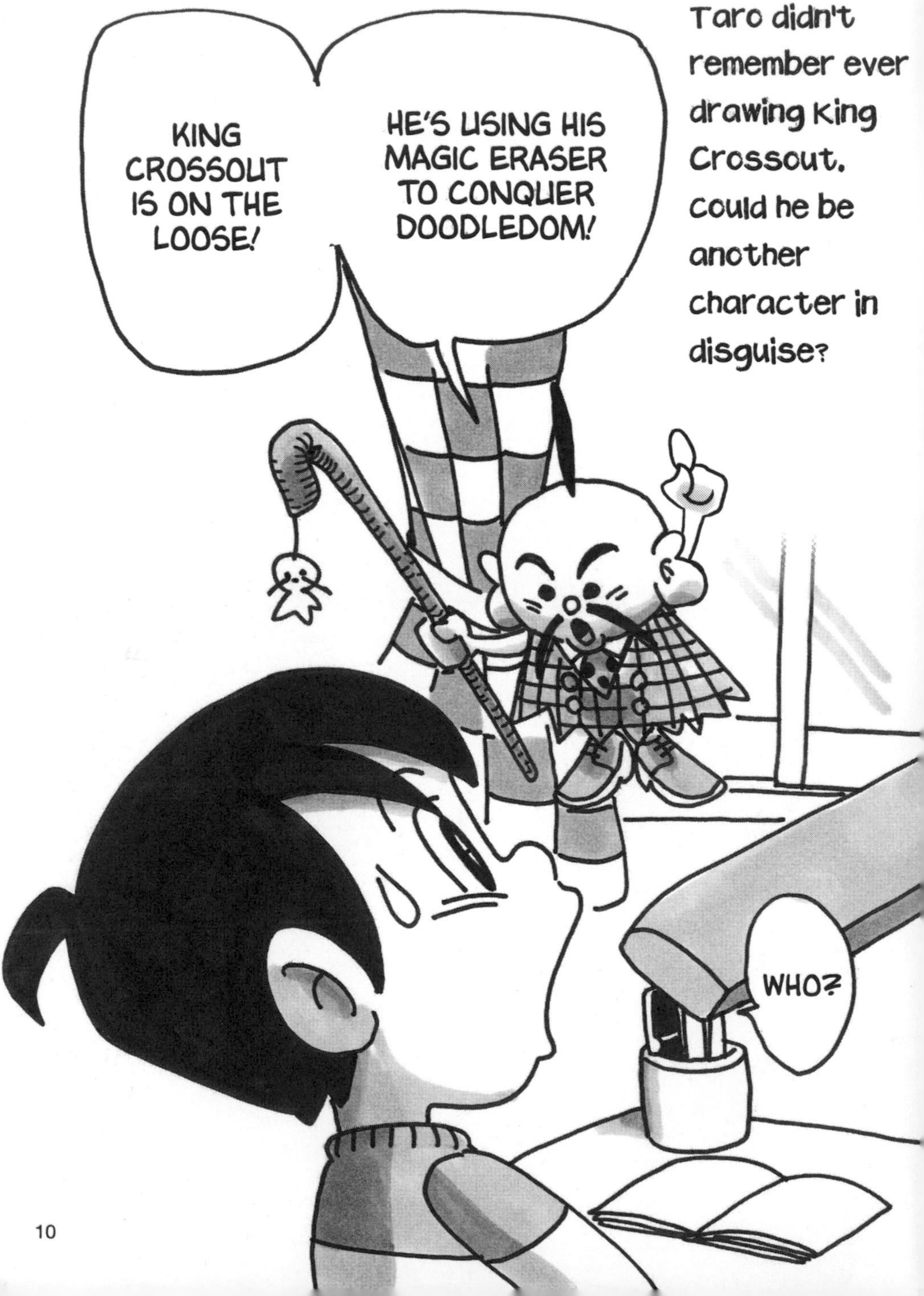
Taro didn't remember ever drawing King Crossout. Could he be another character in disguise?
KING CROSSOUT IS ON THE LOOSE!
HE'S USING HIS MAGIC ERASER TO CONQUER DOODLEDOM!
WHO?

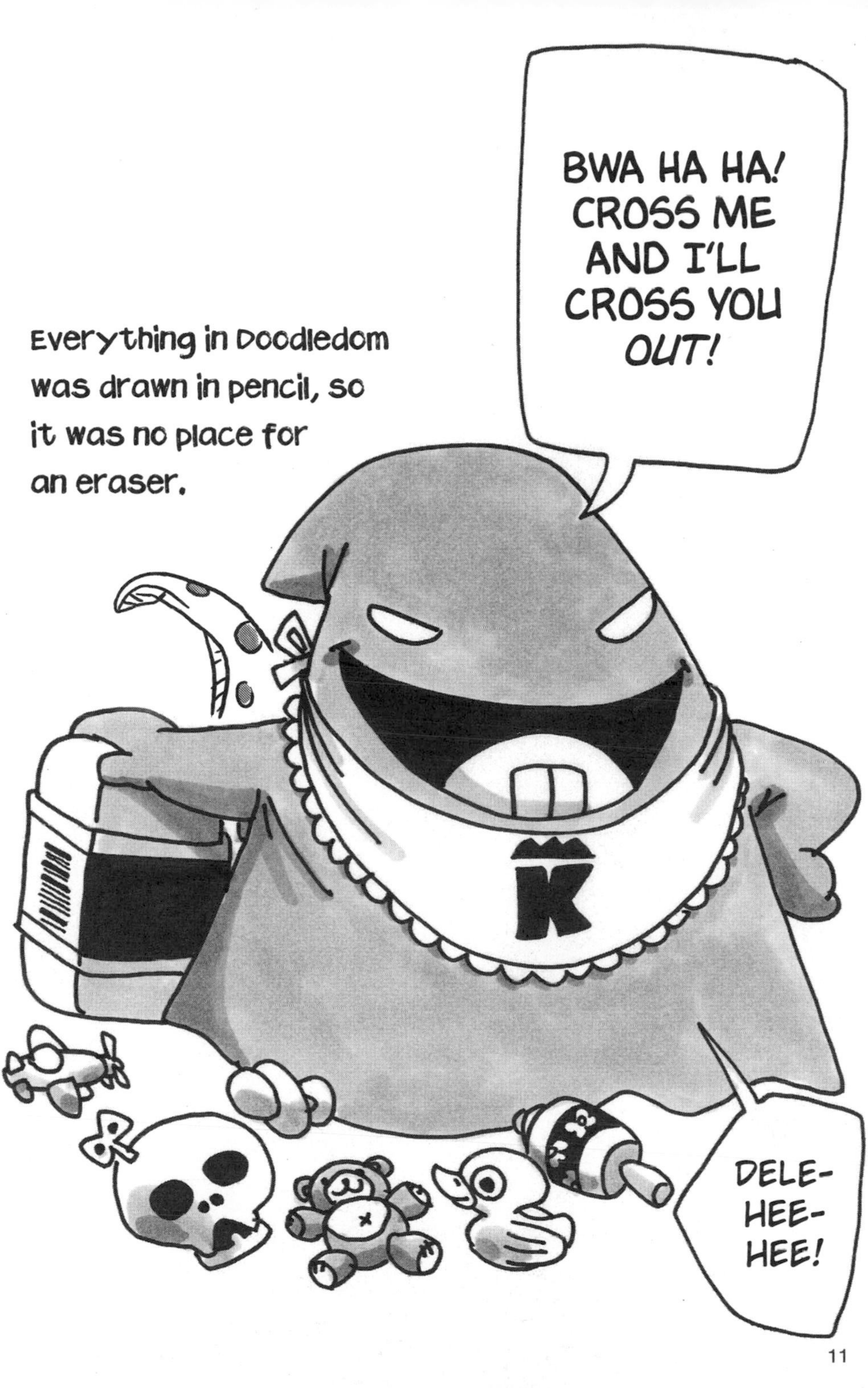
Everything in Doodledom was drawn in pencil, so it was no place for an eraser.
BWA HA HA! CROSS ME AND I'LL CROSS YOU *OUT*!
DELE-HEE-HEE!

The magician explained that Crossout was a bad blankety blanker. With his magic eraser he had wiped out most of the good and lovely things in Doodledom.

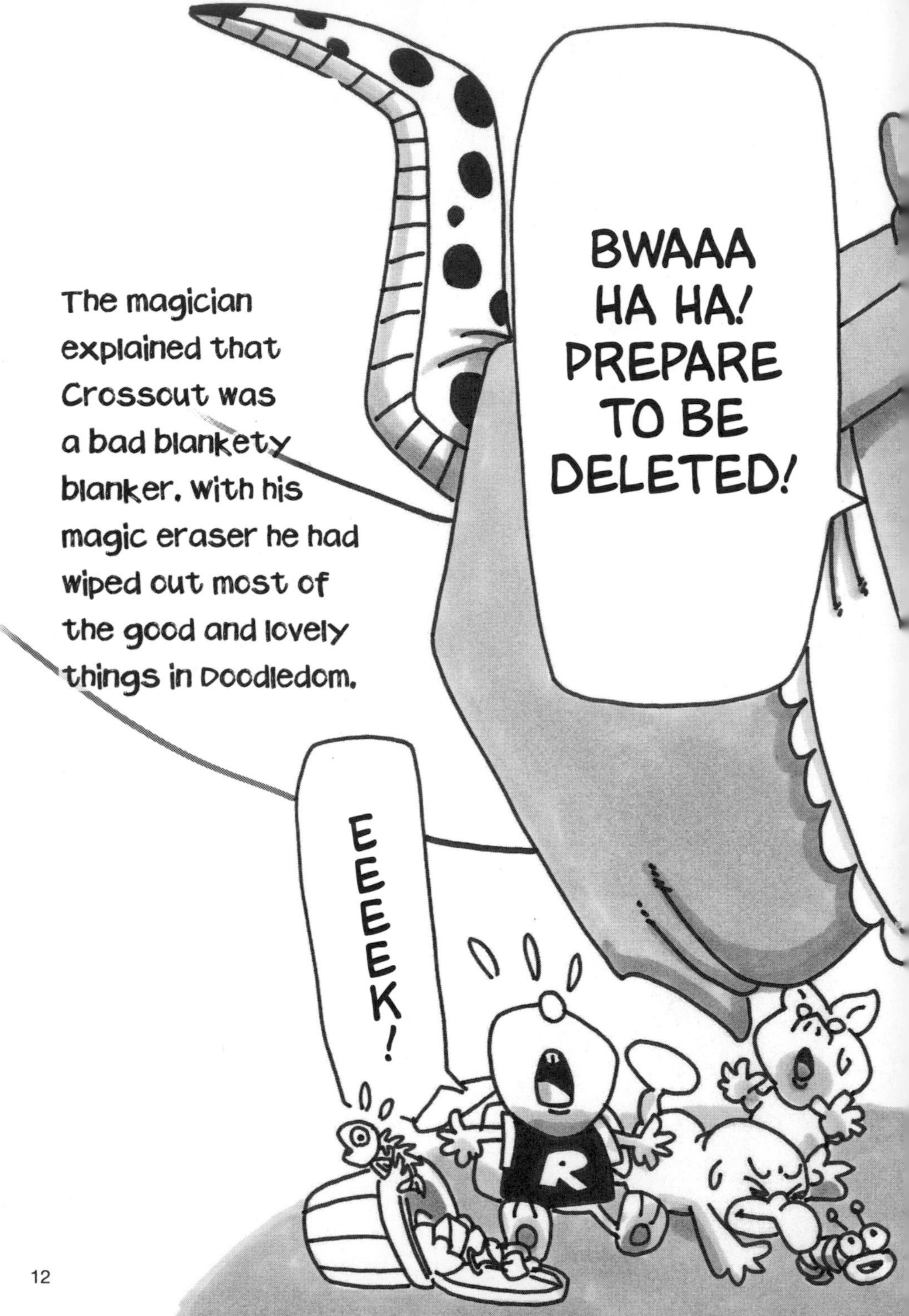
BWAAA HA HA! PREPARE TO BE DELETED!
EEEEEK!

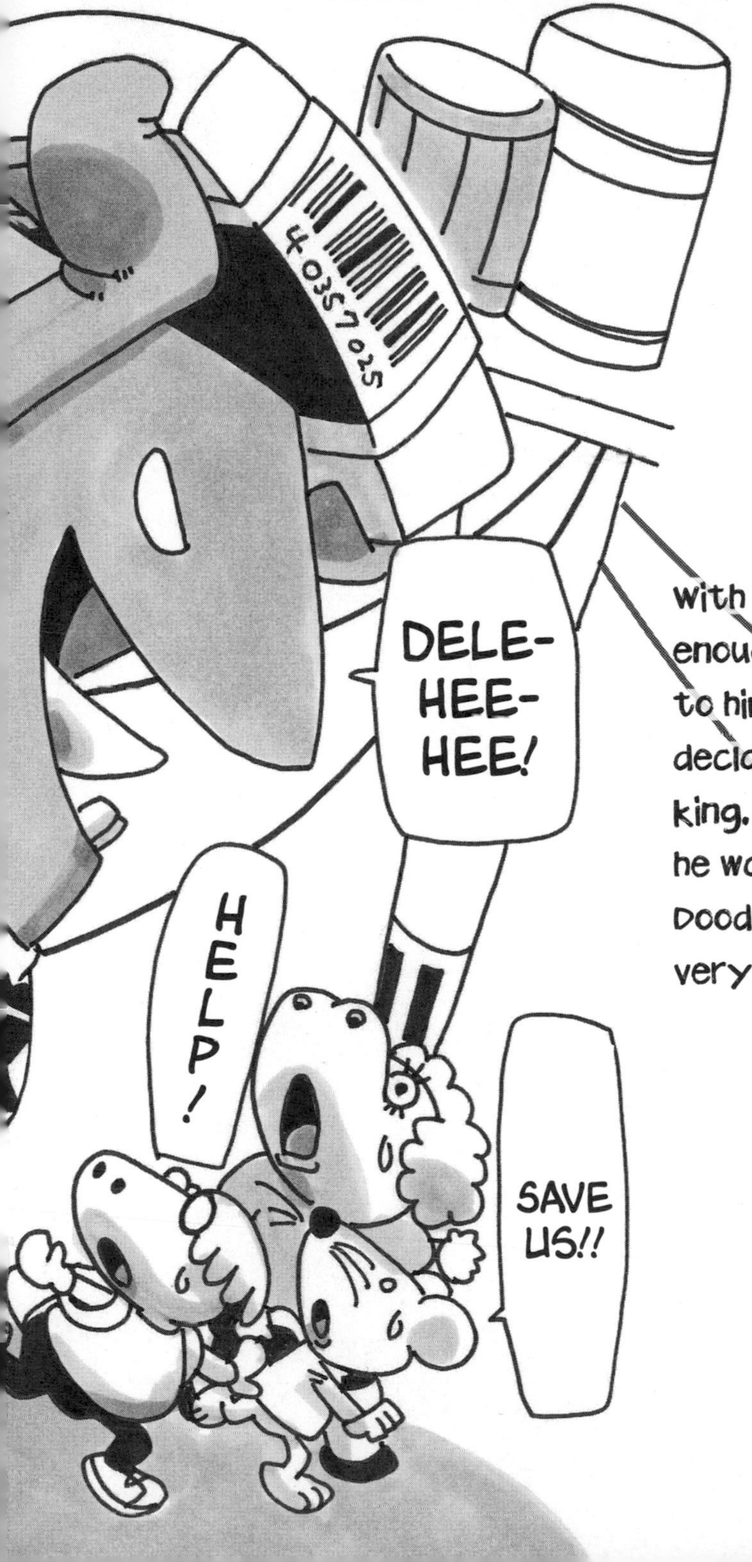
DELE-HEE-HEE!
HELP!
SAVE US!!

With no one brave enough to stand up to him, Crossout declared himself king. Little by little he was turning Doodledom into a very scary place.

The magician's story made Taro fighting mad.

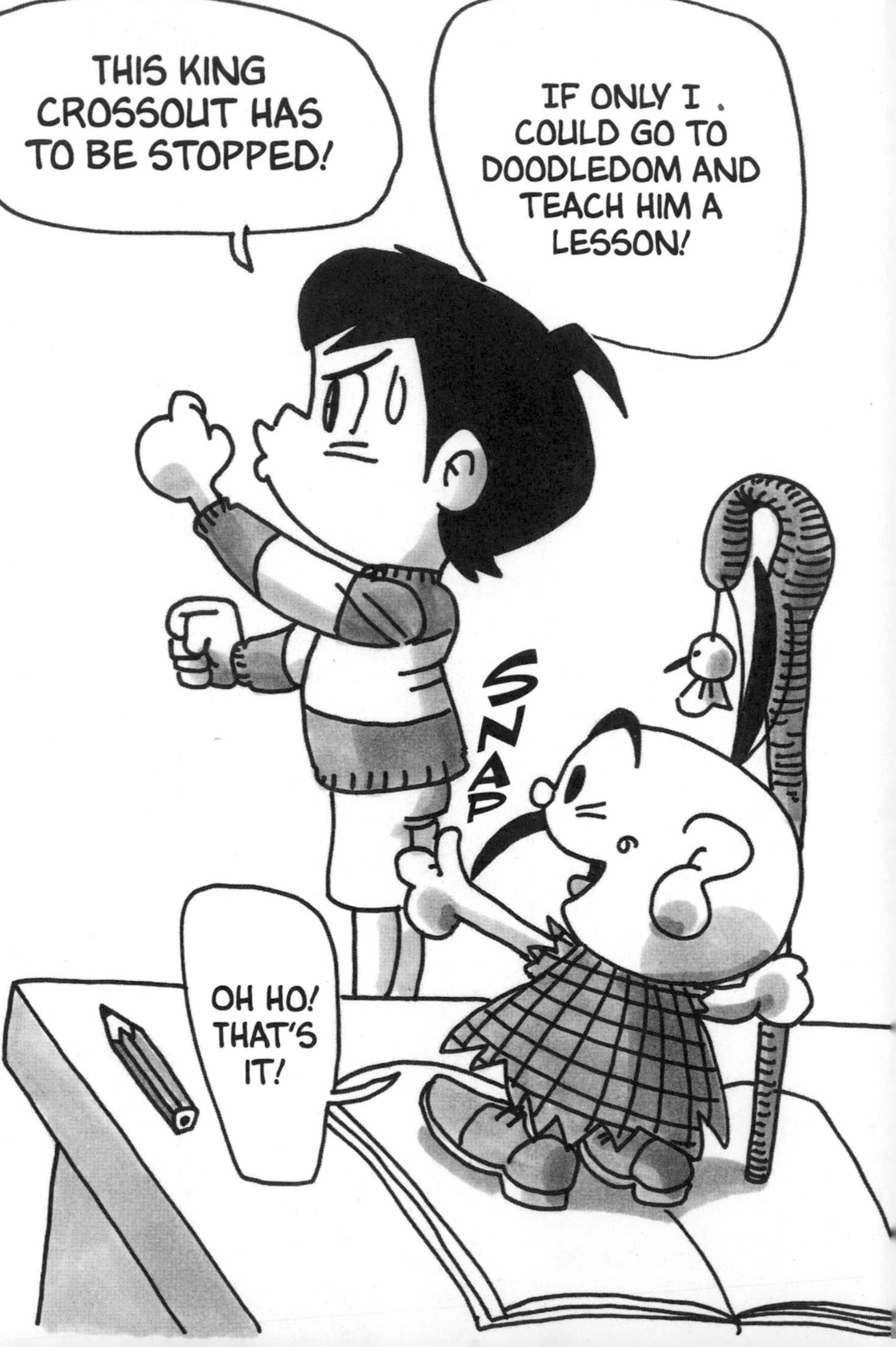
THIS KING CROSSOUT HAS TO BE STOPPED!
IF ONLY I COULD GO TO DOODLEDOM AND TEACH HIM A LESSON!
SNAP
OH HO! THAT'S IT!

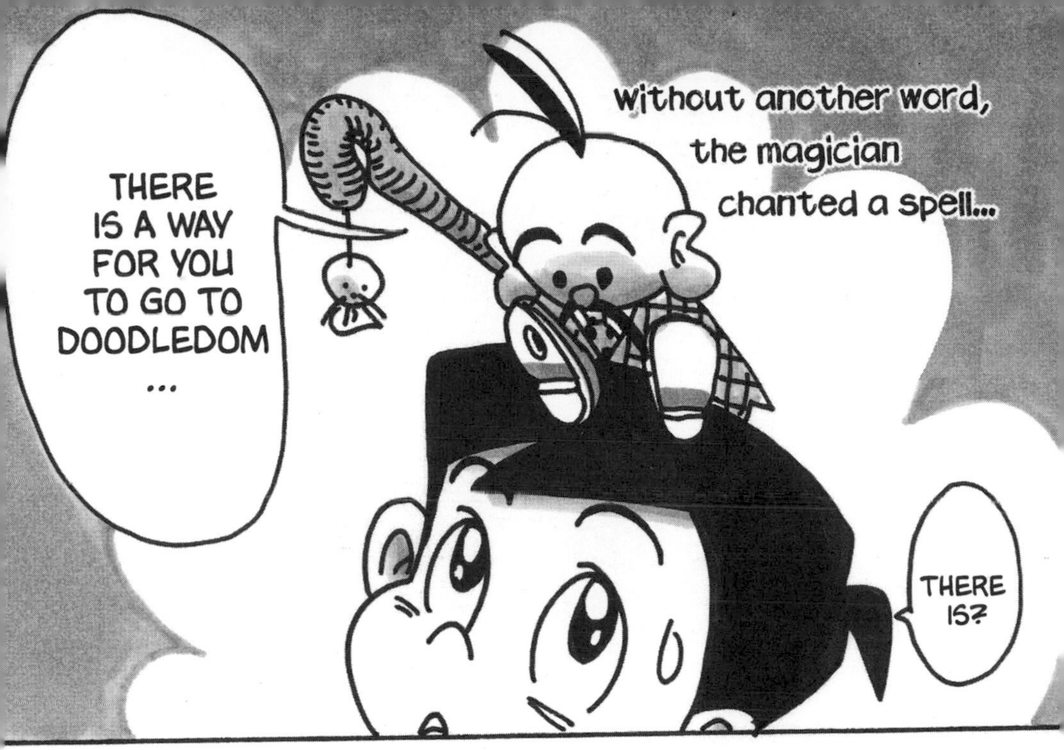
THERE IS A WAY FOR YOU TO GO TO DOODLEDOM ...
THERE IS?
without another word, the magician chanted a spell...
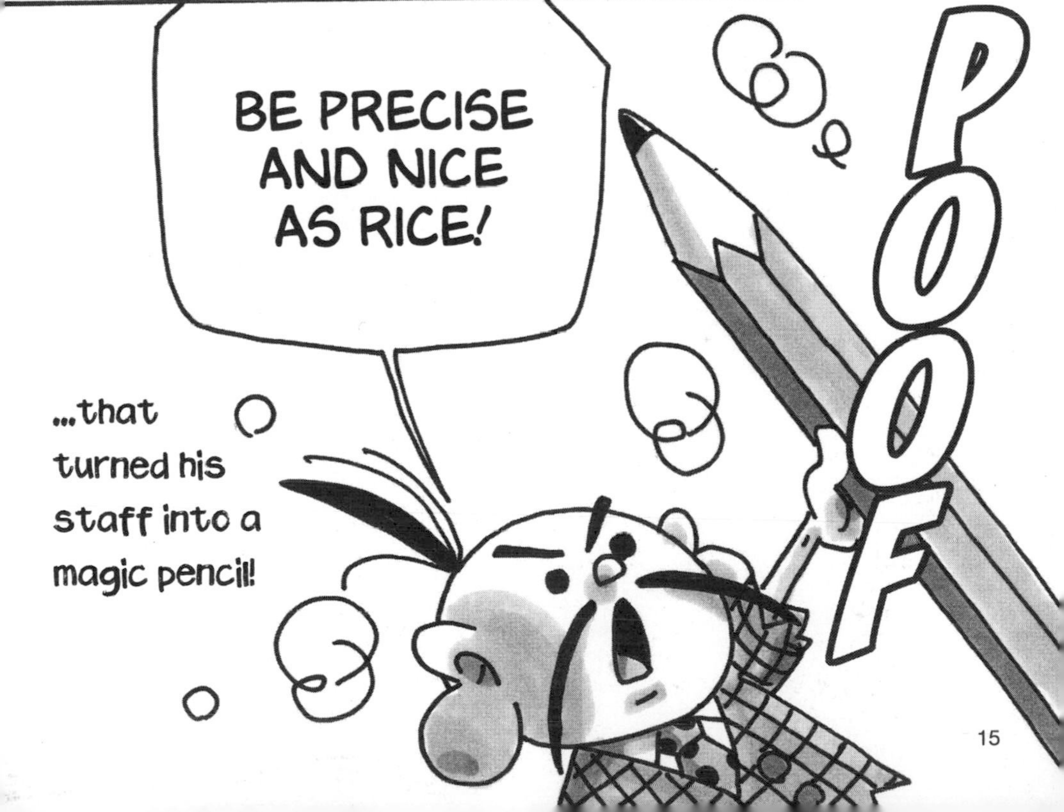
BE PRECISE AND NICE AS RICE!
POOF
...that turned his staff into a magic pencil!

He flew over to Taro and drew on his face.

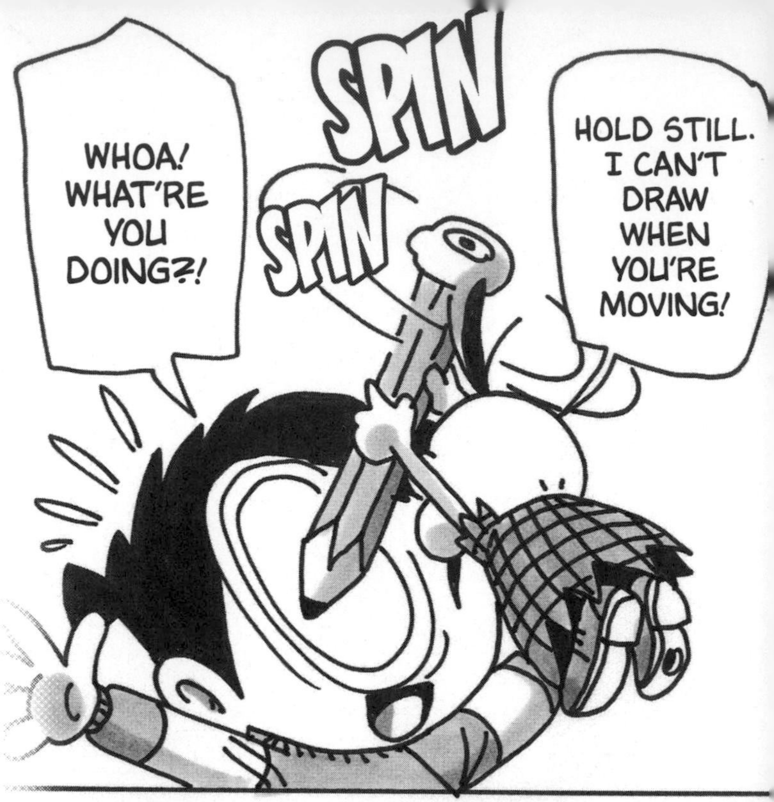
WHOA! WHAT'RE YOU DOING?!
SPIN
SPIN
HOLD STILL. I CAN'T DRAW WHEN YOU'RE MOVING!

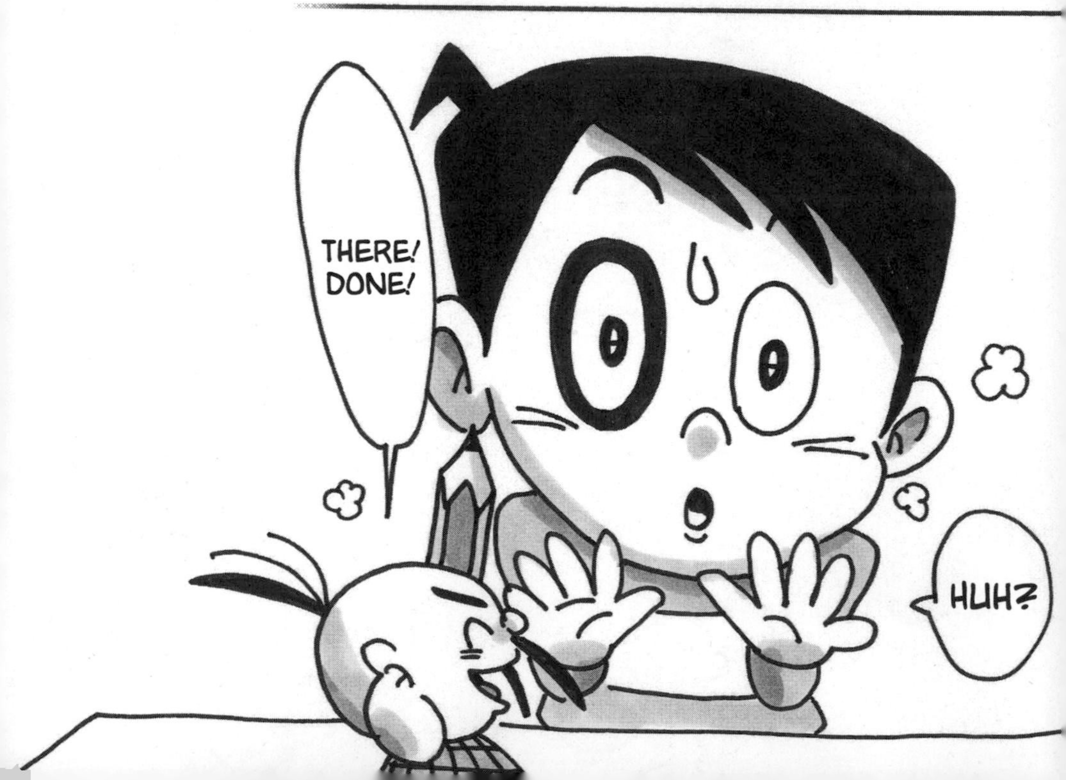
THERE! DONE!
HUH?

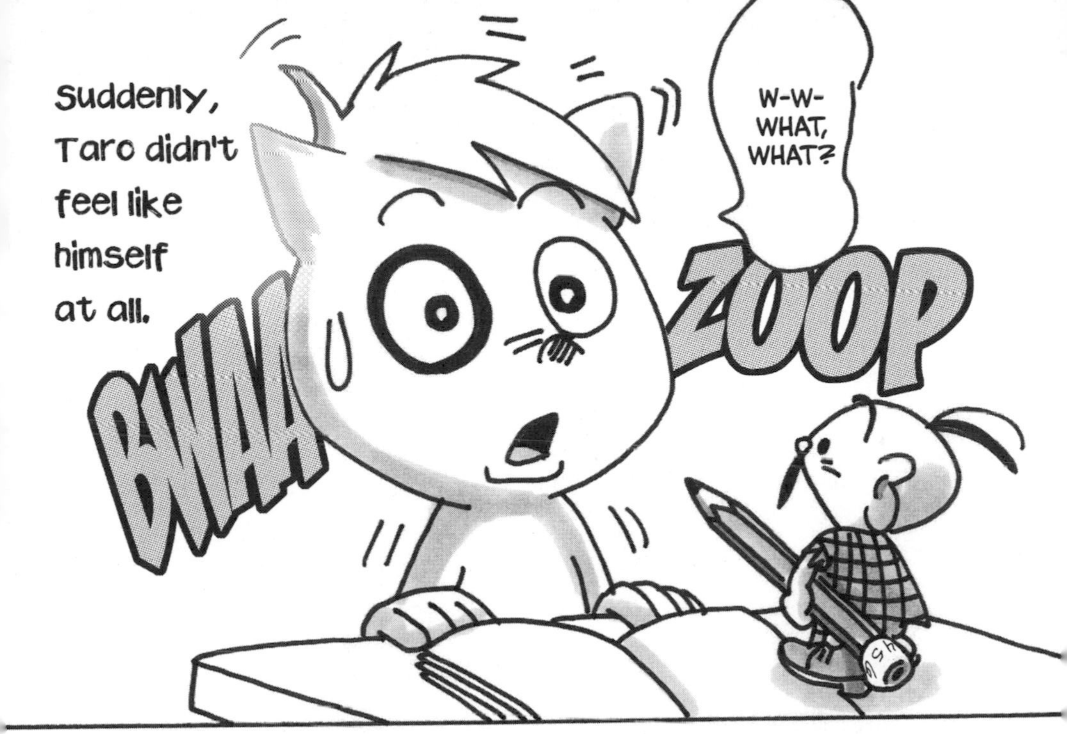
Suddenly, Taro didn't feel like himself at all.
BWAA
W-W-WHAT, WHAT?
ZOOP

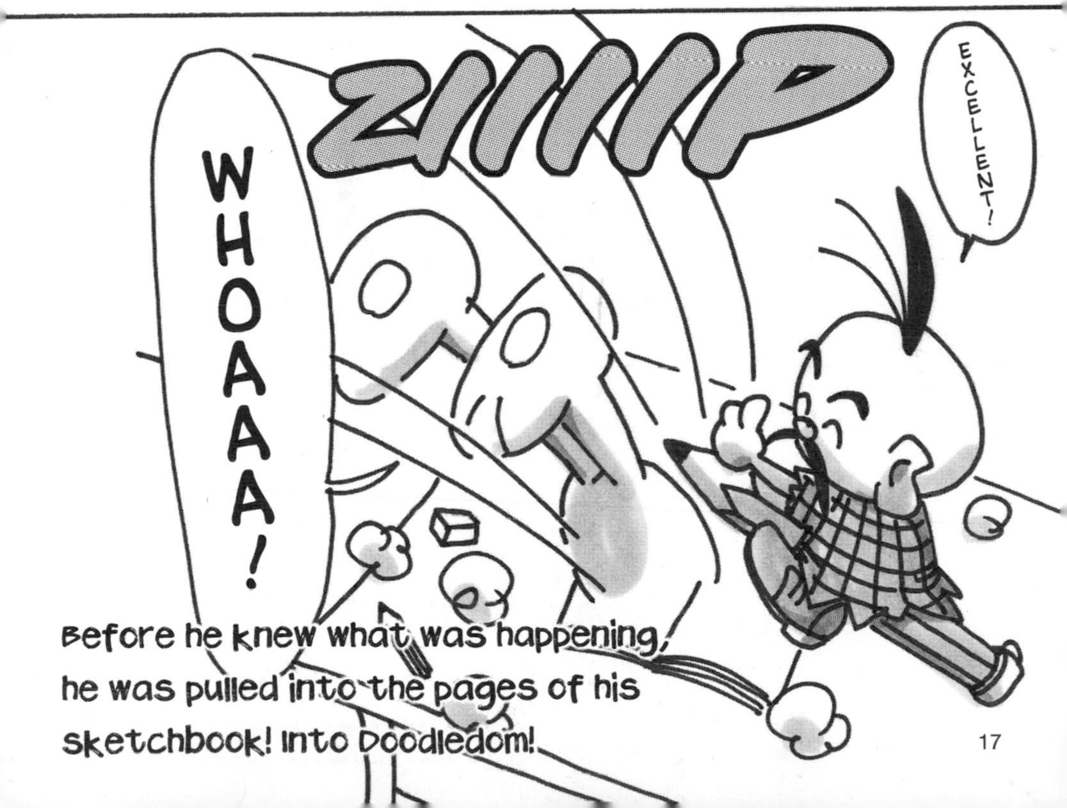
WHOAAA!
ZIIIIP
EXCELLENT!
Before he knew what was happening, he was pulled into the pages of his sketchbook! Into Doodledom!

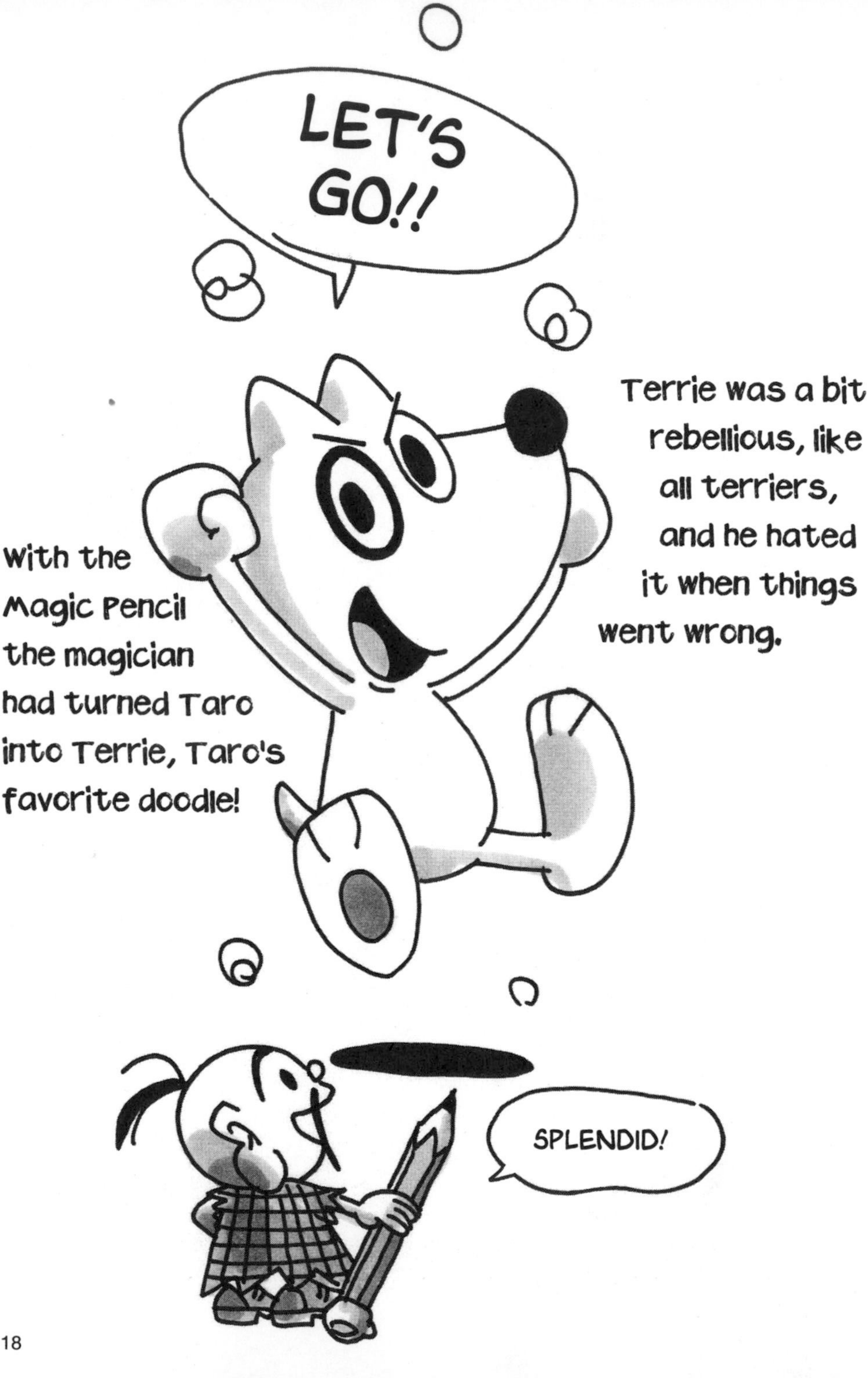
LET'S GO!!
With the Magic Pencil the magician had turned Taro into Terrie, Taro's favorite doodle!
Terrie was a bit rebellious, like all terriers, and he hated it when things went wrong.
SPLENDID!

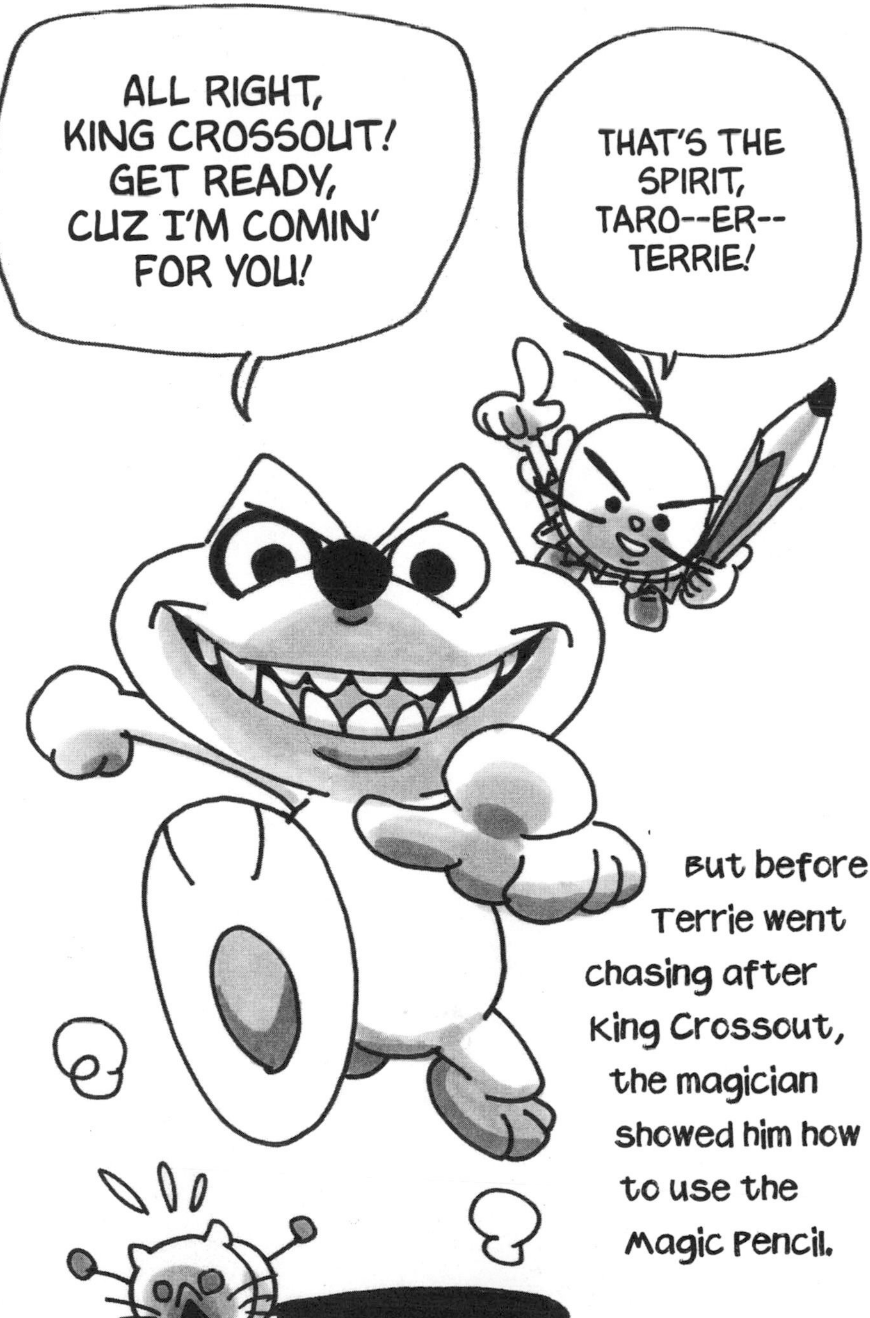
ALL RIGHT, KING CROSSOUT! GET READY, CUZ I'M COMIN' FOR YOU!
THAT'S THE SPIRIT, TARO--ER--TERRIE!
But before Terrie went chasing after King Crossout, the magician showed him how to use the Magic Pencil.

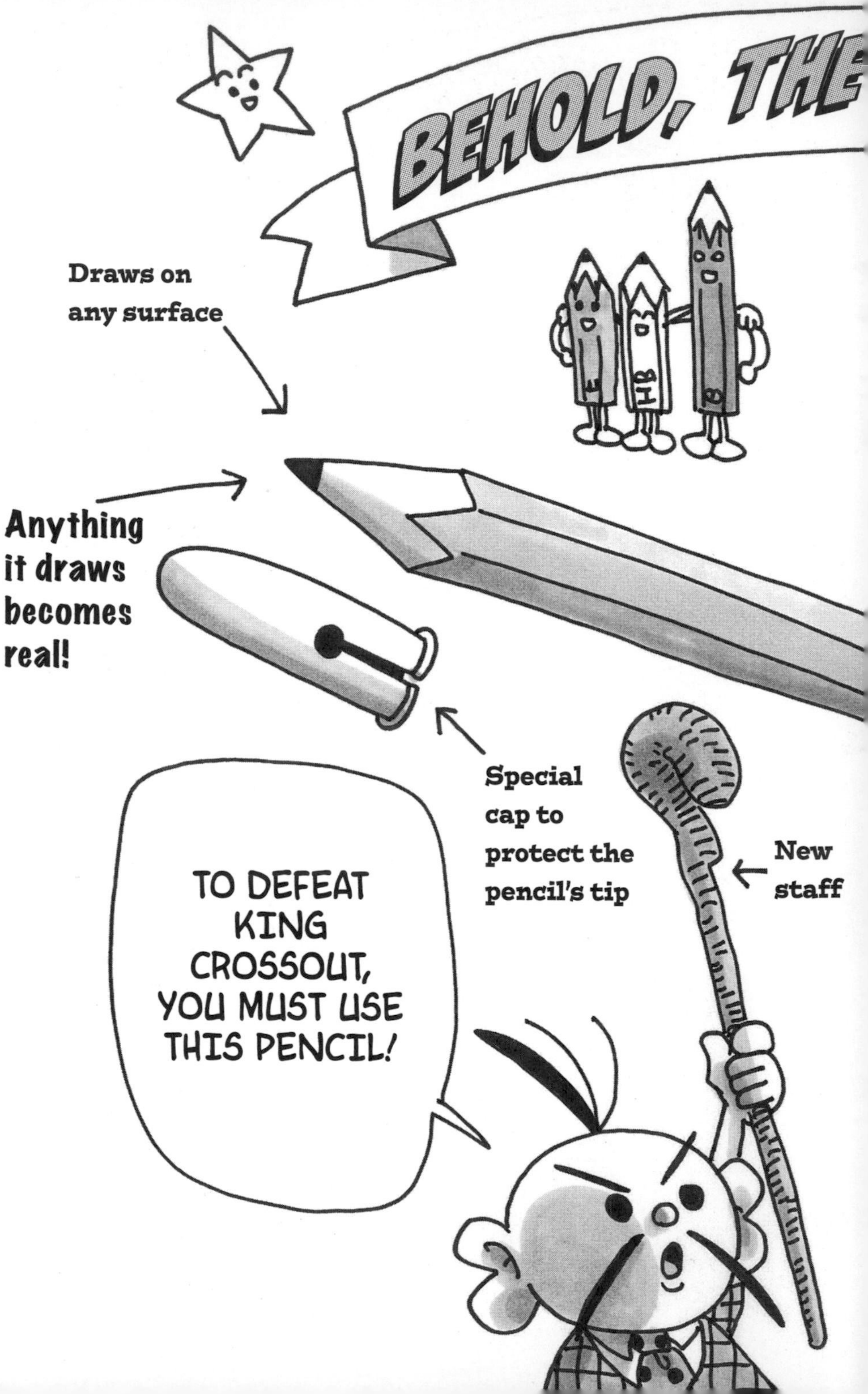
BEHOLD, THE
Draws on any surface
Anything it draws becomes real!
Special cap to protect the pencil's tip
New staff
TO DEFEAT KING CROSSOUT, YOU MUST USE THIS PENCIL!

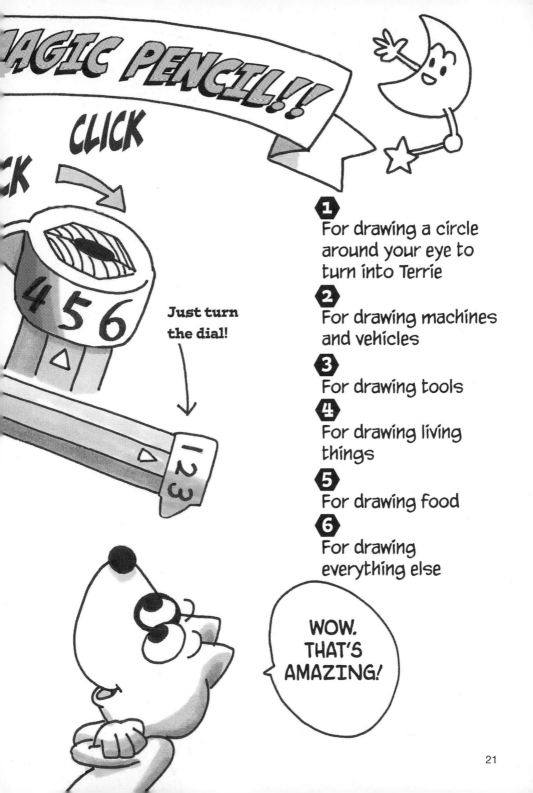

MAGIC PENCIL!!

CLICK

CK CLICK

Just turn the dial!

1 For drawing a circle around your eye to turn into Terrie

2 For drawing machines and vehicles

3 For drawing tools

4 For drawing living things

5 For drawing food

6 For drawing everything else

WOW. THAT'S AMAZING!

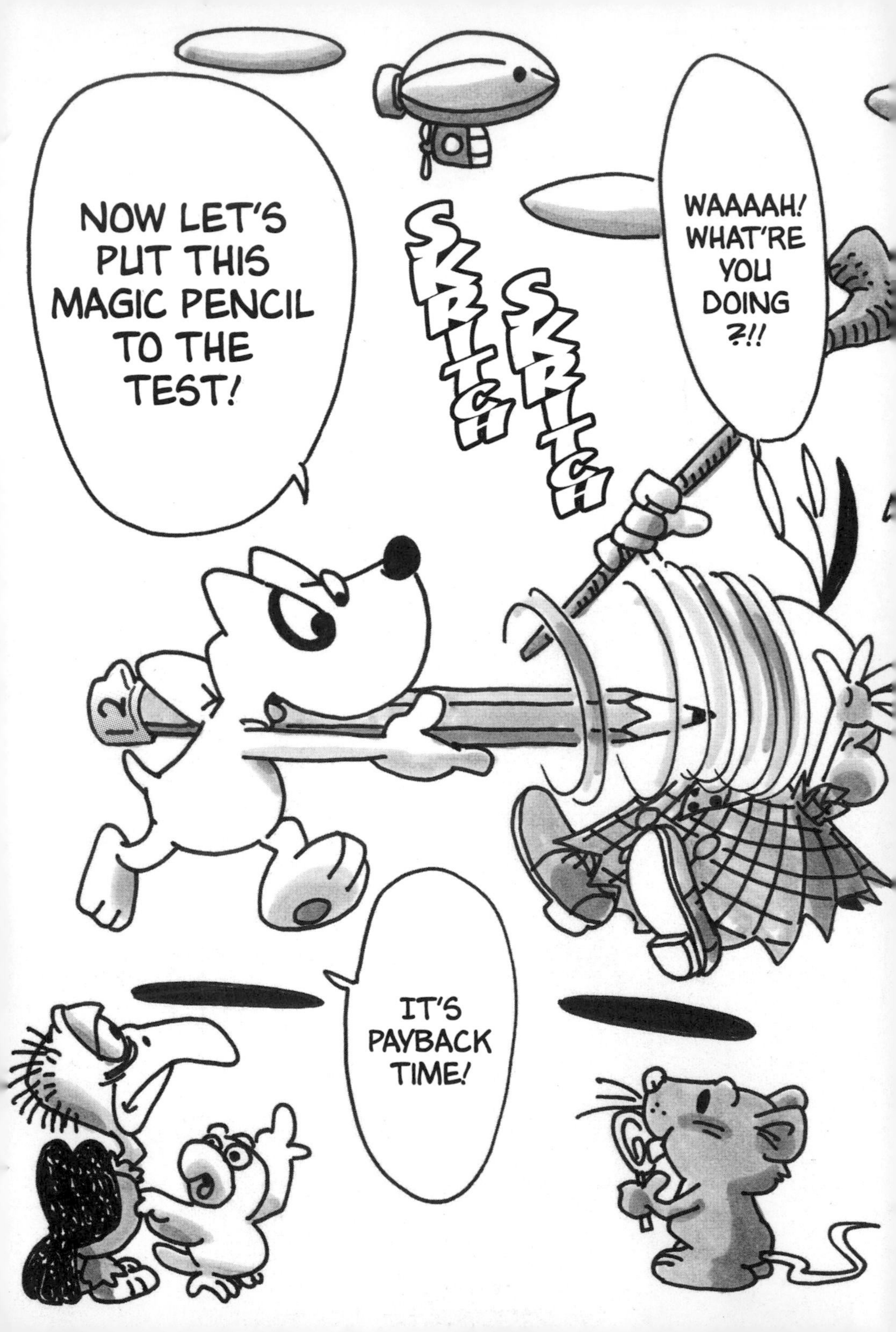
NOW LET'S PUT THIS MAGIC PENCIL TO THE TEST!
SKRITCH SKRITCH
WAAAAH! WHAT'RE YOU DOING ?!!
IT'S PAYBACK TIME!

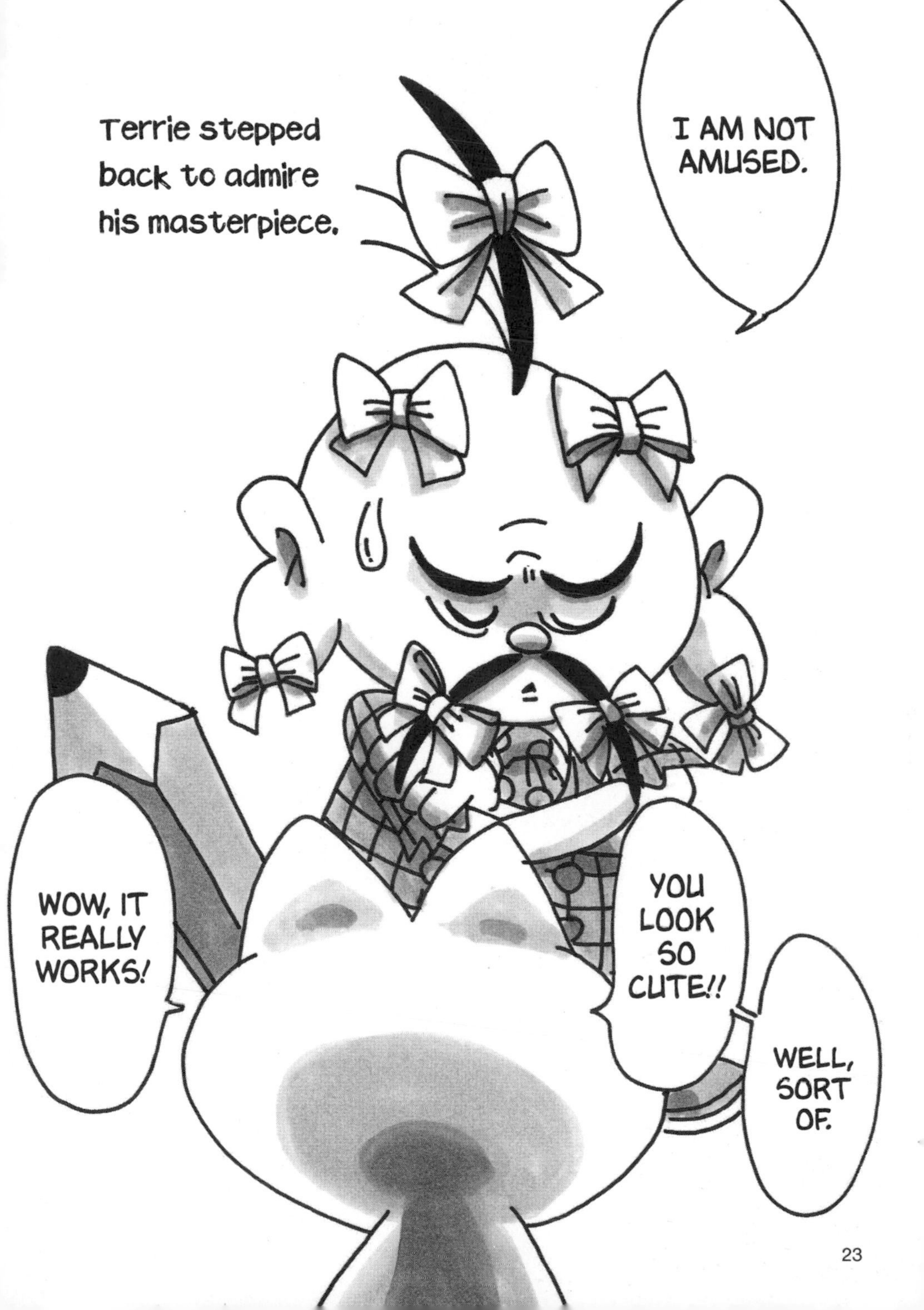
Terrie stepped back to admire his masterpiece.
I AM NOT AMUSED.
WOW, IT REALLY WORKS!
YOU LOOK SO CUTE!!
WELL, SORT OF.

The magician had one more very important thing to tell Terrie.

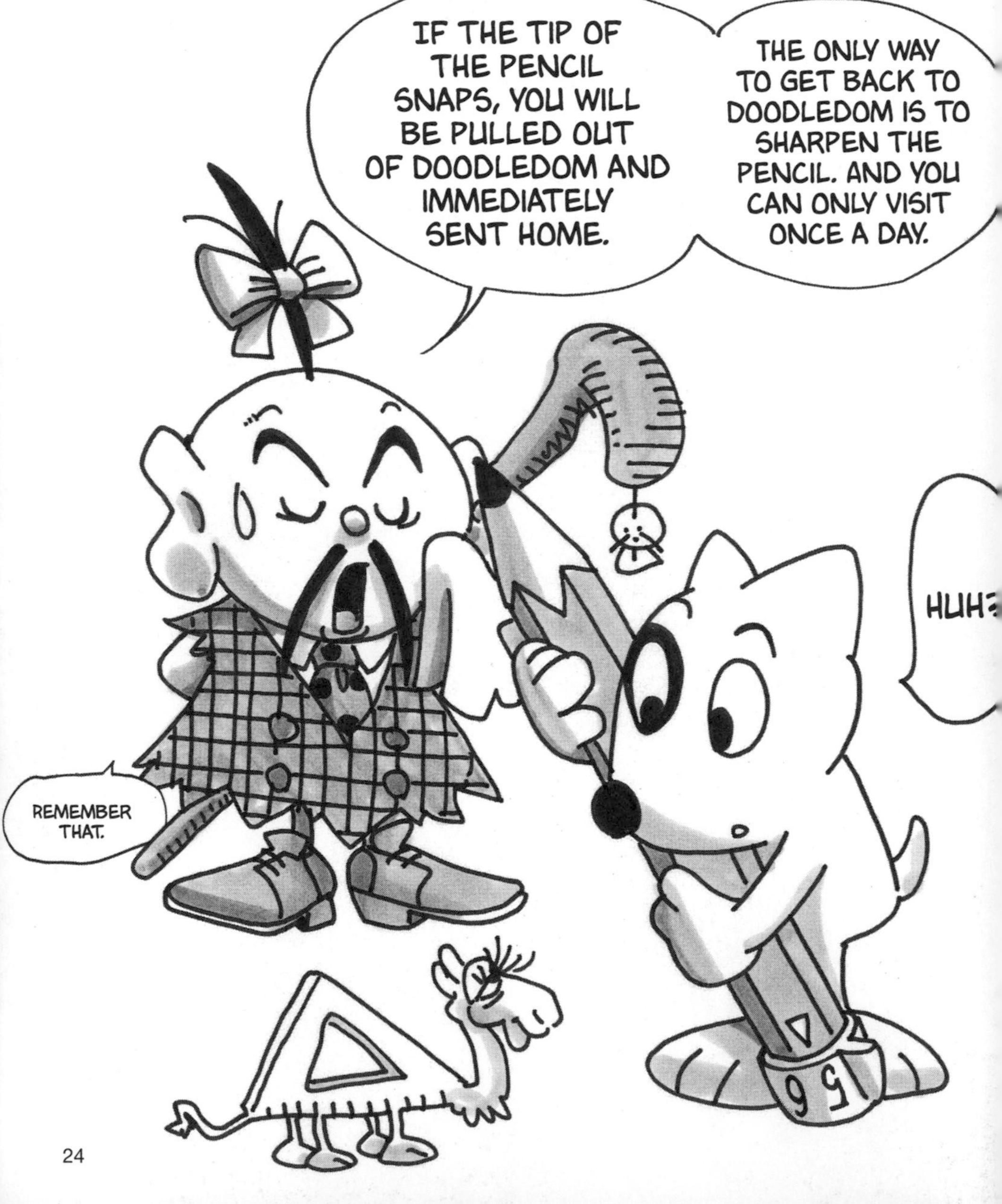
IF THE TIP OF THE PENCIL SNAPS, YOU WILL BE PULLED OUT OF DOODLEDOM AND IMMEDIATELY SENT HOME.
THE ONLY WAY TO GET BACK TO DOODLEDOM IS TO SHARPEN THE PENCIL. AND YOU CAN ONLY VISIT ONCE A DAY.
HUH
REMEMBER THAT.

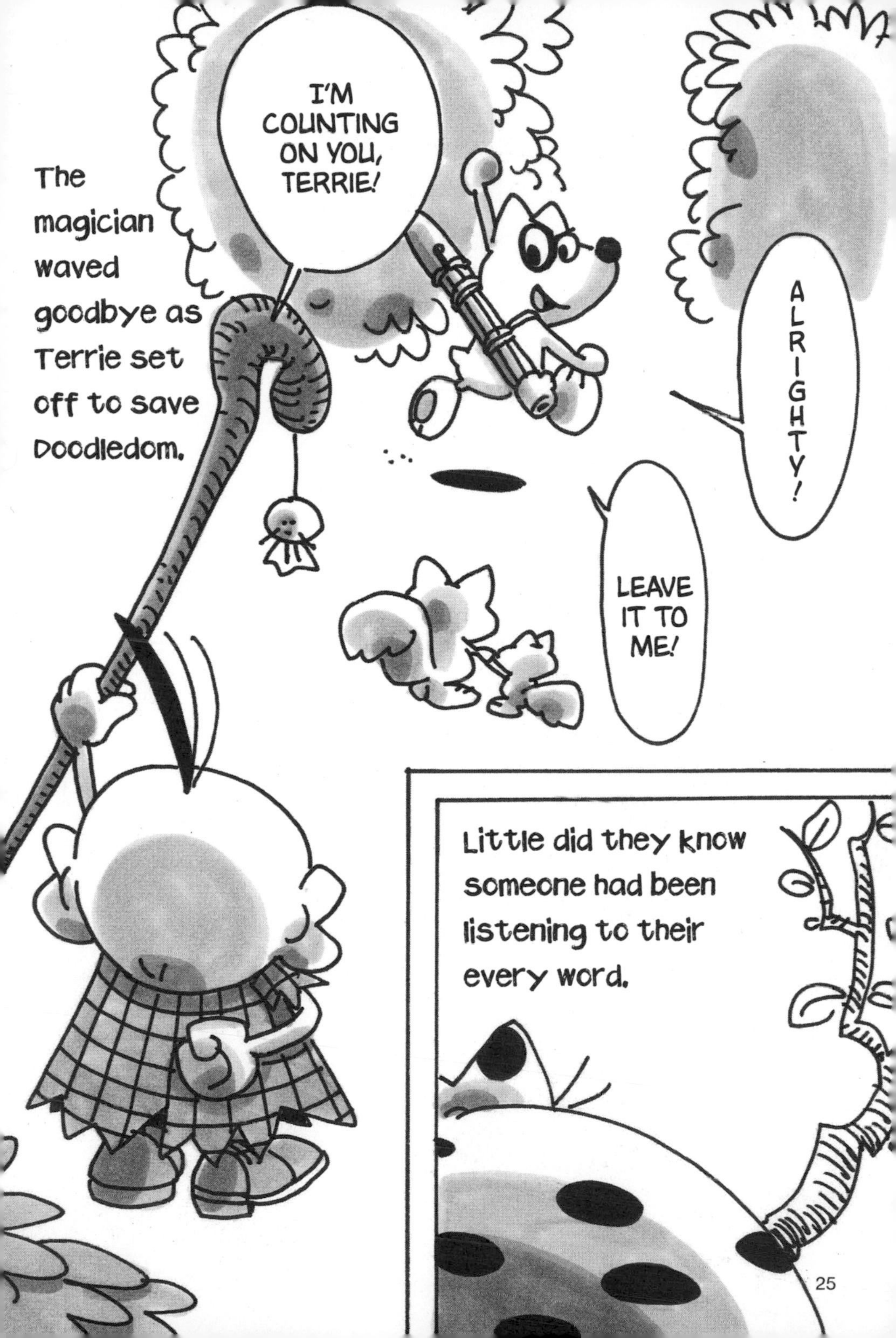
The magician waved goodbye as Terrie set off to save Doodledom.
I'M COUNTING ON YOU, TERRIE!
ALRIGHTY!
LEAVE IT TO ME!
Little did they know someone had been listening to their every word.

The eavesdropper was none other than Tattle-Tail, a sneaky sneak who worked for the king. And there was nothing more Tattle liked than a good secret.

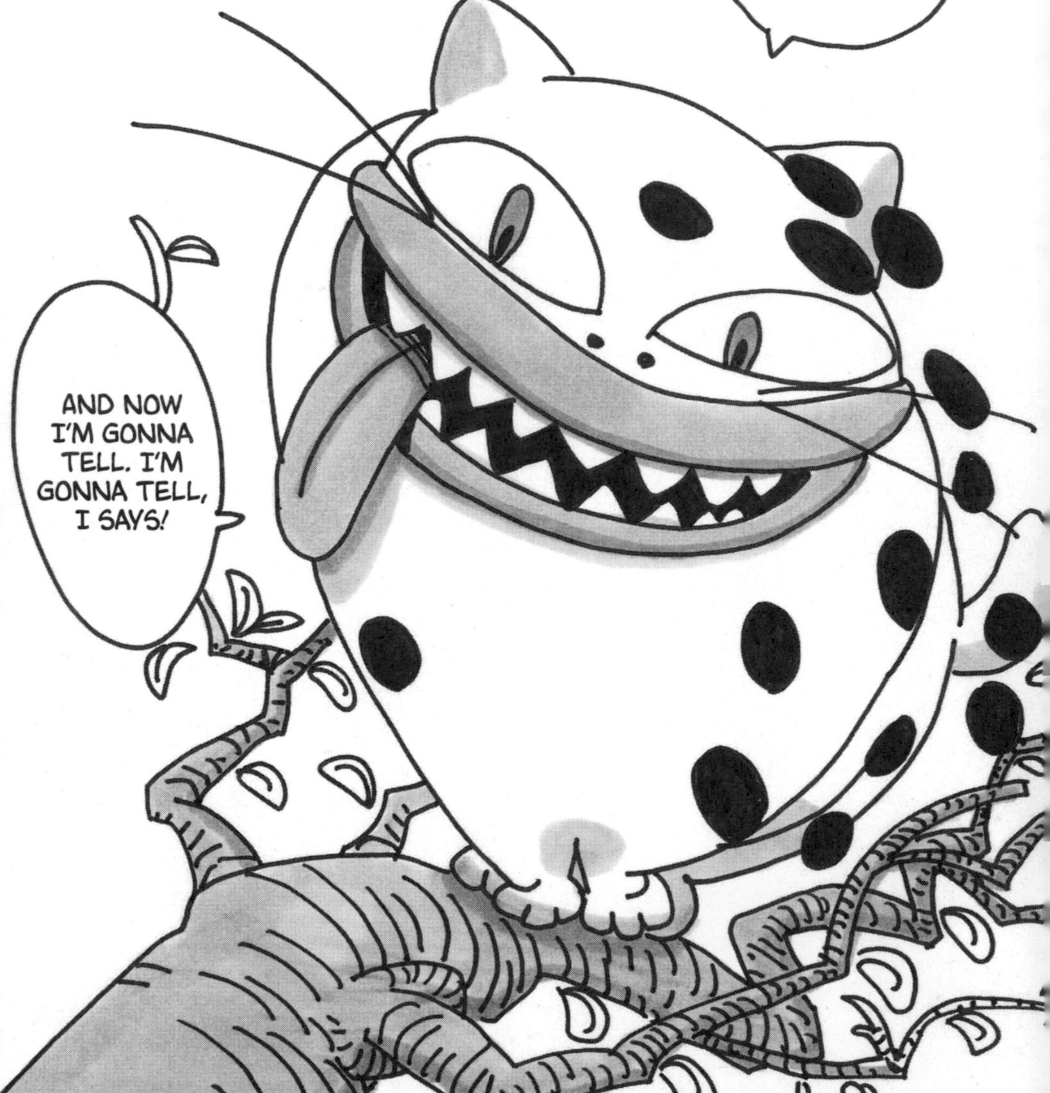
OOOH, WHAT AN INTERESTING BIT OF INFORMATION.
AND NOW I'M GONNA TELL. I'M GONNA TELL, I SAYS!

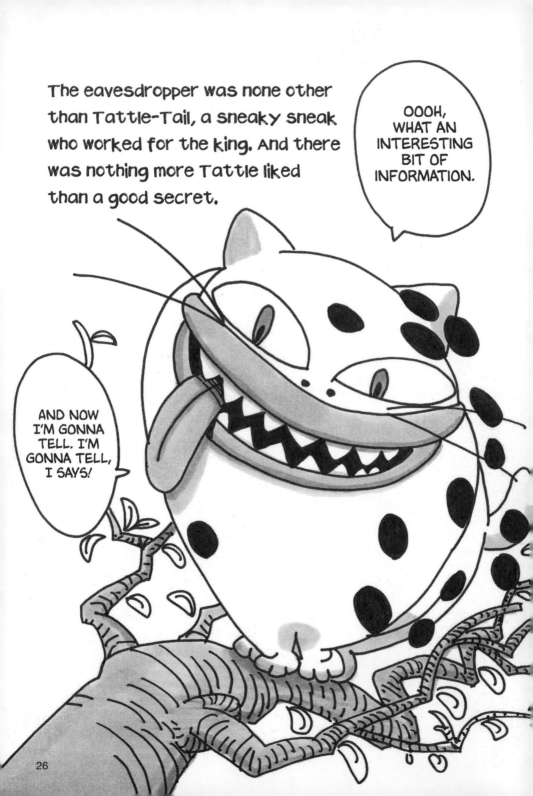

Despite being quite a large fellow, Tattle-Tail hopped lightly from his perch.

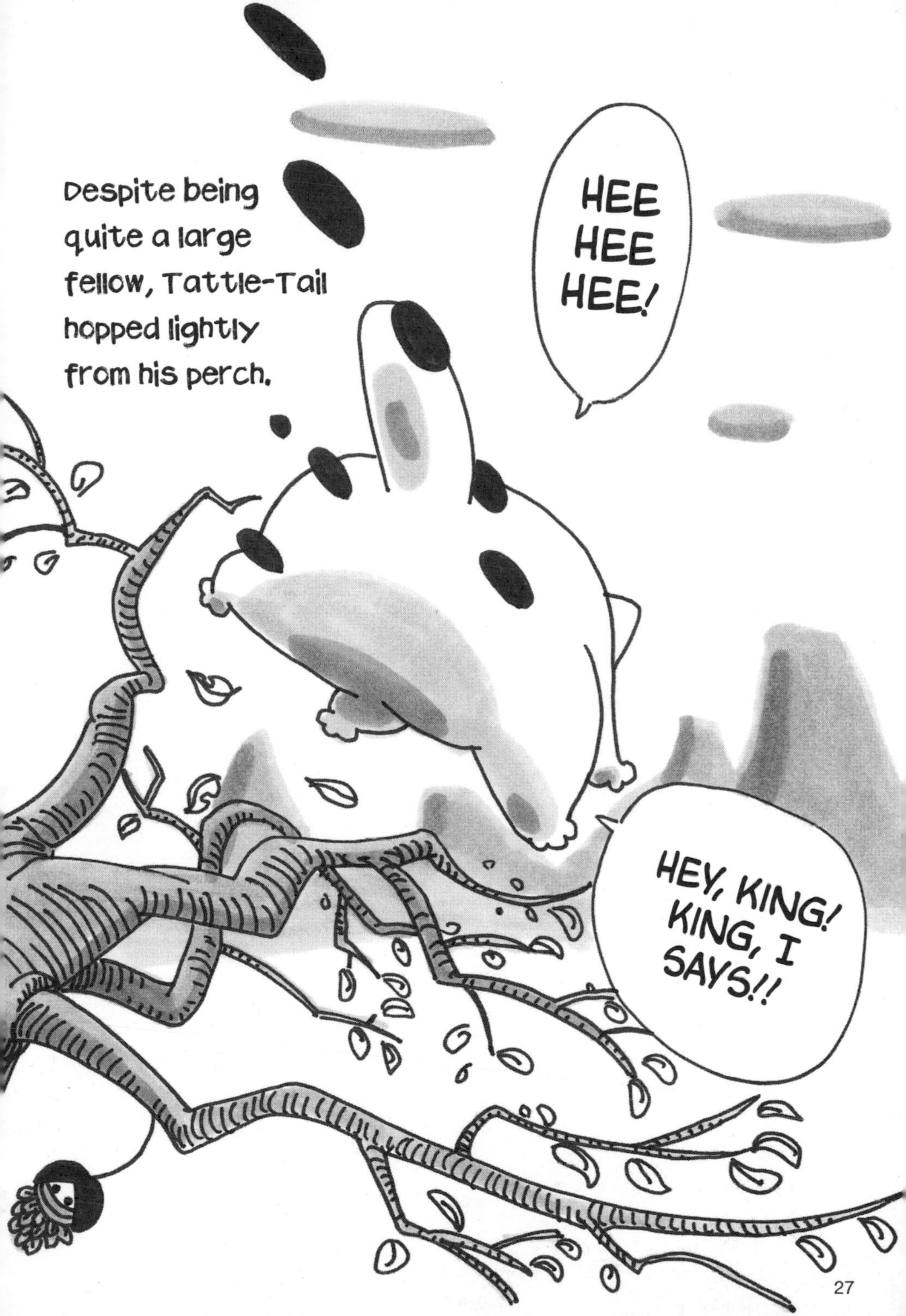
HEE HEE HEE!
HEY, KING! KING, I SAYS!!

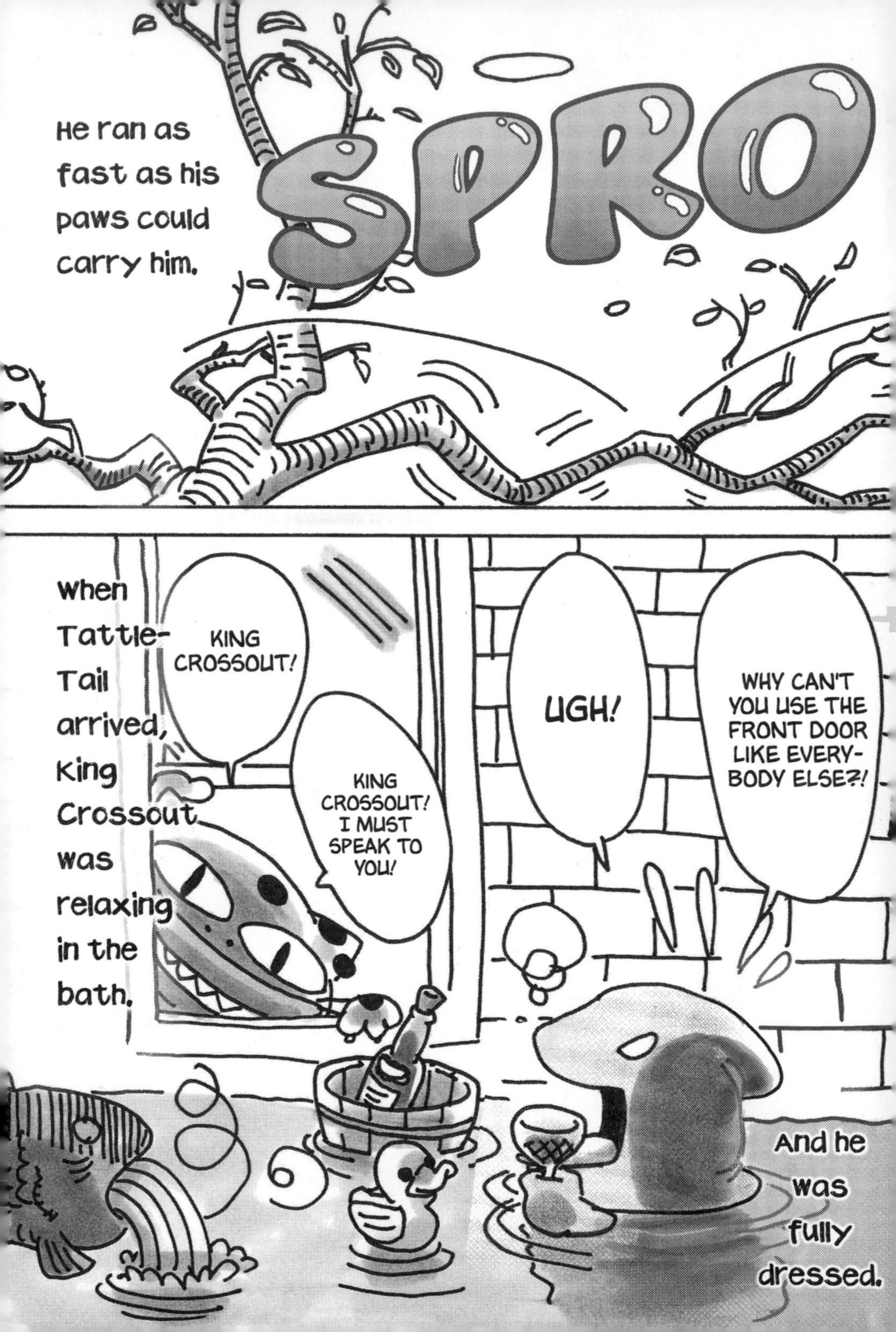
He ran as fast as his paws could carry him.
SPRO
When Tattle-Tail arrived, King Crossout was relaxing in the bath.
KING CROSSOUT!
KING CROSSOUT! I MUST SPEAK TO YOU!
UGH!
WHY CAN'T YOU USE THE FRONT DOOR LIKE EVERY-BODY ELSE?!
And he was fully dressed.

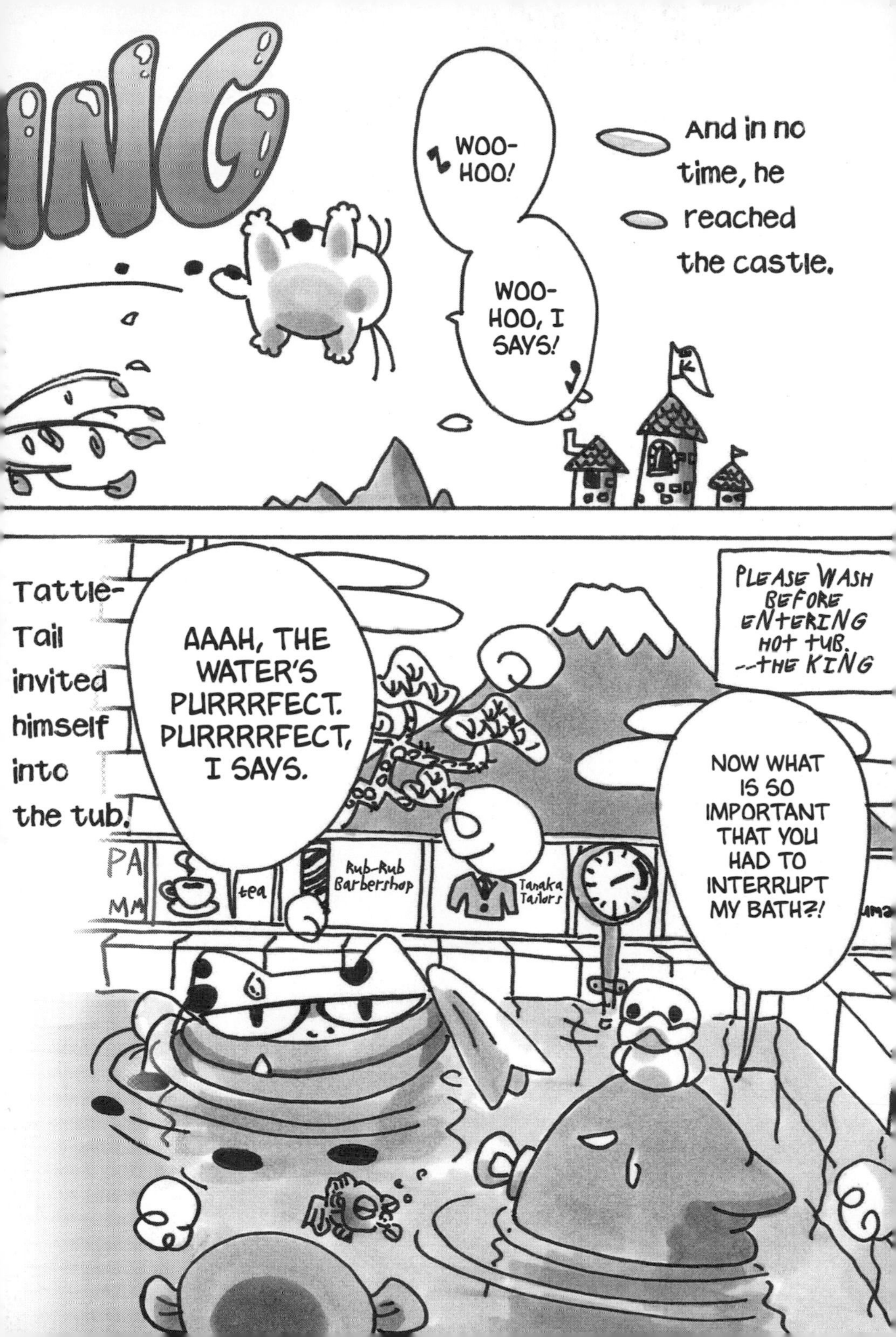

ING
And in no time, he reached the castle.
WOO-HOO!
WOO-HOO, I SAYS!
PLEASE WASH BEFORE ENTERING HOT TUB. --THE KING
NOW WHAT IS SO IMPORTANT THAT YOU HAD TO INTERRUPT MY BATH?!
Tanaka Tailors
Rub-Rub Barbershop
tea
AAAH, THE WATER'S PURRRFECT. PURRRRFECT, I SAYS.
Tattle-Tail invited himself into the tub.

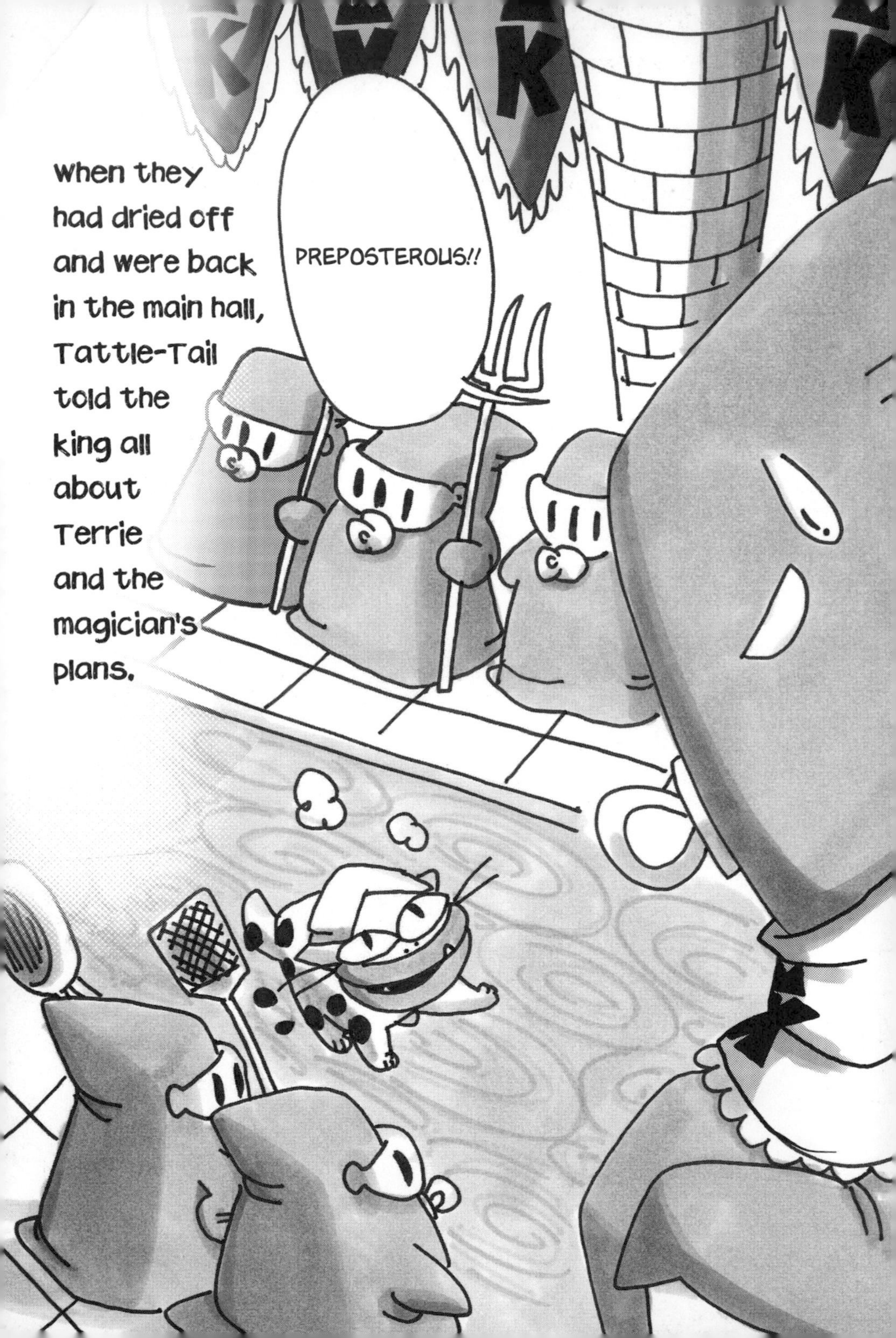
When they had dried off and were back in the main hall, Tattle-Tail told the king all about Terrie and the magician's plans.
PREPOSTEROUS!!

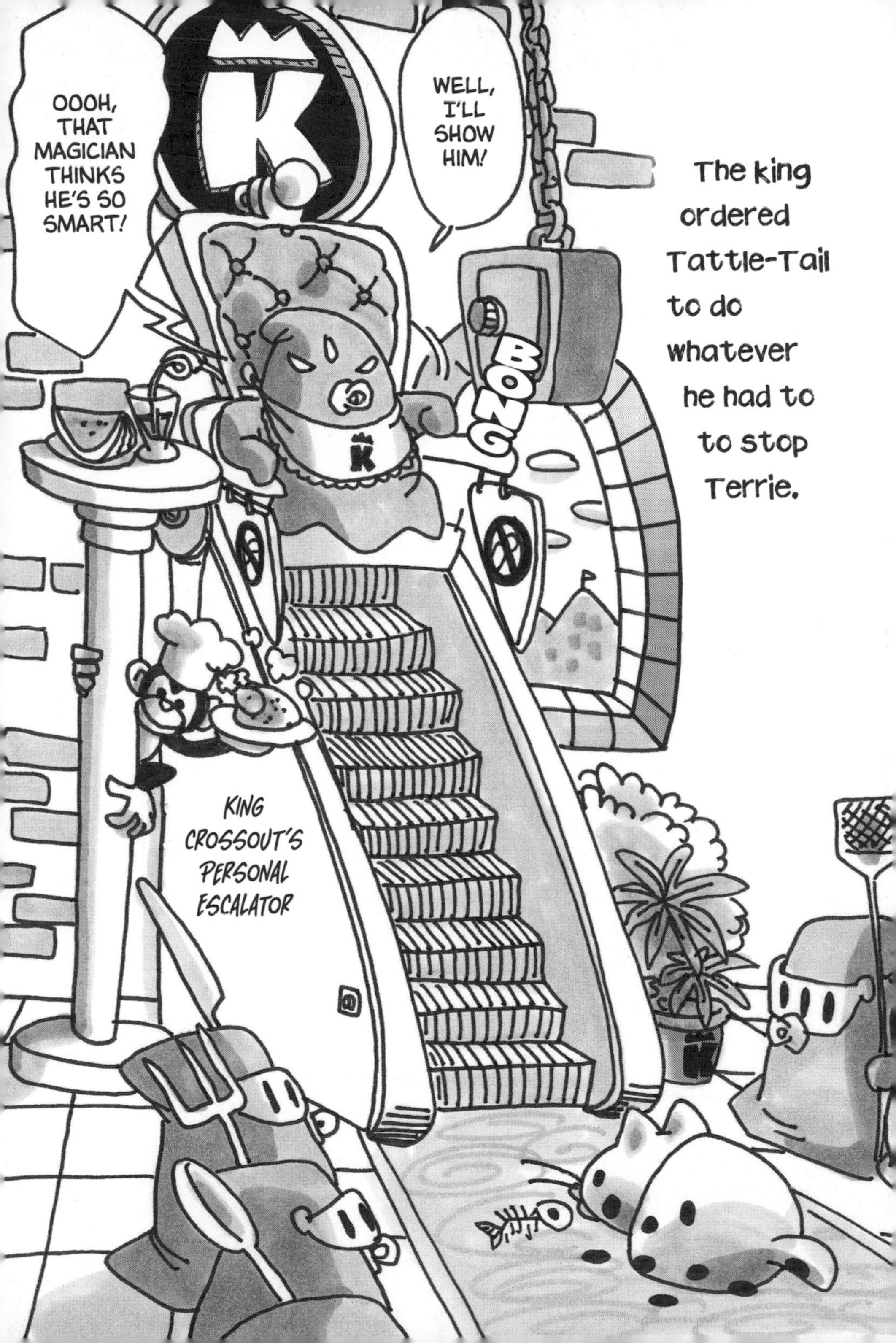
The king ordered Tattle-Tail to do whatever he had to to stop Terrie.
WELL, I'LL SHOW HIM!
OOOH, THAT MAGICIAN THINKS HE'S SO SMART!
BONG
KING CROSSOUT'S PERSONAL ESCALATOR

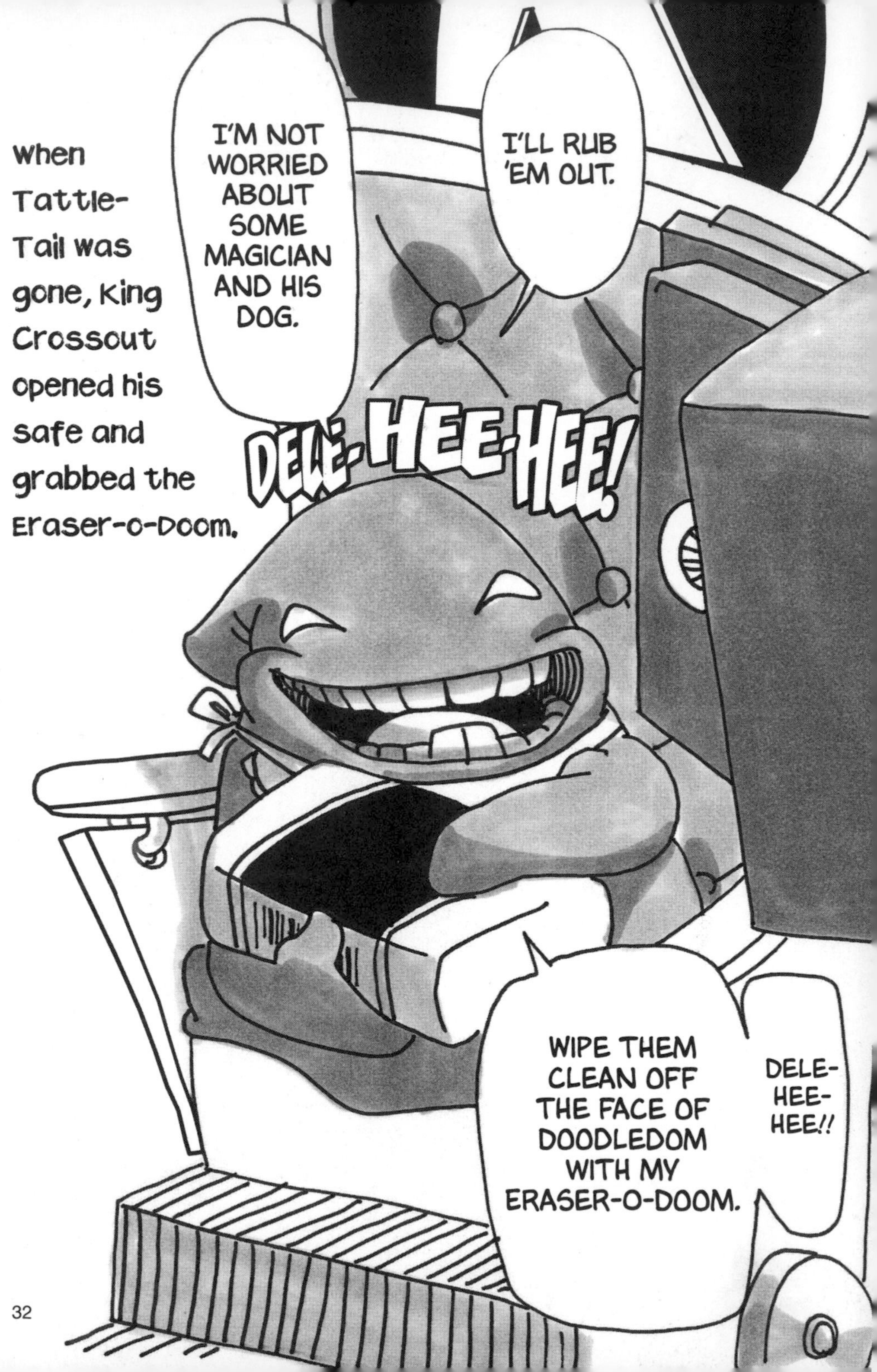
When Tattle-Tail was gone, King Crossout opened his safe and grabbed the Eraser-o-Doom.
I'M NOT WORRIED ABOUT SOME MAGICIAN AND HIS DOG.
I'LL RUB 'EM OUT.
DELE-HEE-HEE!
WIPE THEM CLEAN OFF THE FACE OF DOODLEDOM WITH MY ERASER-O-DOOM.
DELE-HEE-HEE!!

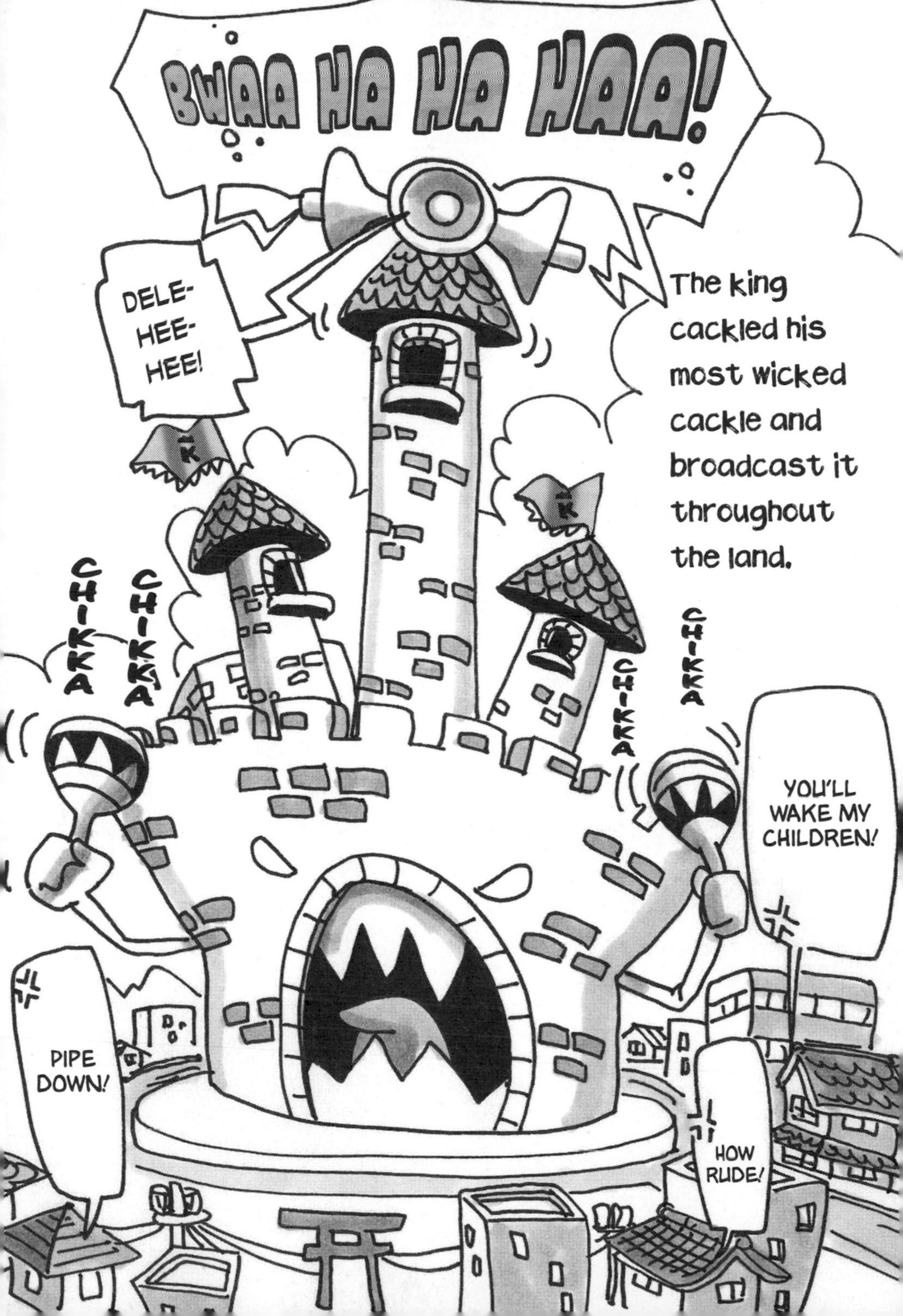
BWAA HA HA HAA!
The king cackled his most wicked cackle and broadcast it throughout the land.
DELE-HEE-HEE!
CHIKKA
CHIKKA
CHIKKA
CHIKKA
YOU'LL WAKE MY CHILDREN!
HOW RUDE!
PIPE DOWN!

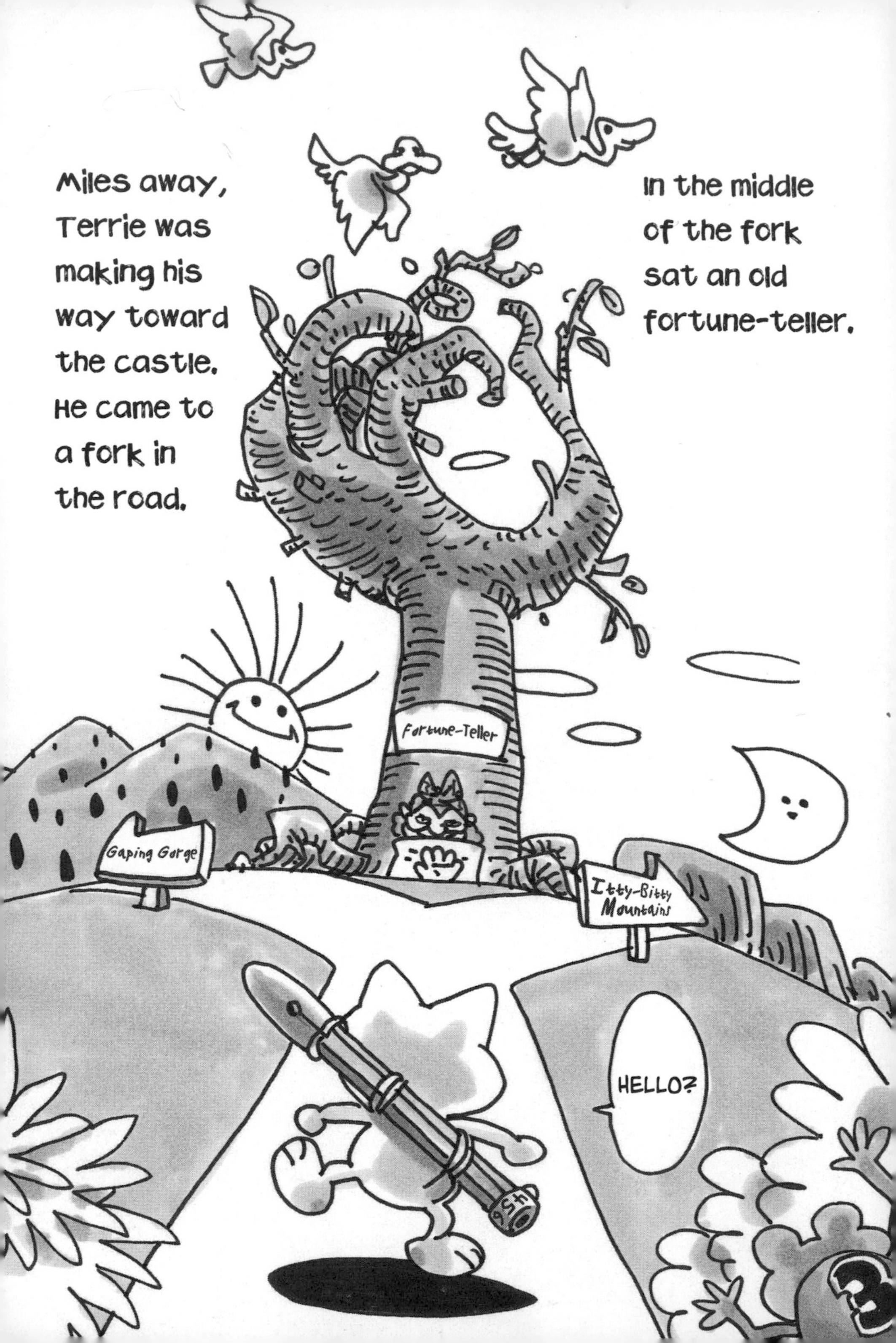
Miles away, Terrie was making his way toward the castle. He came to a fork in the road.
In the middle of the fork sat an old fortune-teller.
Fortune-Teller
Gaping Gorge
Itty-Bitty Mountains
HELLO?

The fortune-teller's voice cracked when she spoke.

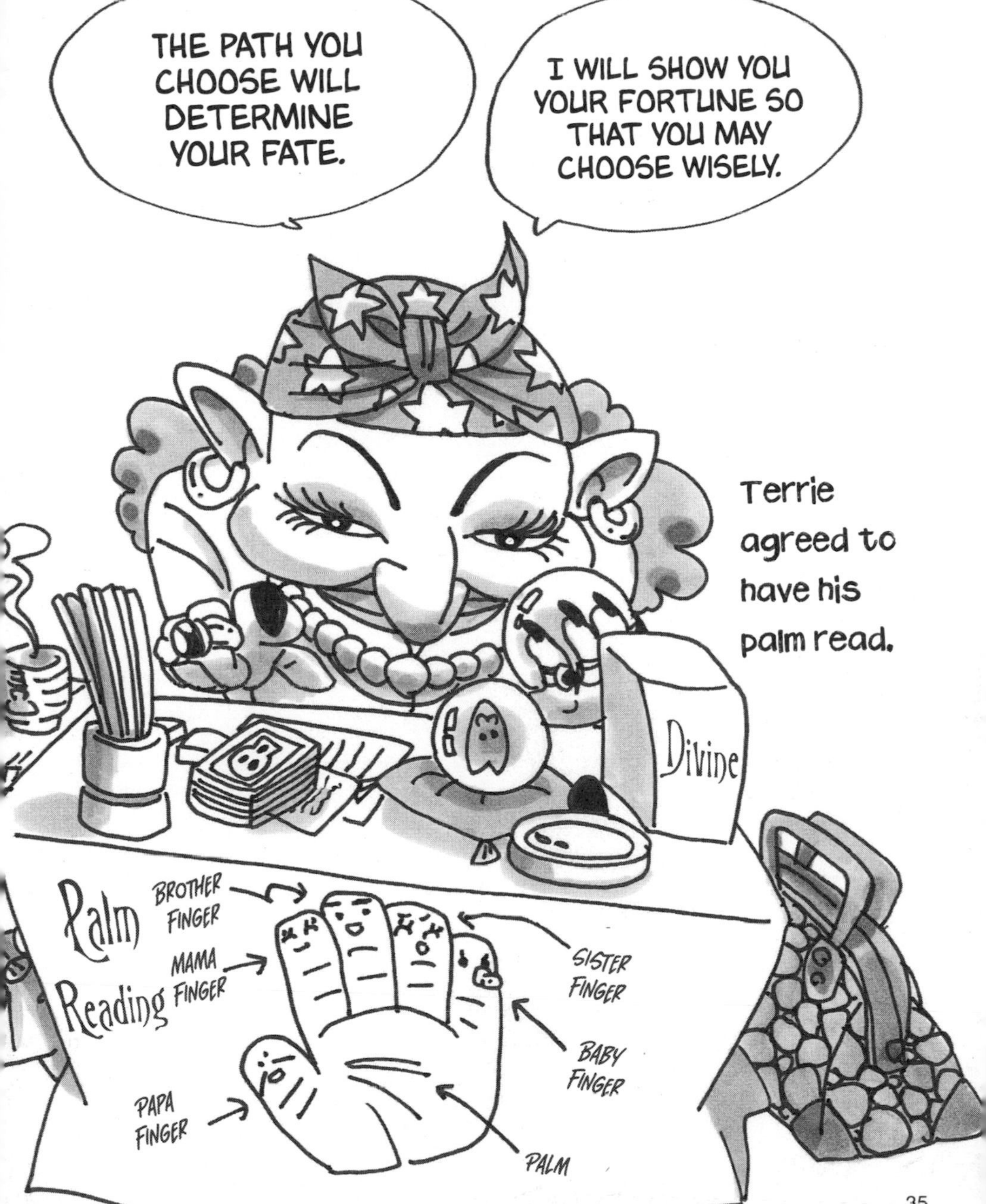
THE PATH YOU CHOOSE WILL DETERMINE YOUR FATE.
I WILL SHOW YOU YOUR FORTUNE SO THAT YOU MAY CHOOSE WISELY.
Divine
Palm Reading
BROTHER FINGER
MAMA FINGER
SISTER FINGER
BABY FINGER
PAPA FINGER
PALM

Terrie agreed to have his palm read.

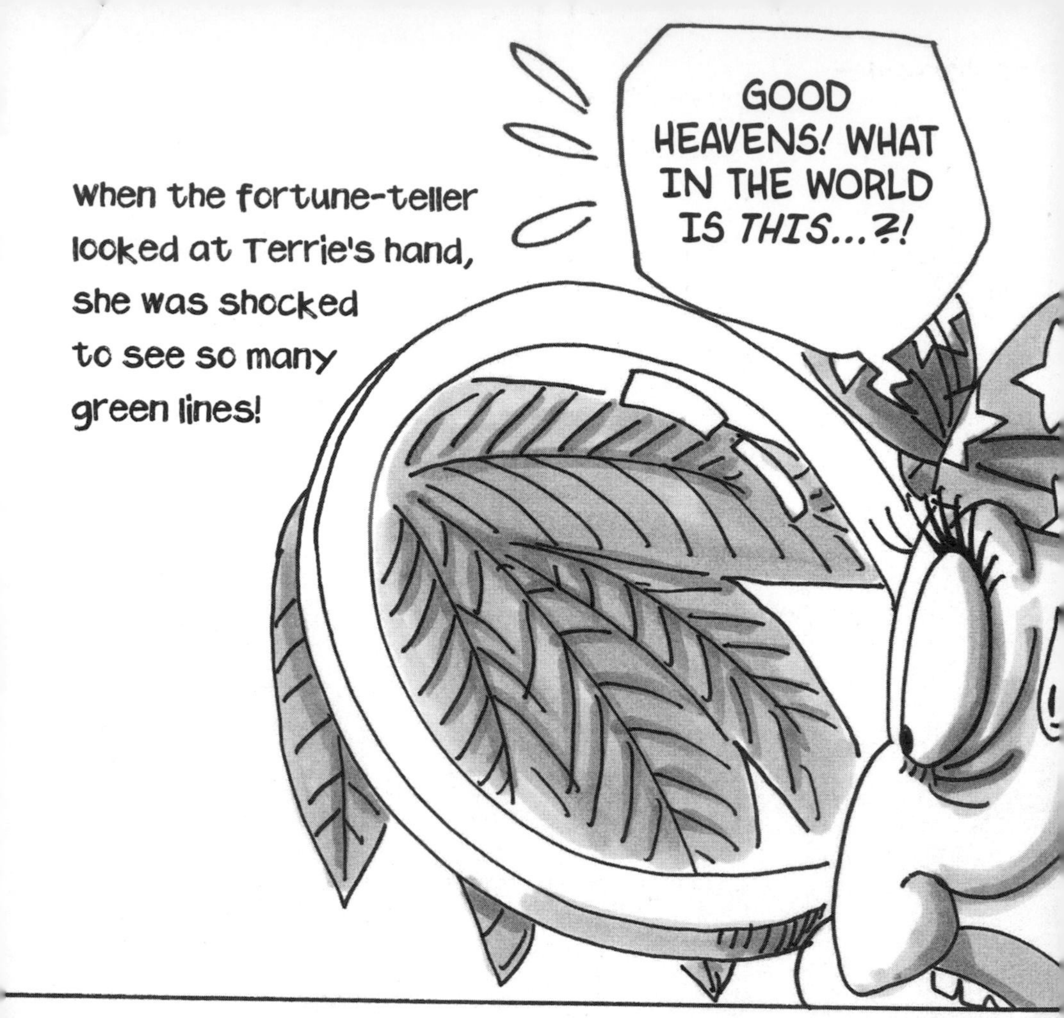
When the fortune-teller looked at Terrie's hand, she was shocked to see so many green lines!
GOOD HEAVENS! WHAT IN THE WORLD IS *THIS*...?!
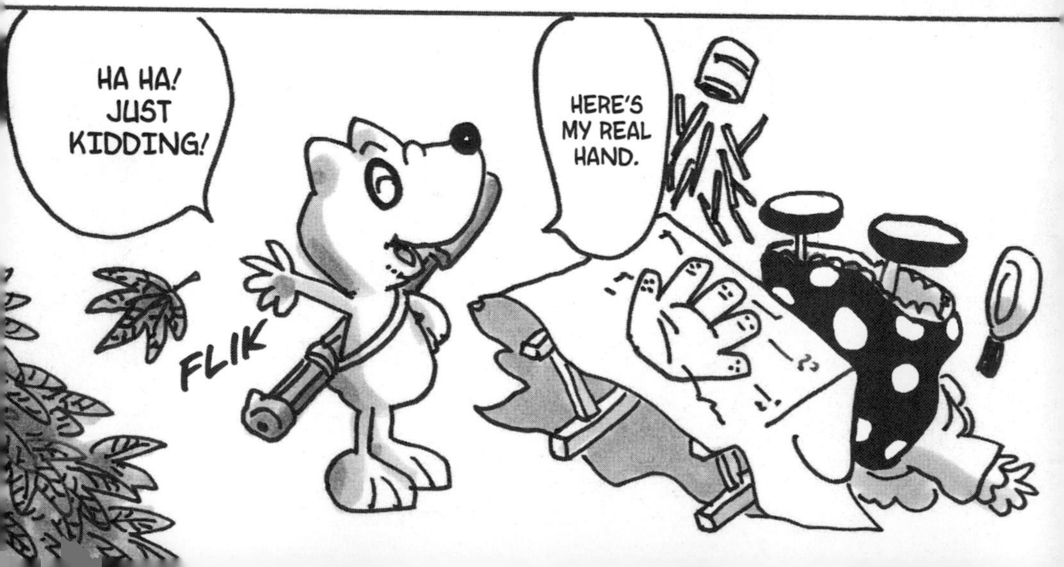
HA HA! JUST KIDDING!
HERE'S MY REAL HAND.
FLIK

The fortune-teller looked closely at Terrie's paw.

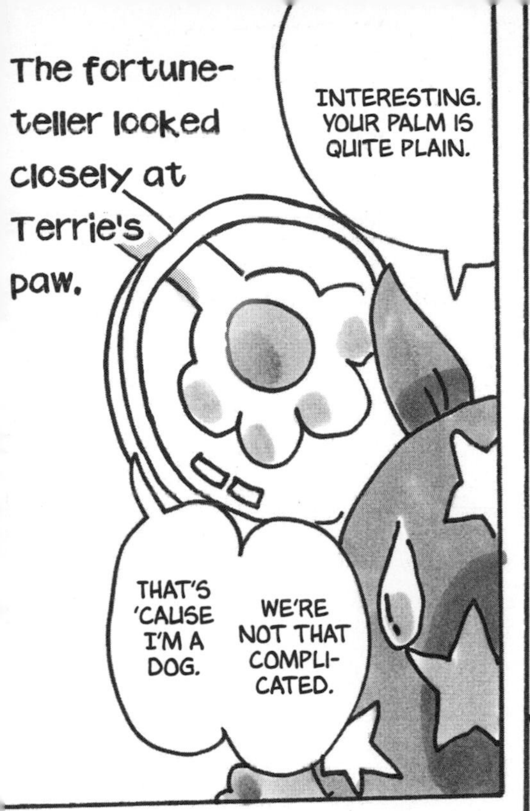
INTERESTING. YOUR PALM IS QUITE PLAIN.
THAT'S 'CAUSE I'M A DOG.
WE'RE NOT THAT COMPLICATED.

Now, Terrie didn't like strangers telling him what to do, but he did like the sound of Gaping Gorge.

He set off in the direction the fortune-teller pointed, hoping for an adventure.

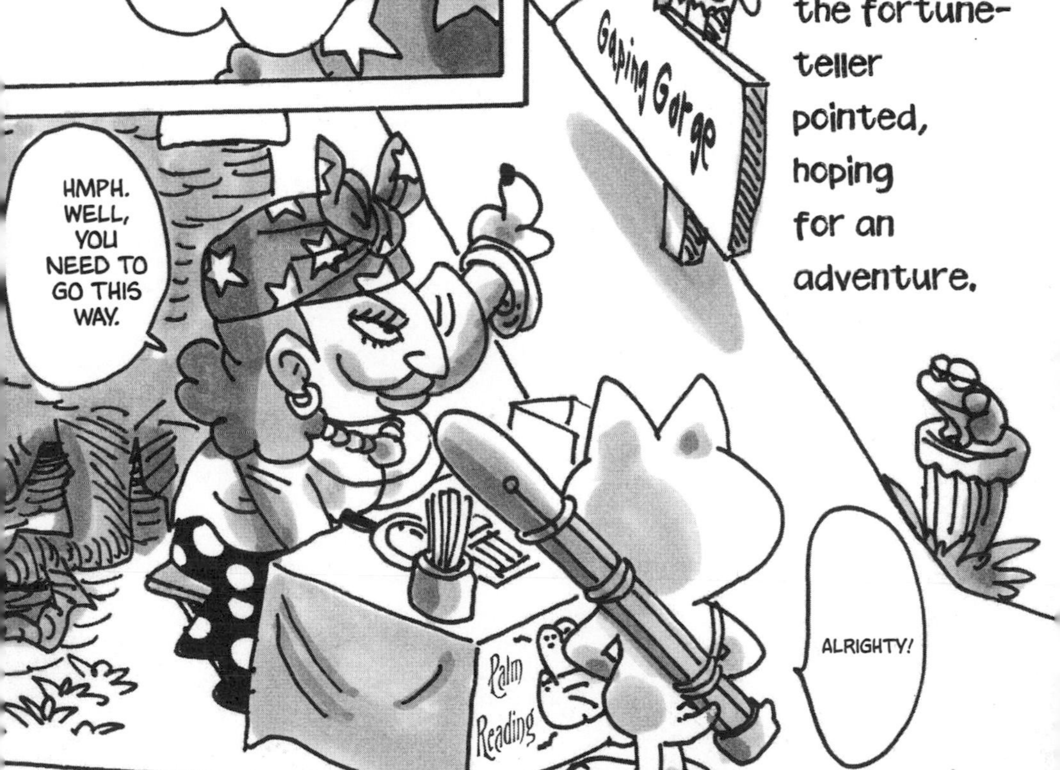
HMPH. WELL, YOU NEED TO GO THIS WAY.
Gaping Gorge
Palm Reading
ALRIGHTY!

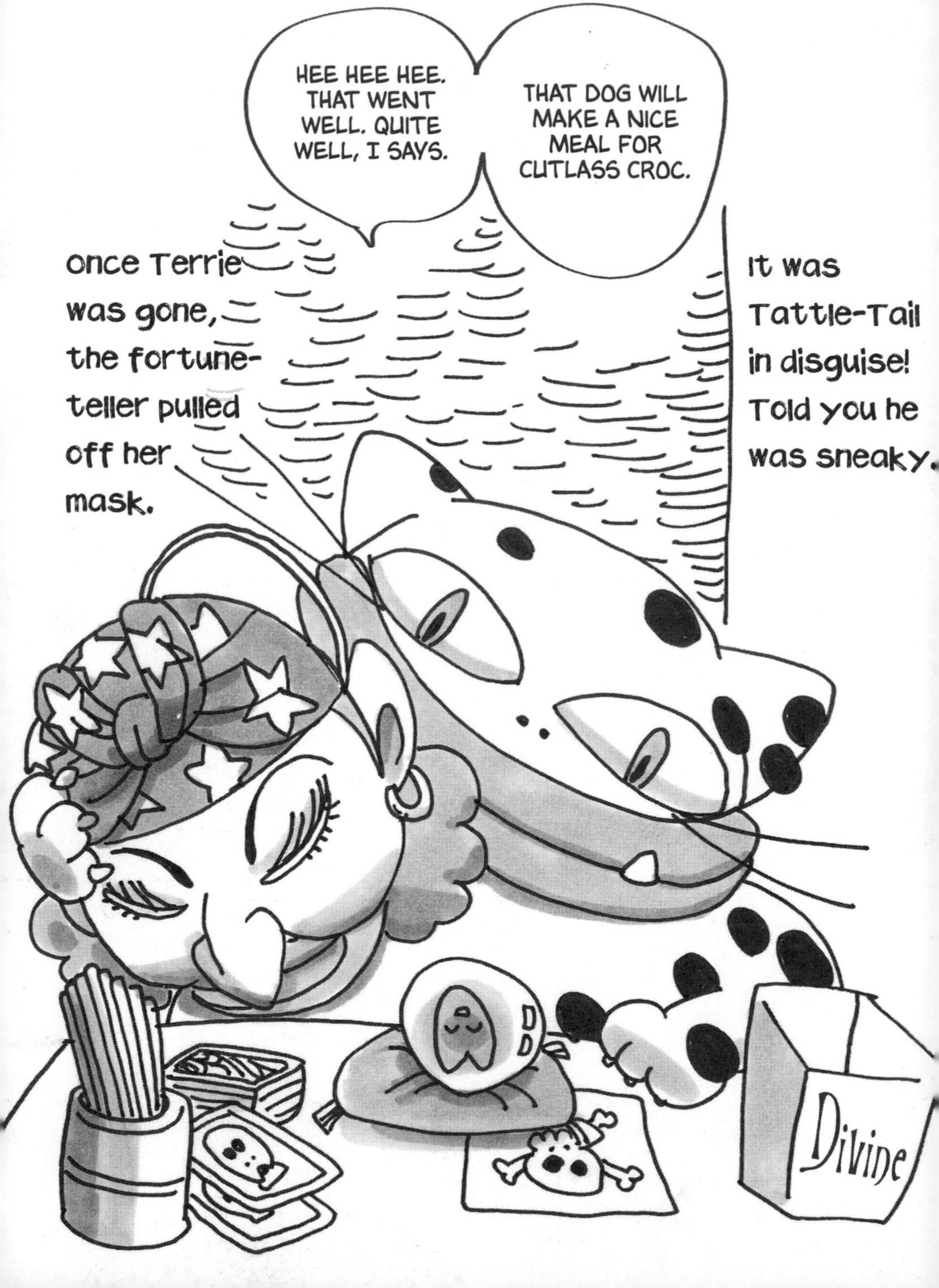
once Terrie was gone, the fortune-teller pulled off her mask.
HEE HEE HEE. THAT WENT WELL. QUITE WELL, I SAYS.
THAT DOG WILL MAKE A NICE MEAL FOR CUTLASS CROC.
It was Tattle-Tail in disguise! Told you he was sneaky.
Divine

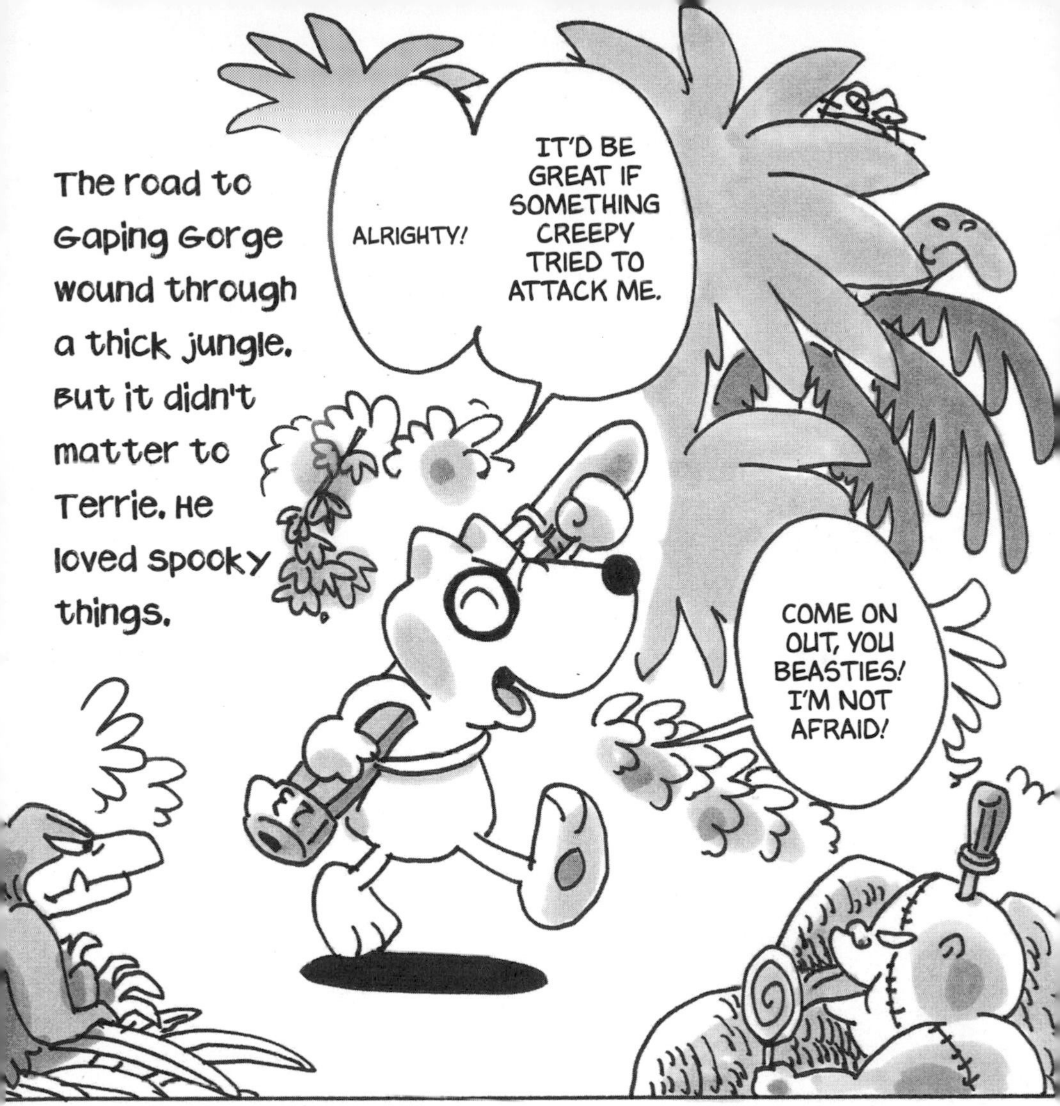
The road to Gaping Gorge wound through a thick jungle. But it didn't matter to Terrie. He loved spooky things.
ALRIGHTY!
IT'D BE GREAT IF SOMETHING CREEPY TRIED TO ATTACK ME.
COME ON OUT, YOU BEASTIES! I'M NOT AFRAID!

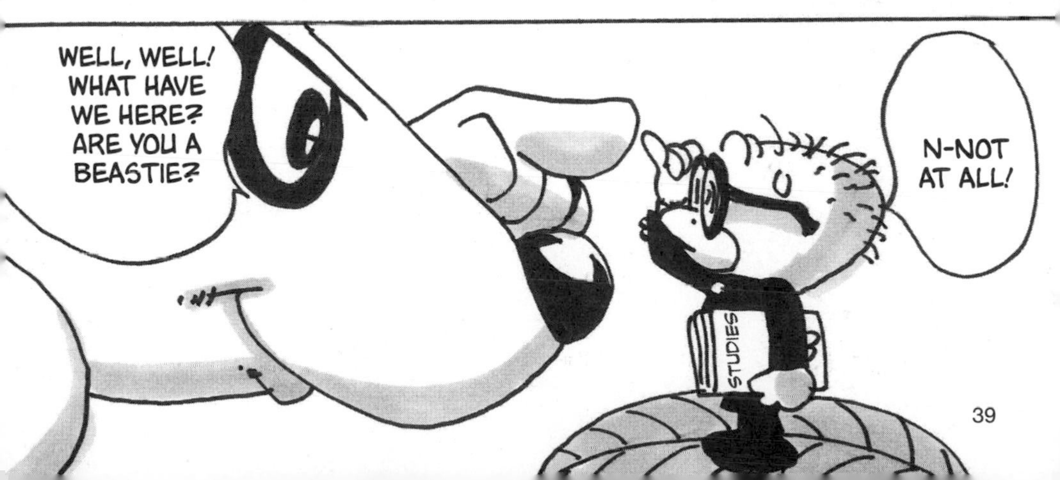
WELL, WELL! WHAT HAVE WE HERE? ARE YOU A BEASTIE?
N-NOT AT ALL!
STUDIES

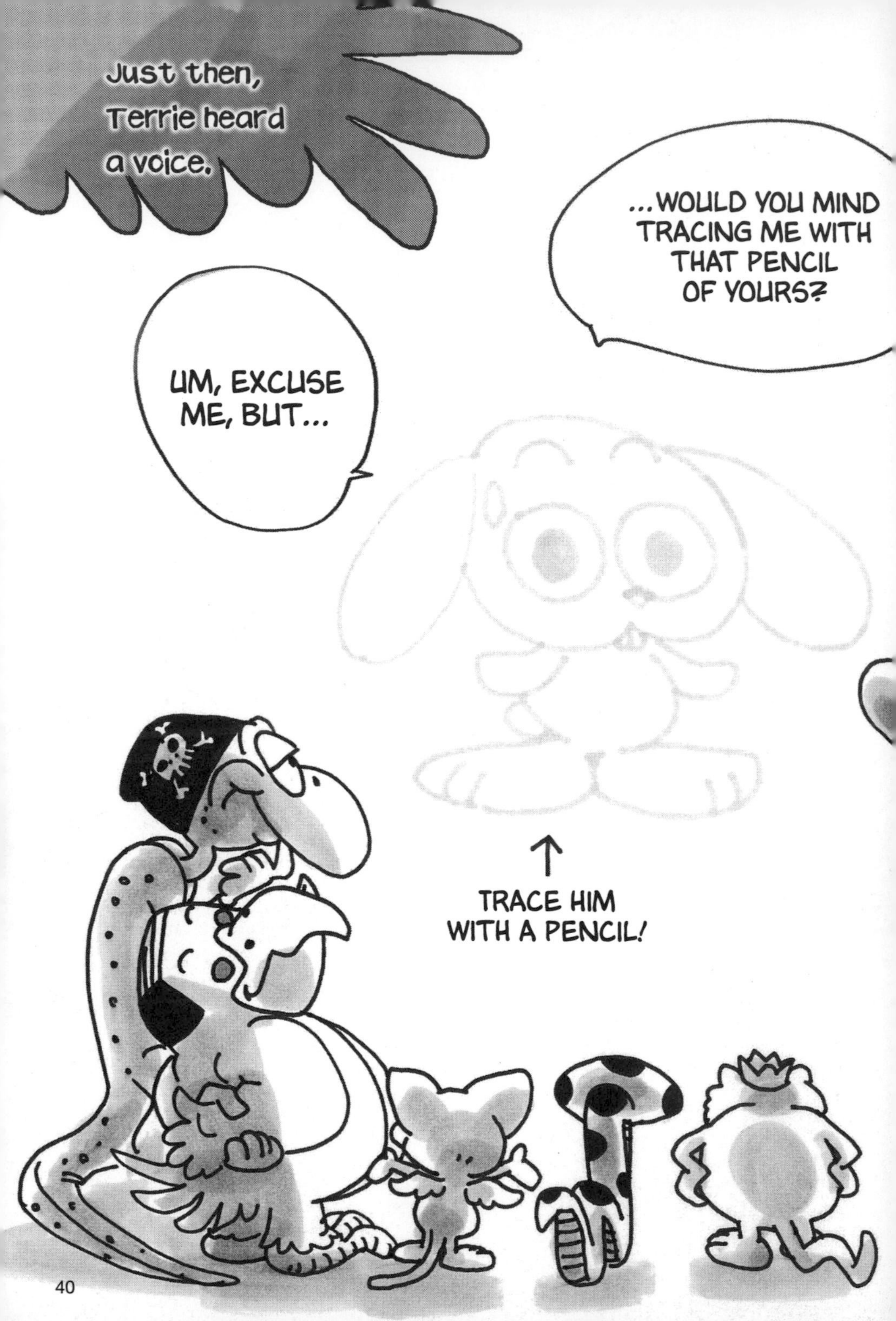
Just then,
Terrie heard
a voice.
UM, EXCUSE ME, BUT...
...WOULD YOU MIND TRACING ME WITH THAT PENCIL OF YOURS?
TRACE HIM WITH A PENCIL!

He had to look very carefully to find where the voice had come from. The creature who had spoken looked as if it had been almost completely erased.

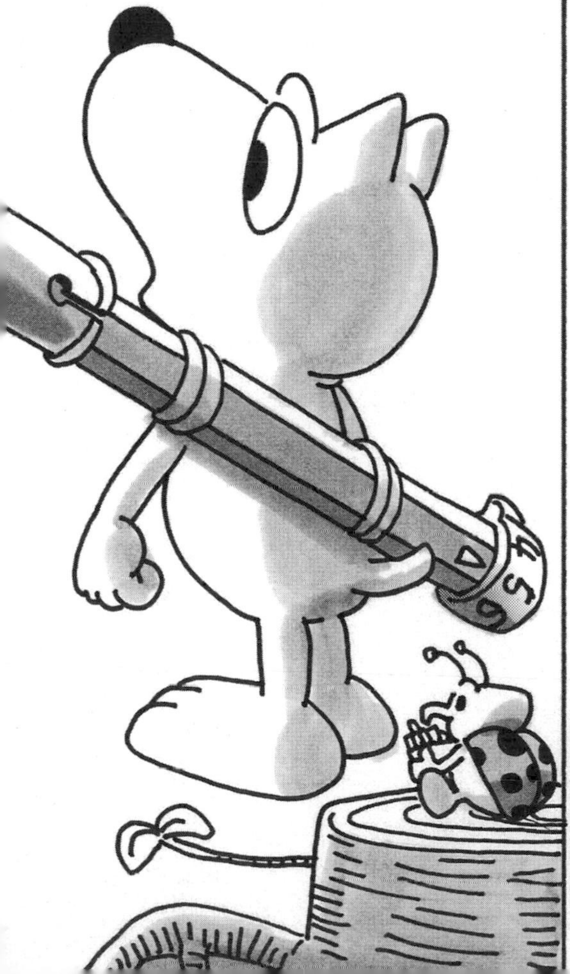

With the Magic Pencil, Terrie traced the creature...

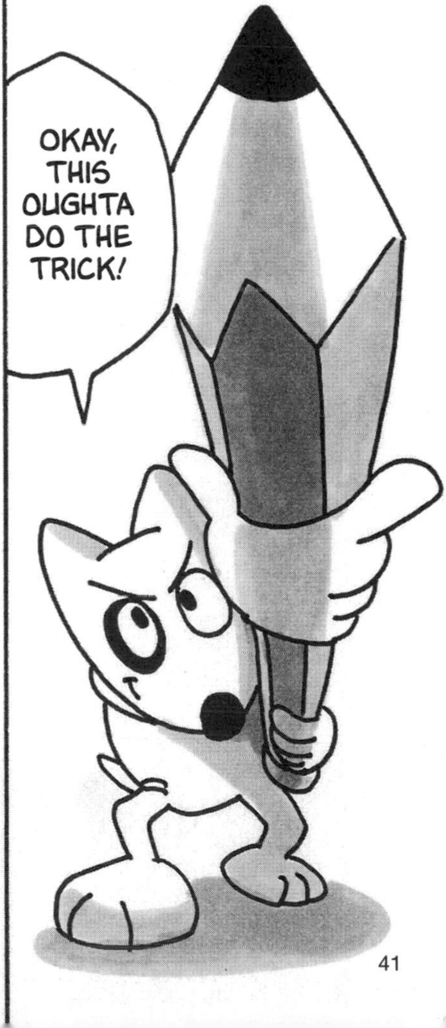
OKAY, THIS OUGHTA DO THE TRICK!

...and revealed a timid-looking rabbit!

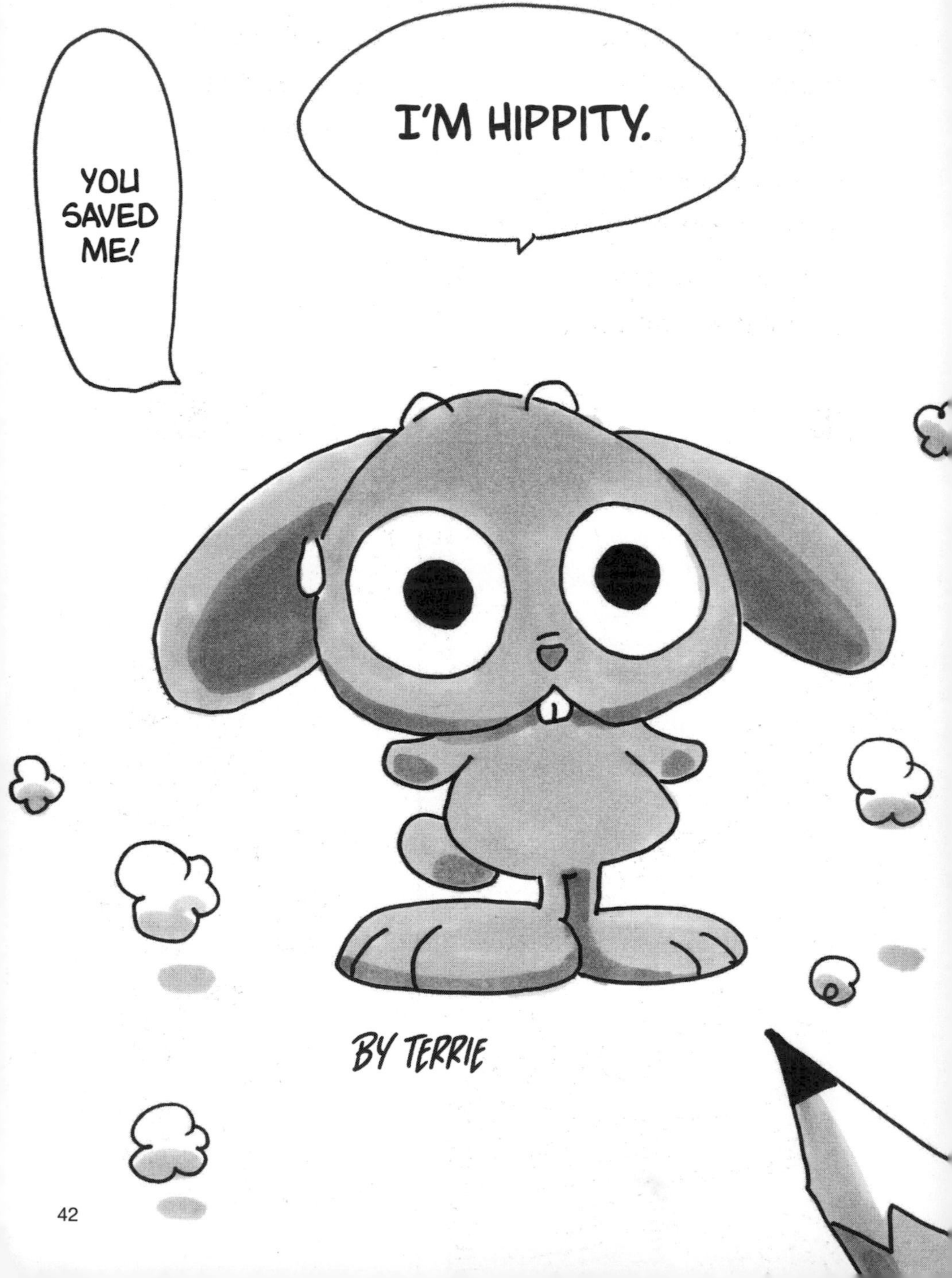
I'M HIPPITY.
YOU SAVED ME!
BY TERRIE

Hippity may have looked timid, but he was one brave bunny. He had tried to stand up to King Crossout, but the king, having no patience for defiance, had erased Hippity with the Eraser-o-Doom.

But now that Hippity was back to his old self, he was ready to join Terrie on his quest.

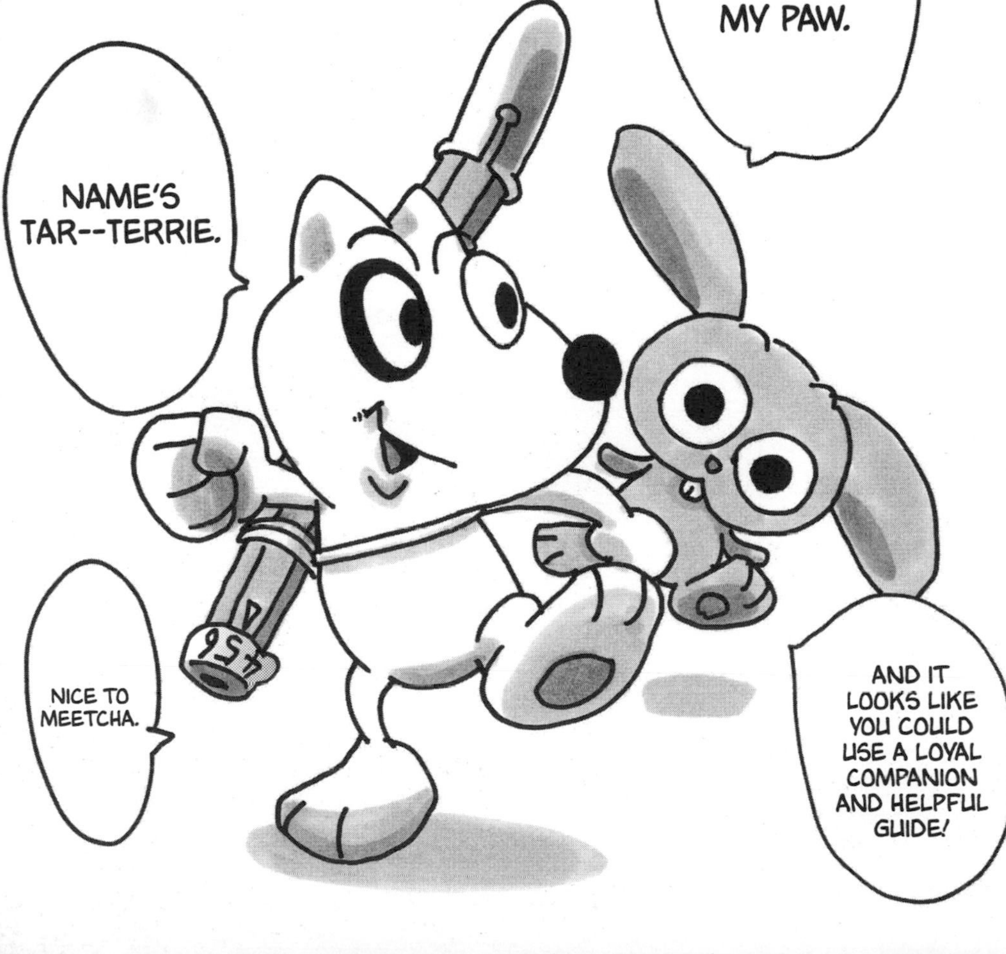
I KNOW THIS PLACE LIKE THE BACK OF MY PAW.
AND IT LOOKS LIKE YOU COULD USE A LOYAL COMPANION AND HELPFUL GUIDE!
NAME'S TAR--TERRIE.
NICE TO MEETCHA.

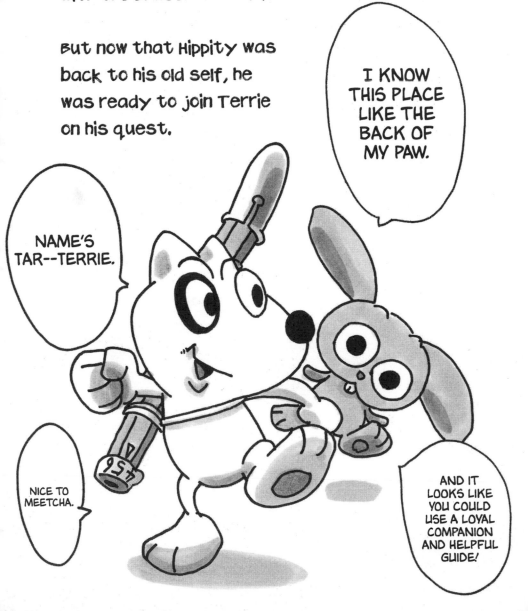

Battle at Gaping Gorge

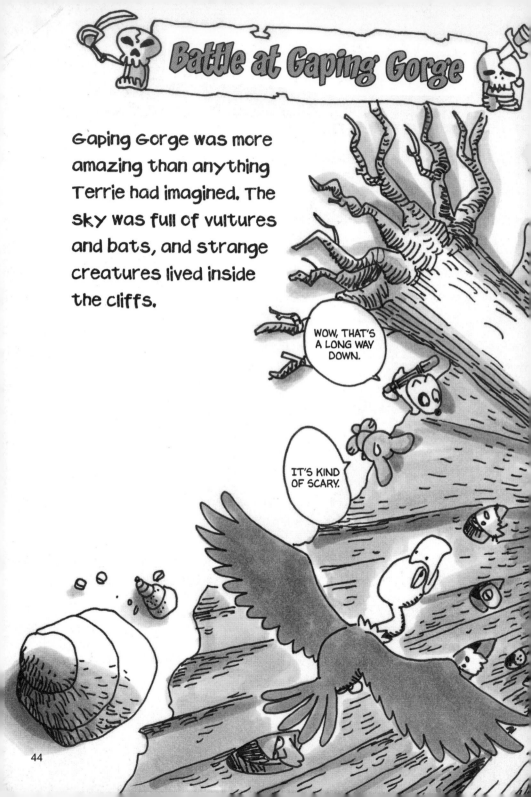

Gaping Gorge was more amazing than anything Terrie had imagined. The sky was full of vultures and bats, and strange creatures lived inside the cliffs.

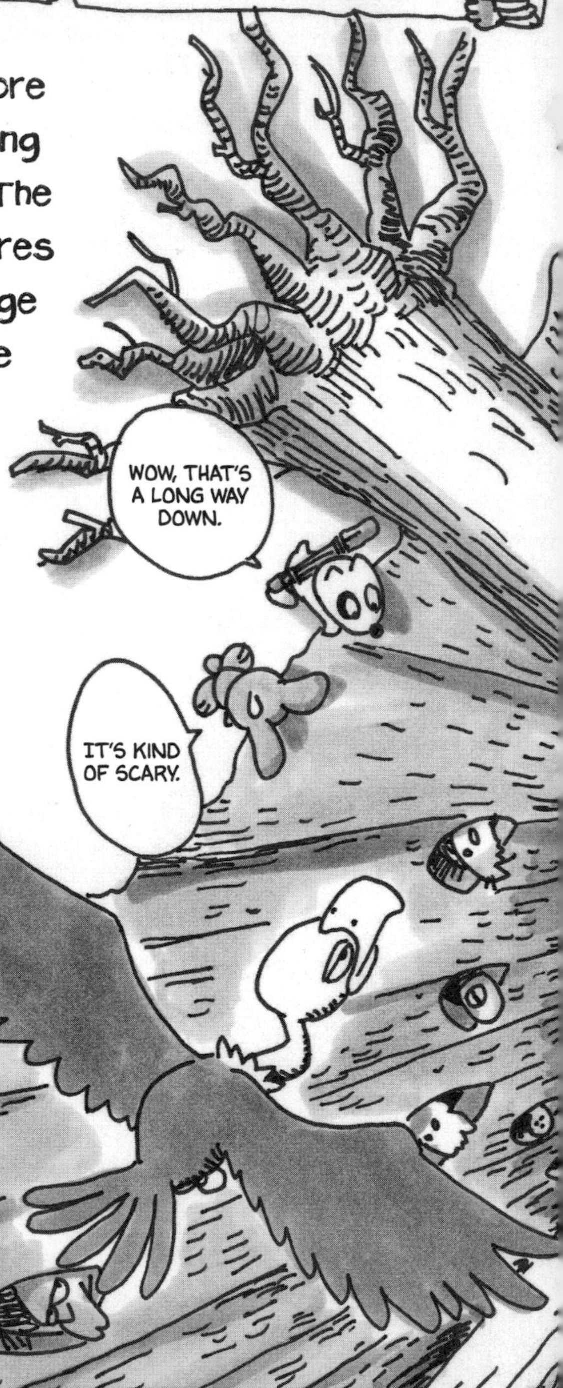
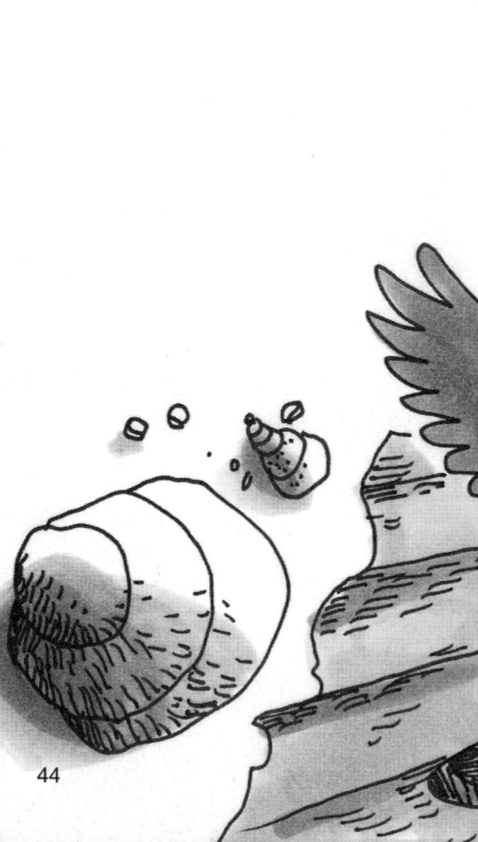
WOW, THAT'S A LONG WAY DOWN.
IT'S KIND OF SCARY.

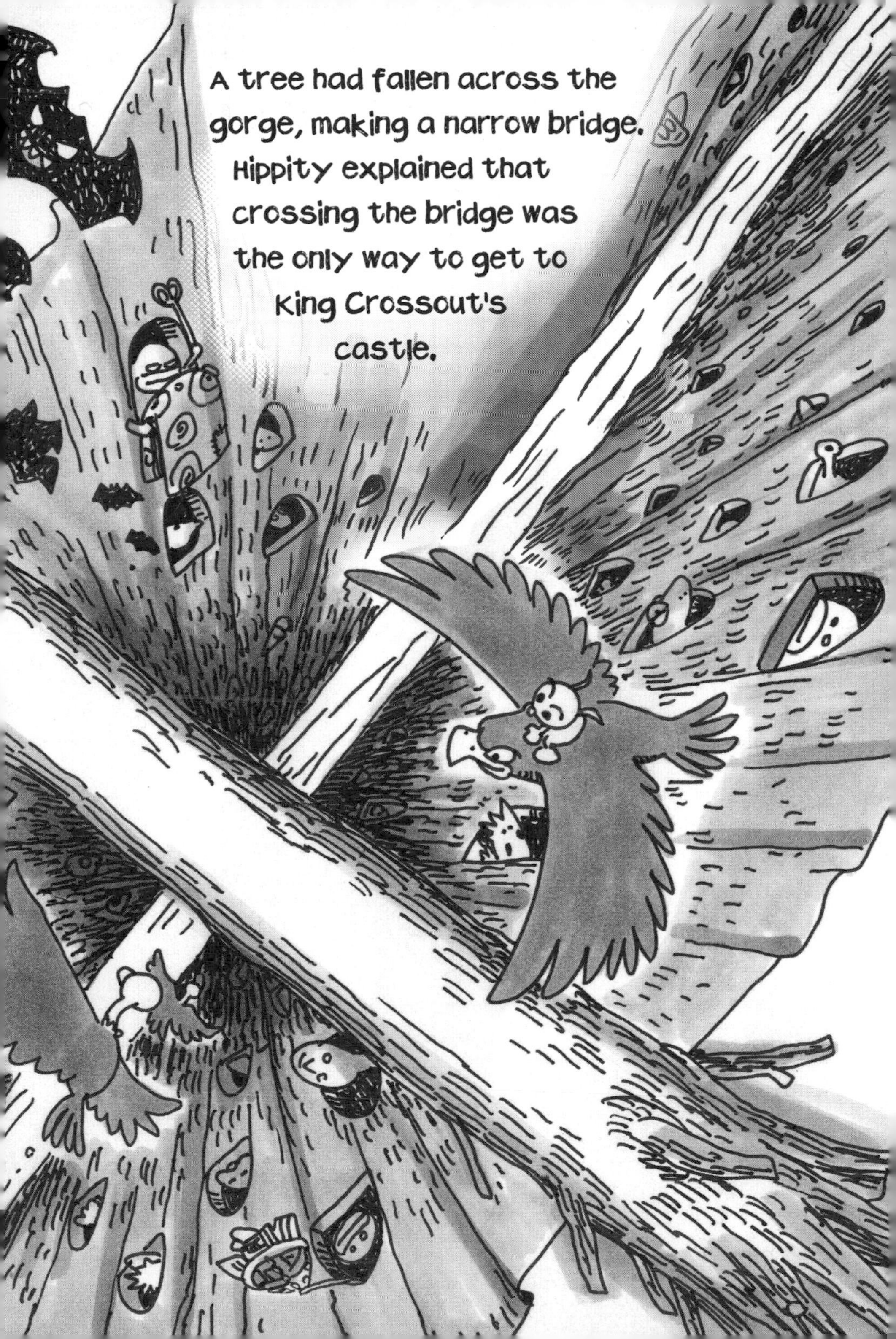
A tree had fallen across the gorge, making a narrow bridge. Hippity explained that crossing the bridge was the only way to get to King Crossout's castle.

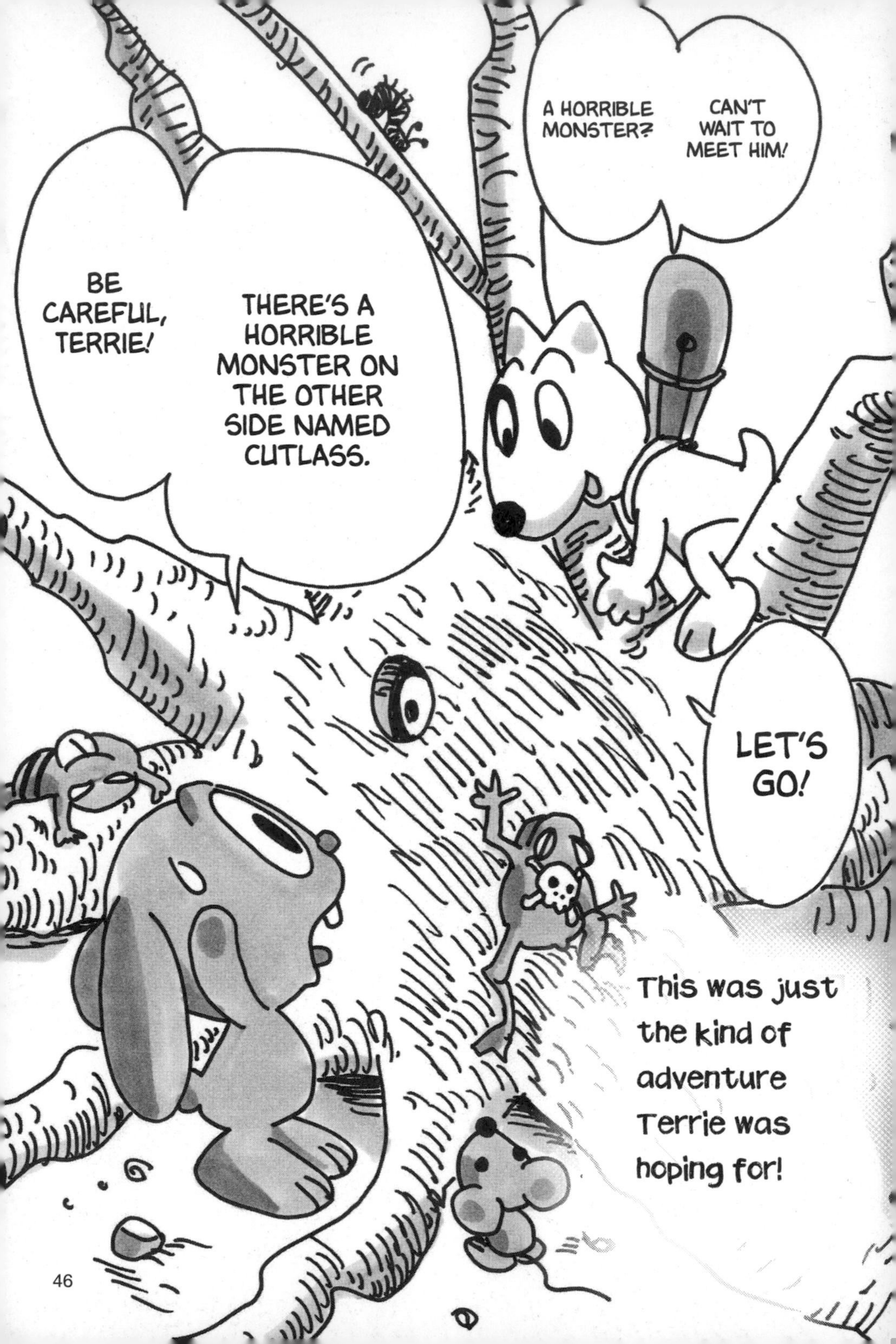
BE CAREFUL, TERRIE!
THERE'S A HORRIBLE MONSTER ON THE OTHER SIDE NAMED CUTLASS.
A HORRIBLE MONSTER?
CAN'T WAIT TO MEET HIM!
LET'S GO!
This was just the kind of adventure Terrie was hoping for!

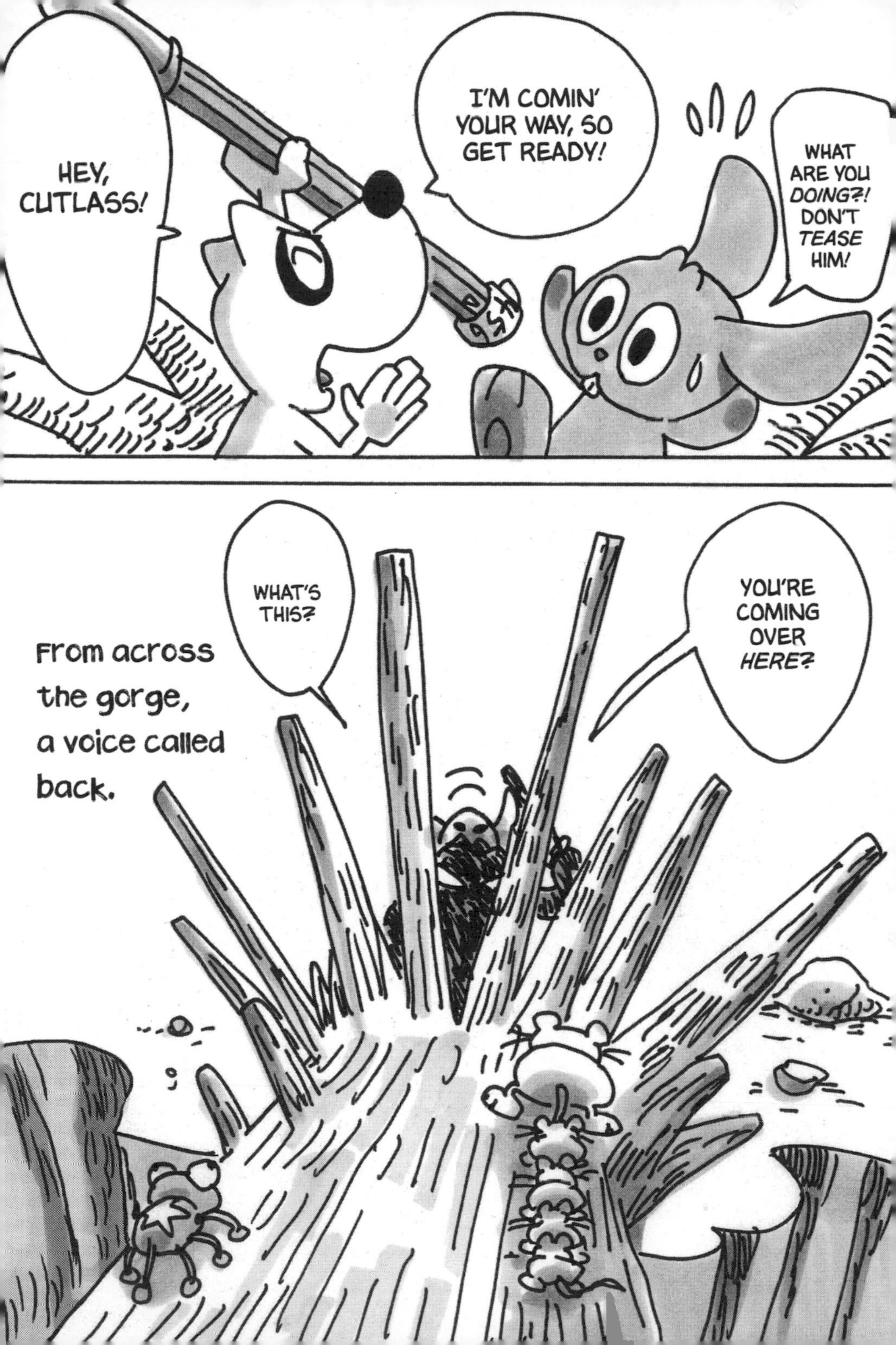
HEY, CUTLASS!
I'M COMIN' YOUR WAY, SO GET READY!
WHAT ARE YOU *DOING?!* DON'T *TEASE* HIM!
From across the gorge, a voice called back.
WHAT'S THIS?
YOU'RE COMING OVER *HERE?*

Cutlass Croc was a bad baddie. He never lost a battle, and he tossed everyone he defeated into the gorge.

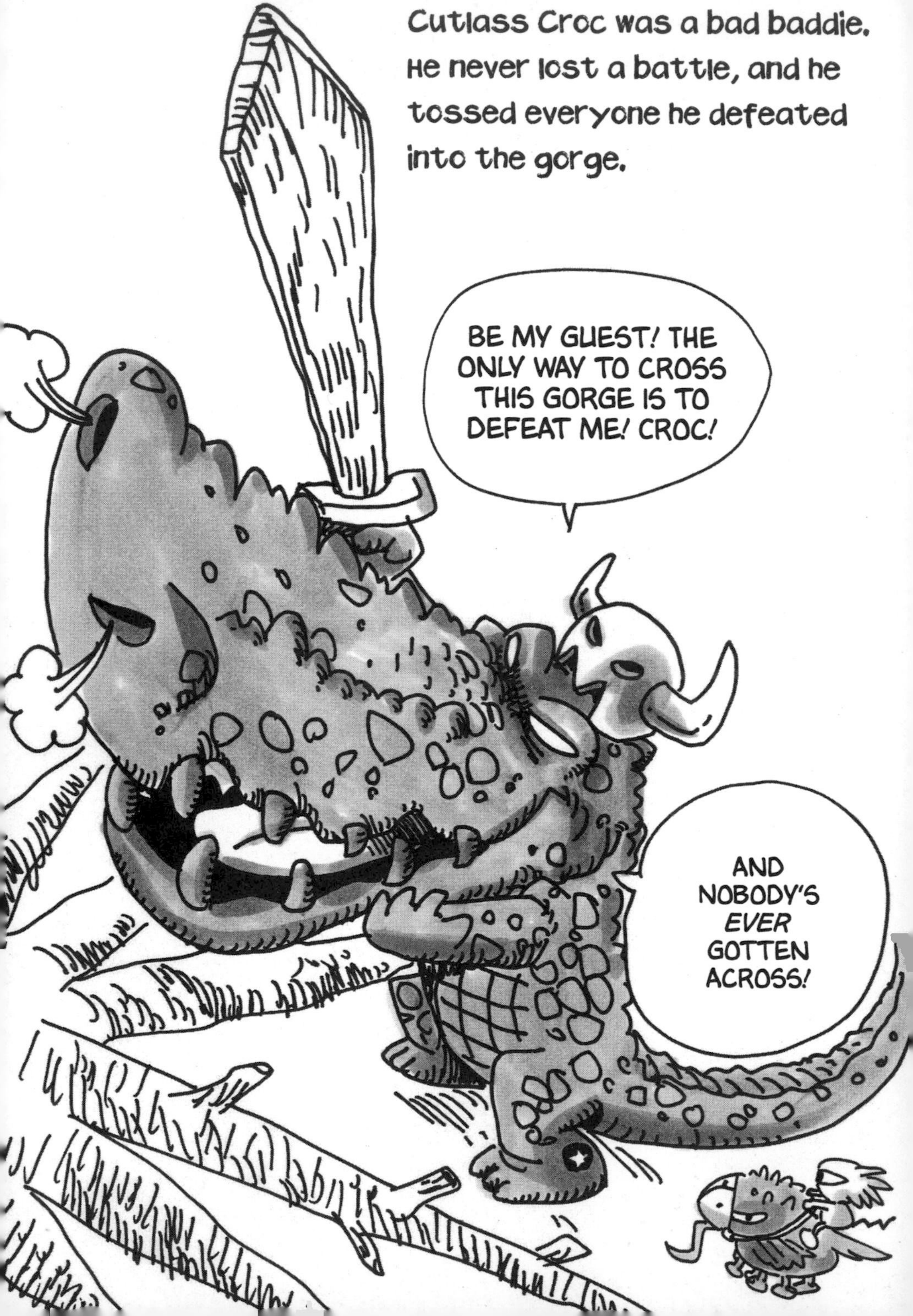
BE MY GUEST! THE ONLY WAY TO CROSS THIS GORGE IS TO DEFEAT ME! CROC!
AND NOBODY'S *EVER* GOTTEN ACROSS!

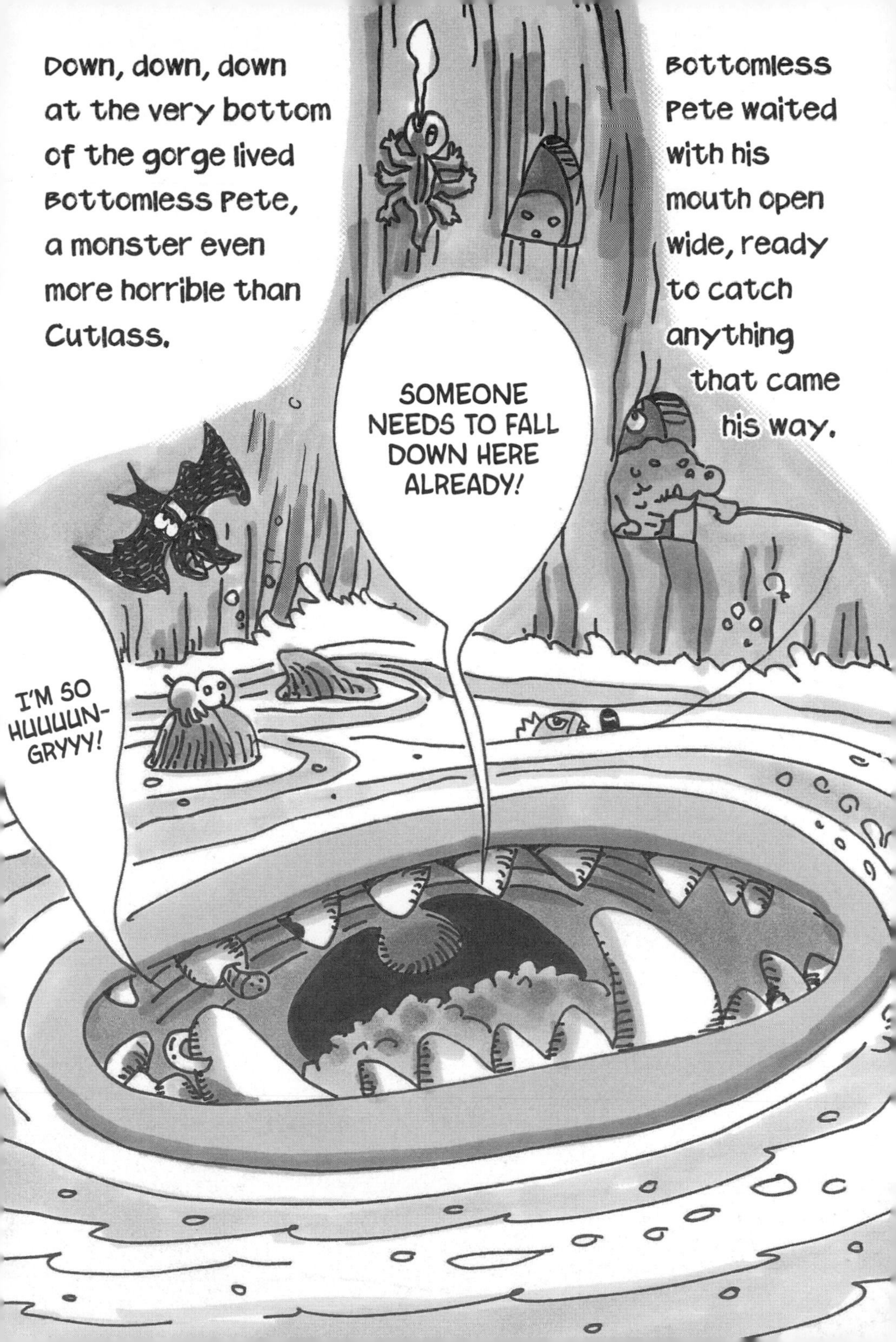
Down, down, down at the very bottom of the gorge lived Bottomless Pete, a monster even more horrible than Cutlass.
Bottomless Pete waited with his mouth open wide, ready to catch anything that came his way.
SOMEONE NEEDS TO FALL DOWN HERE ALREADY!
I'M SO HUUUUN-GRYYY!

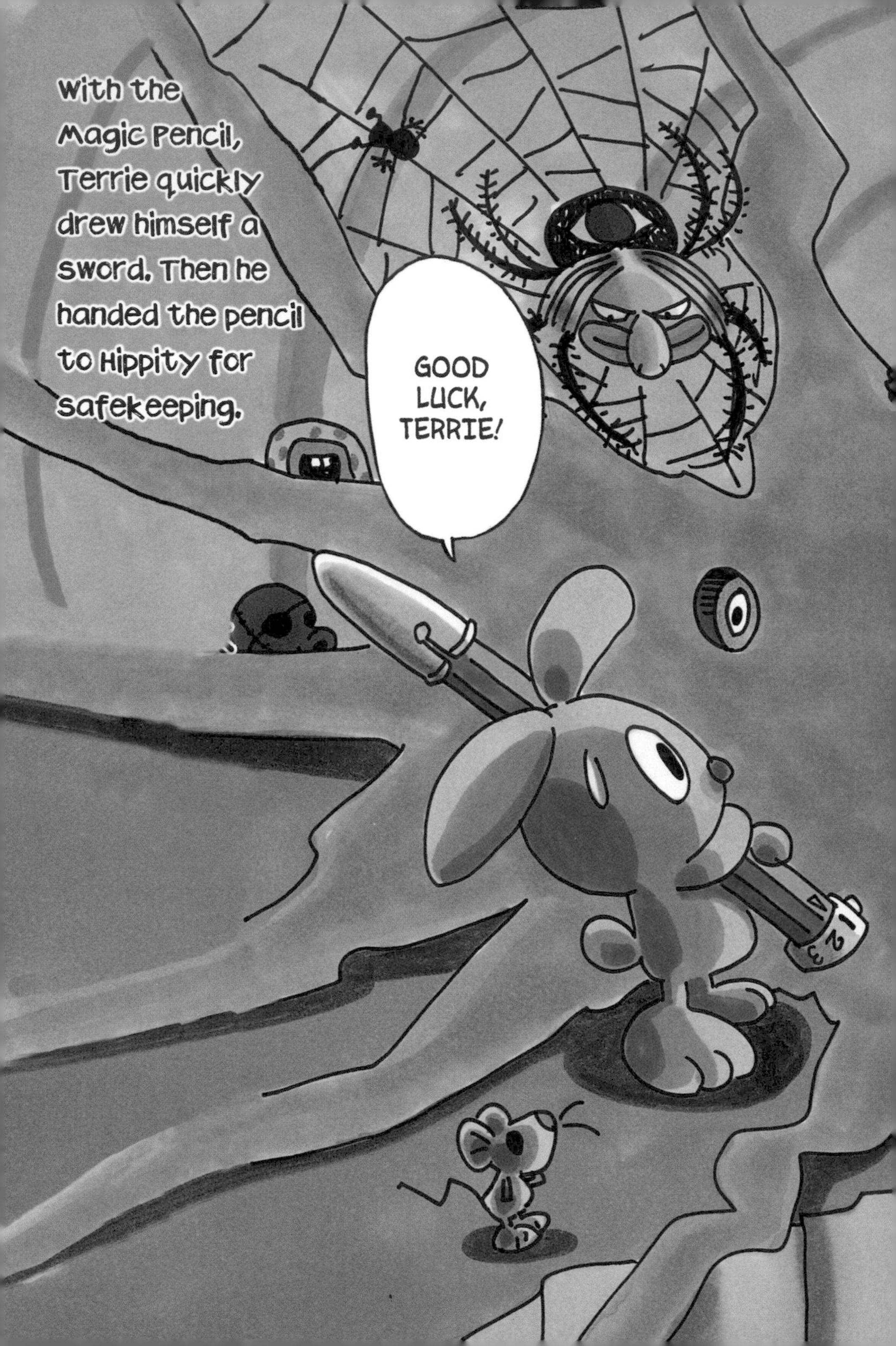
With the Magic Pencil, Terrie quickly drew himself a sword. Then he handed the pencil to Hippity for safekeeping.
GOOD LUCK, TERRIE!

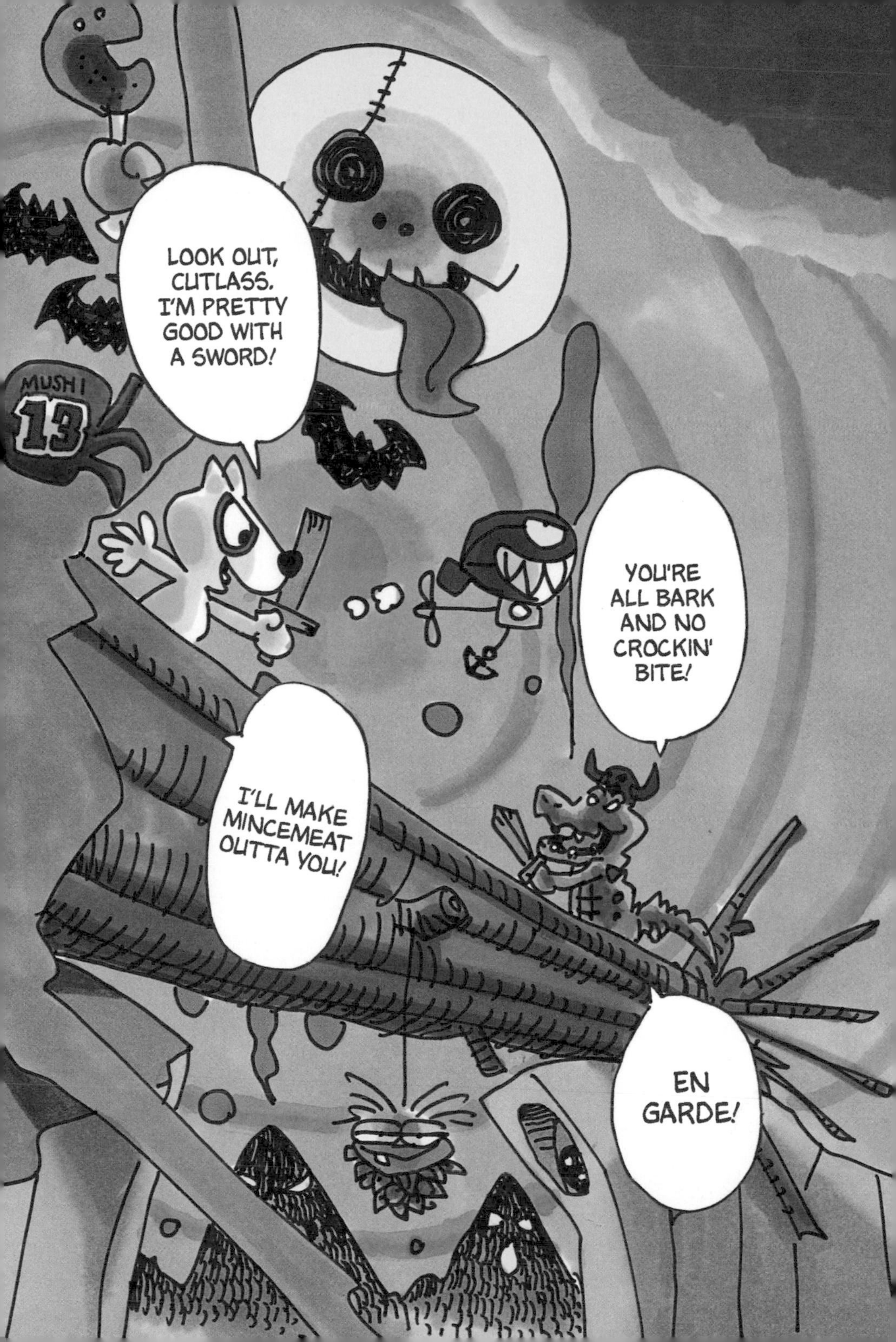
MUSHI 13
LOOK OUT, CUTLASS. I'M PRETTY GOOD WITH A SWORD!
YOU'RE ALL BARK AND NO CROCKIN' BITE!
I'LL MAKE MINCEMEAT OUTTA YOU!
EN GARDE!

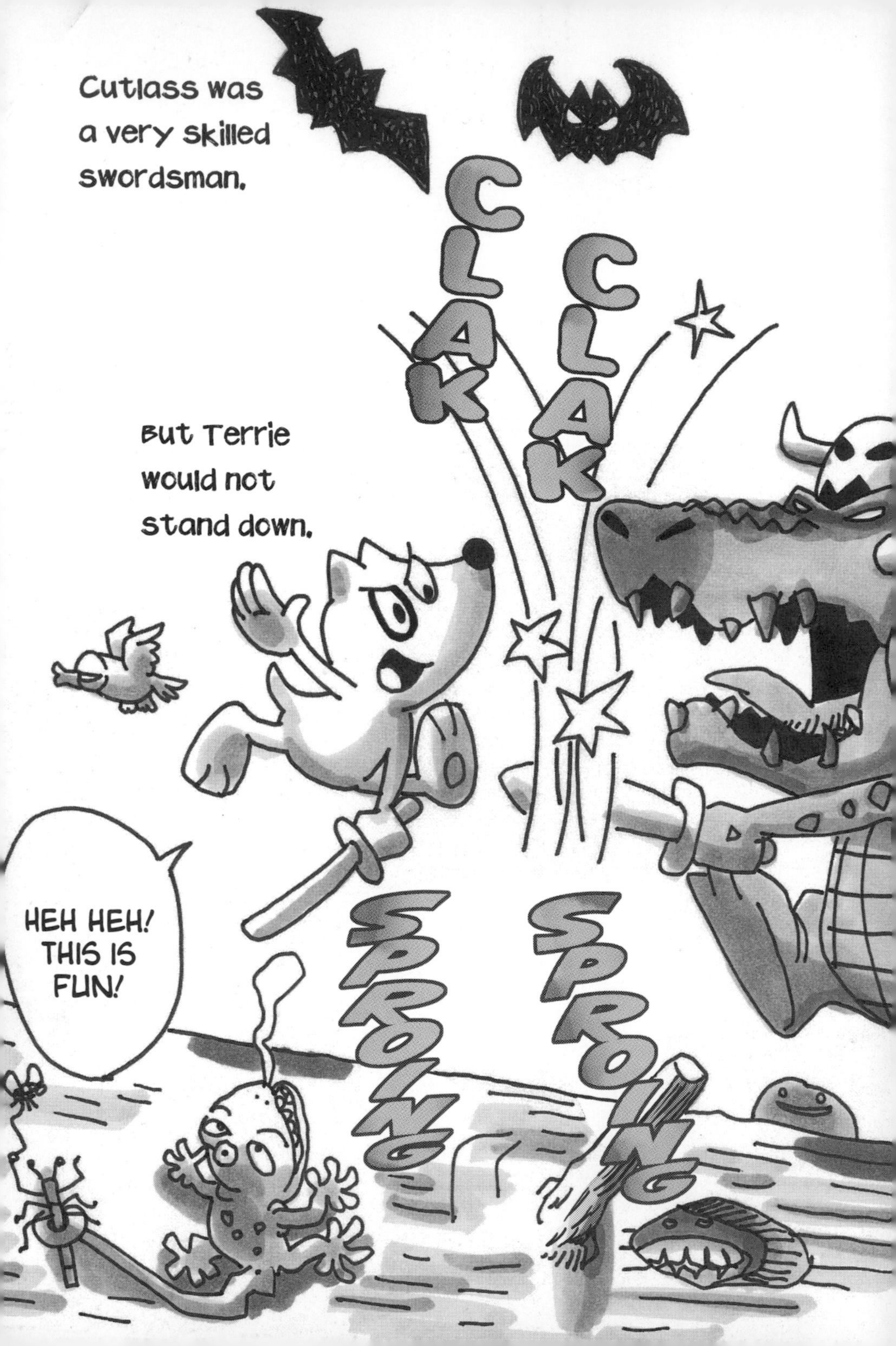
Cutlass was a very skilled swordsman.
CLAK CLAK
But Terrie would not stand down.
HEH HEH! THIS IS FUN!
SPROING SPROING

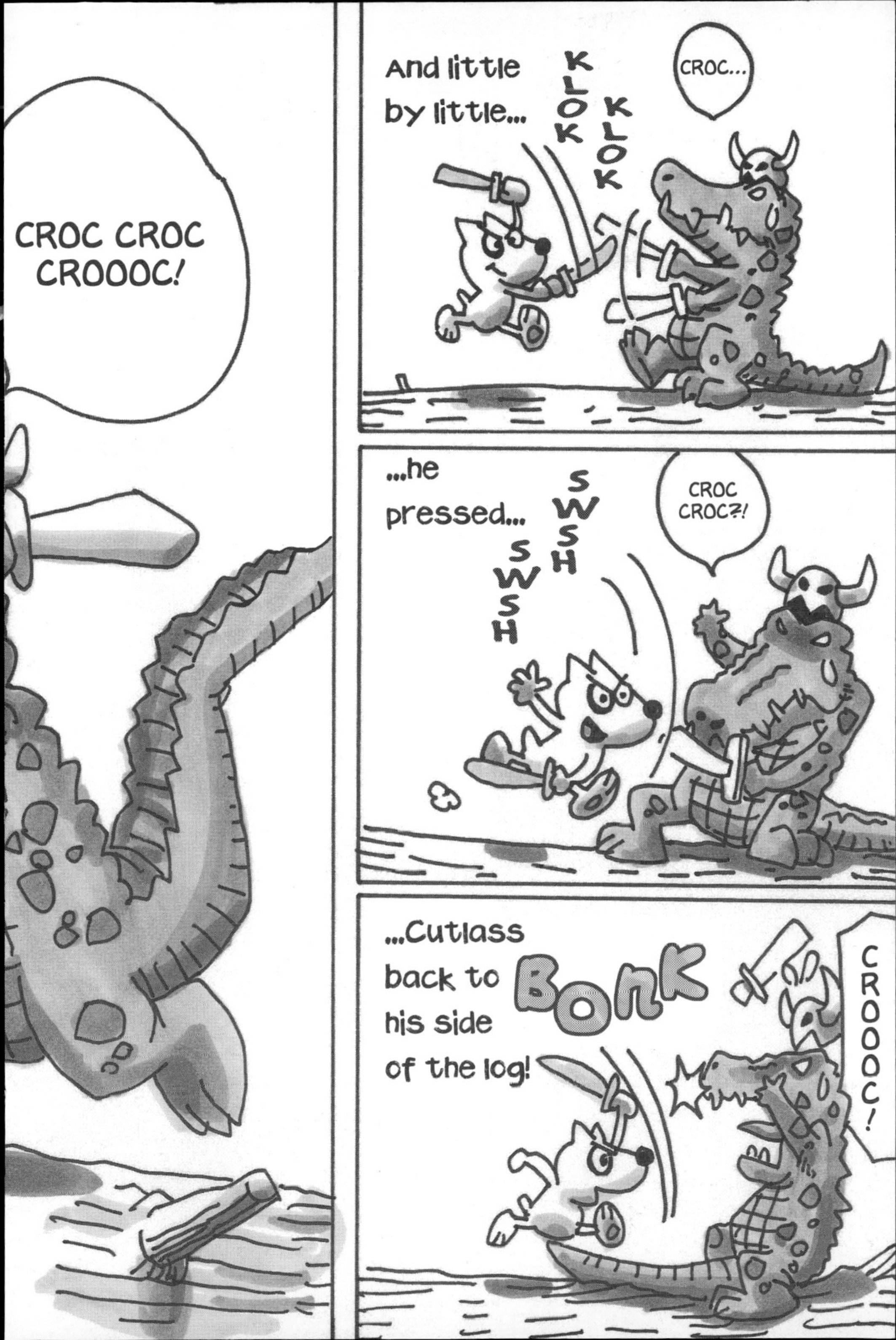
CROC...
KLOK KLOK
And little by little...
CROC CROC?!
SWSH SWSH
...he pressed...
CROOOOC!
BONK
...Cutlass back to his side of the log!
CROC CROC CROOOC!

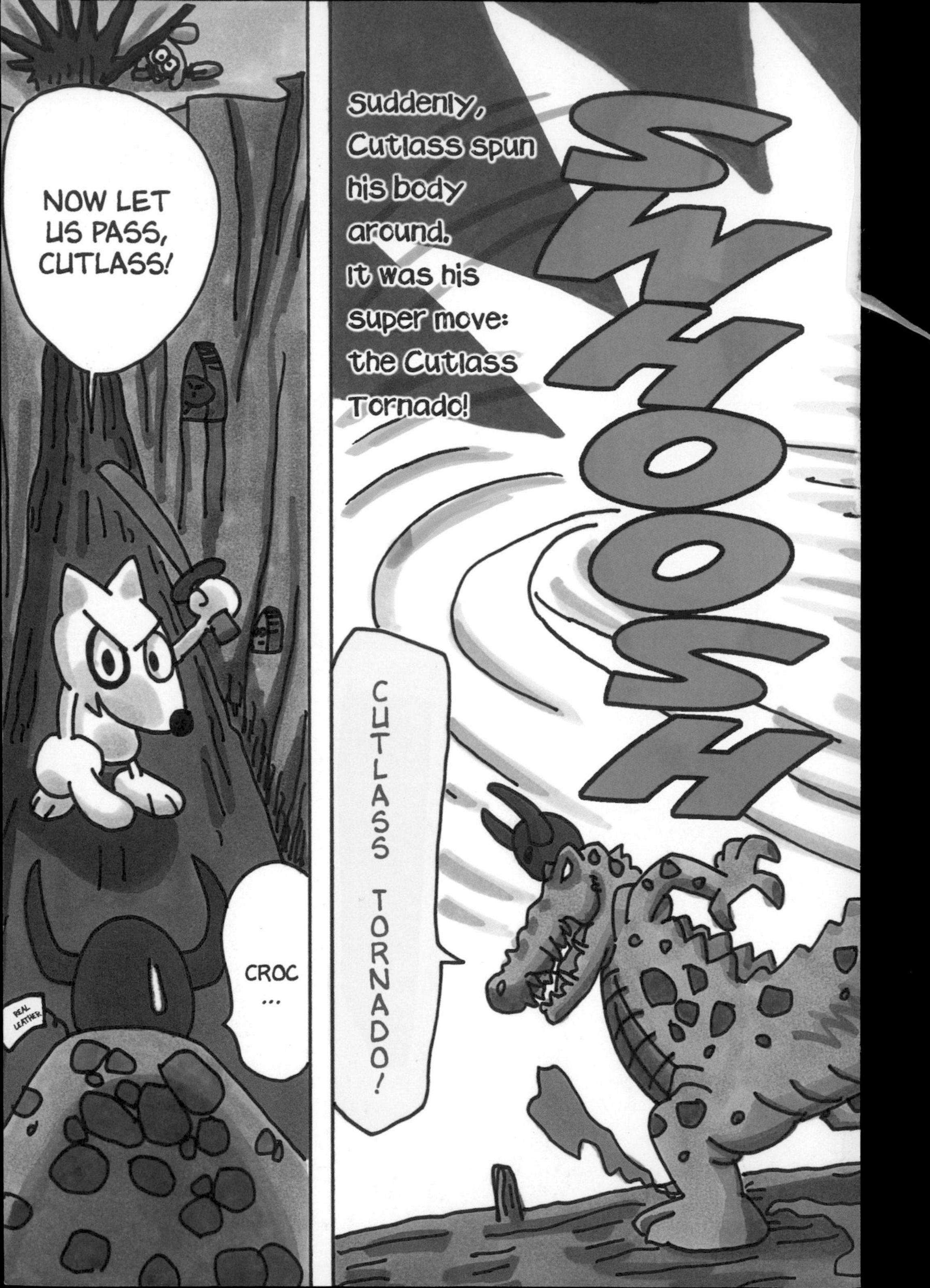
NOW LET US PASS, CUTLASS!
REAL LEATHER
CROC ...
Suddenly, Cutlass spun his body around. It was his super move: the Cutlass Tornado!
SWHOOSH
CUTLASS TORNADO!

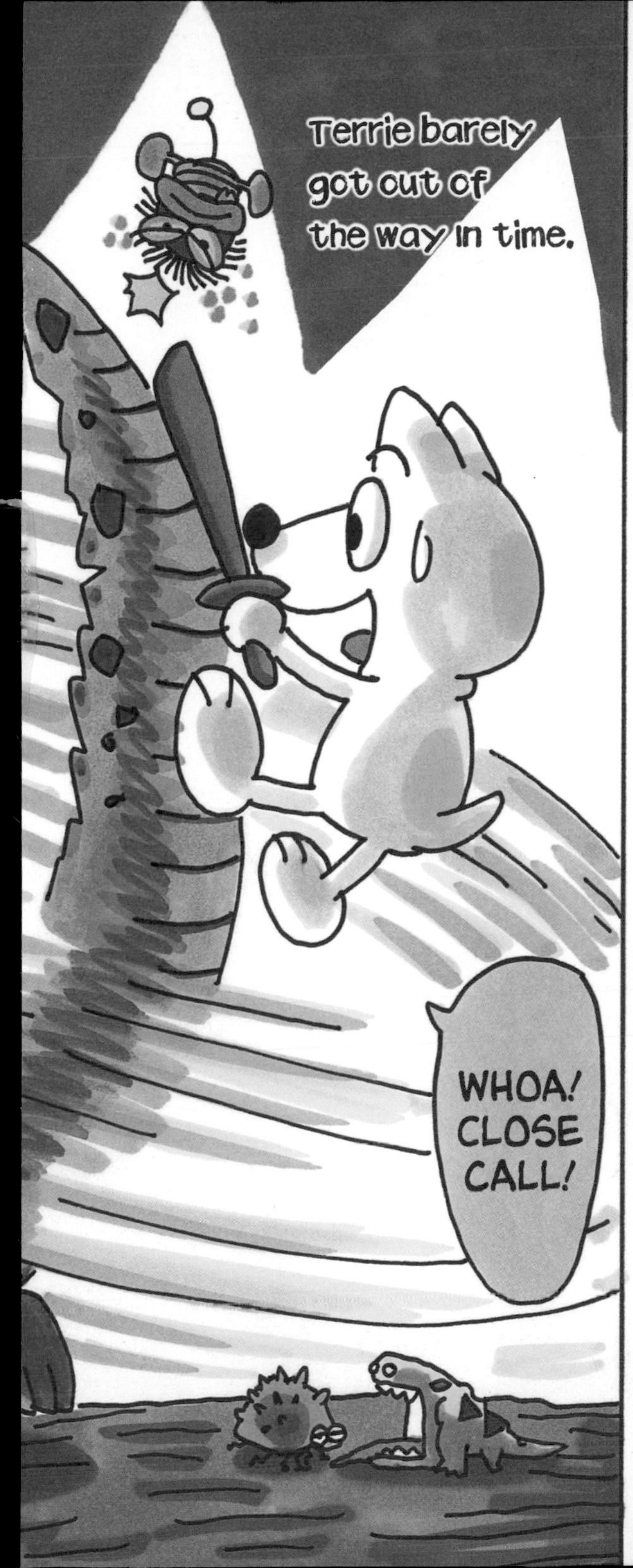
Terrie barely got out of the way in time.
WHOA! CLOSE CALL!
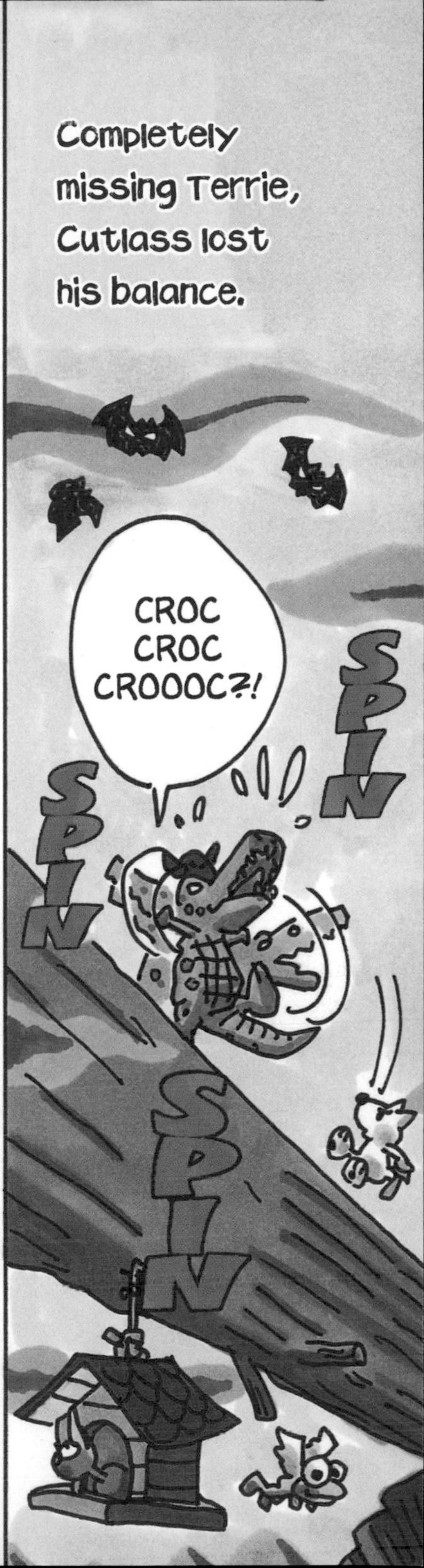
Completely missing Terrie, Cutlass lost his balance.
CROC CROC CROOOC?!
SPIN
SPIN
SPIN

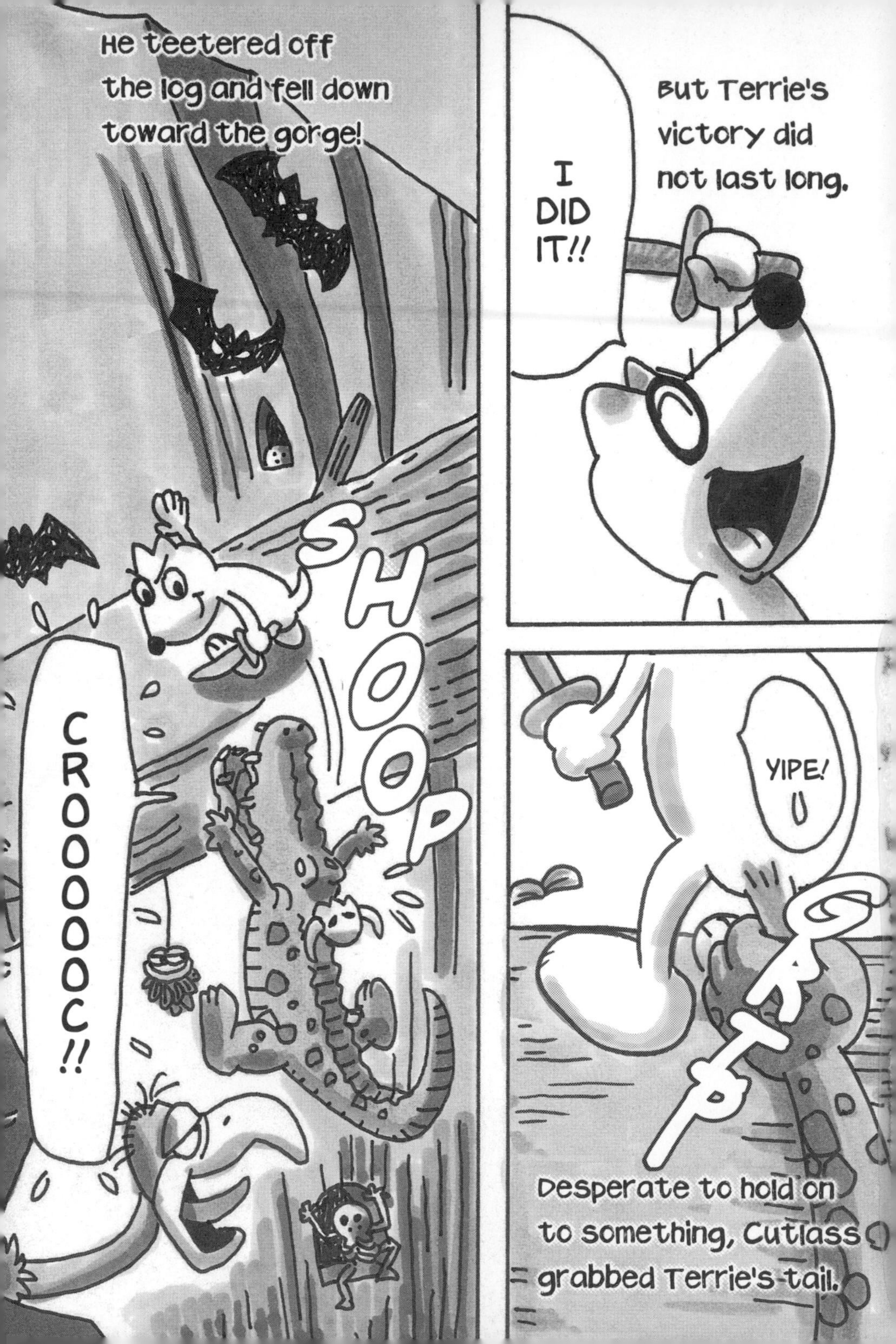
He teetered off the log and fell down toward the gorge!
SHOOP
CROOOOOOC!!
I DID IT!!
But Terrie's victory did not last long.
YIPE!
GRIP
Desperate to hold on to something, Cutlass grabbed Terrie's tail.

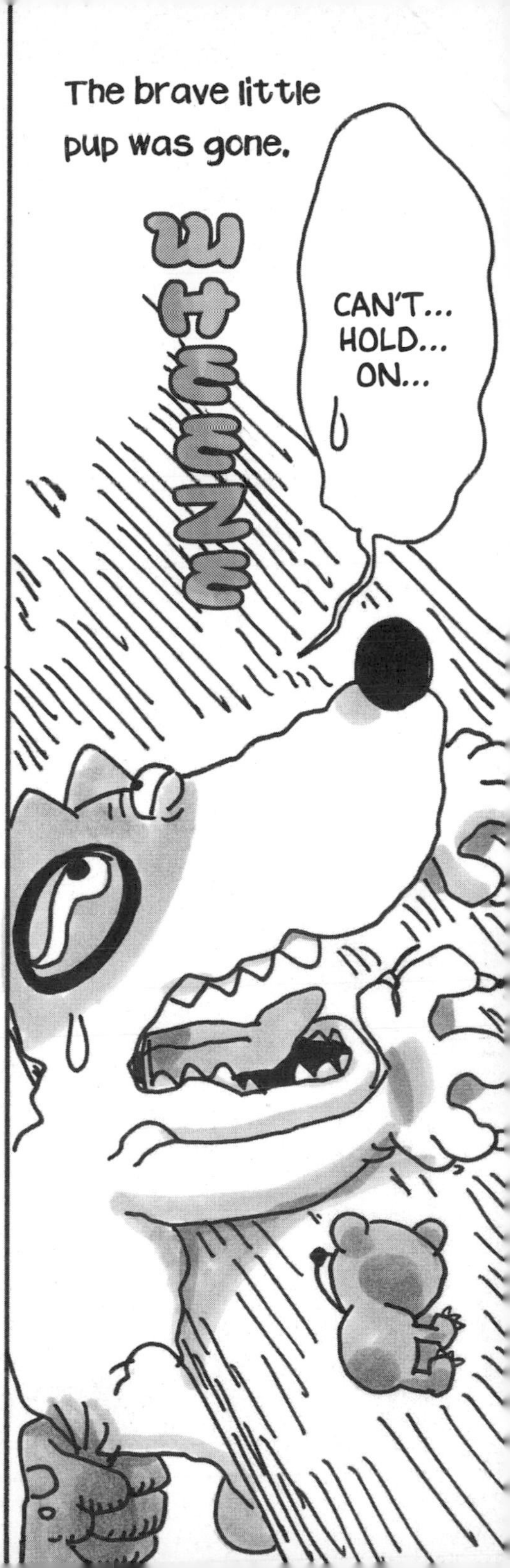
The brave little pup was gone.
WHEENE
CAN'T... HOLD... ON...
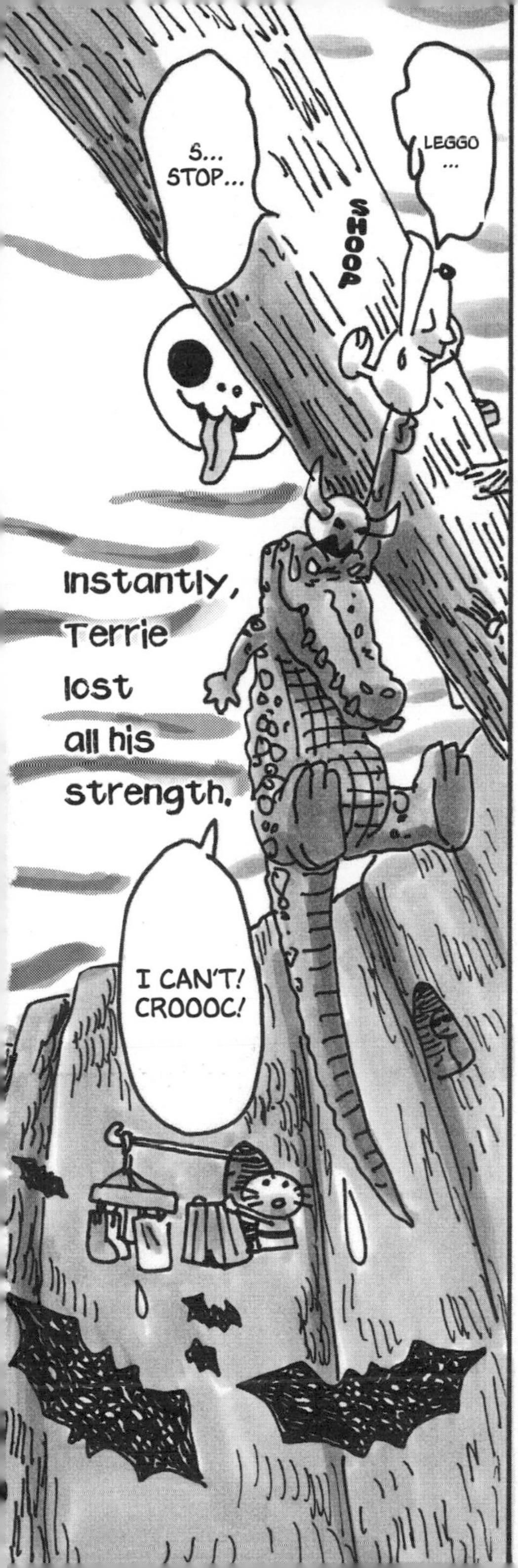
LEGGO ...
SHOOP
S... STOP...
Instantly, Terrie lost all his strength.
I CAN'T! CROOOC!

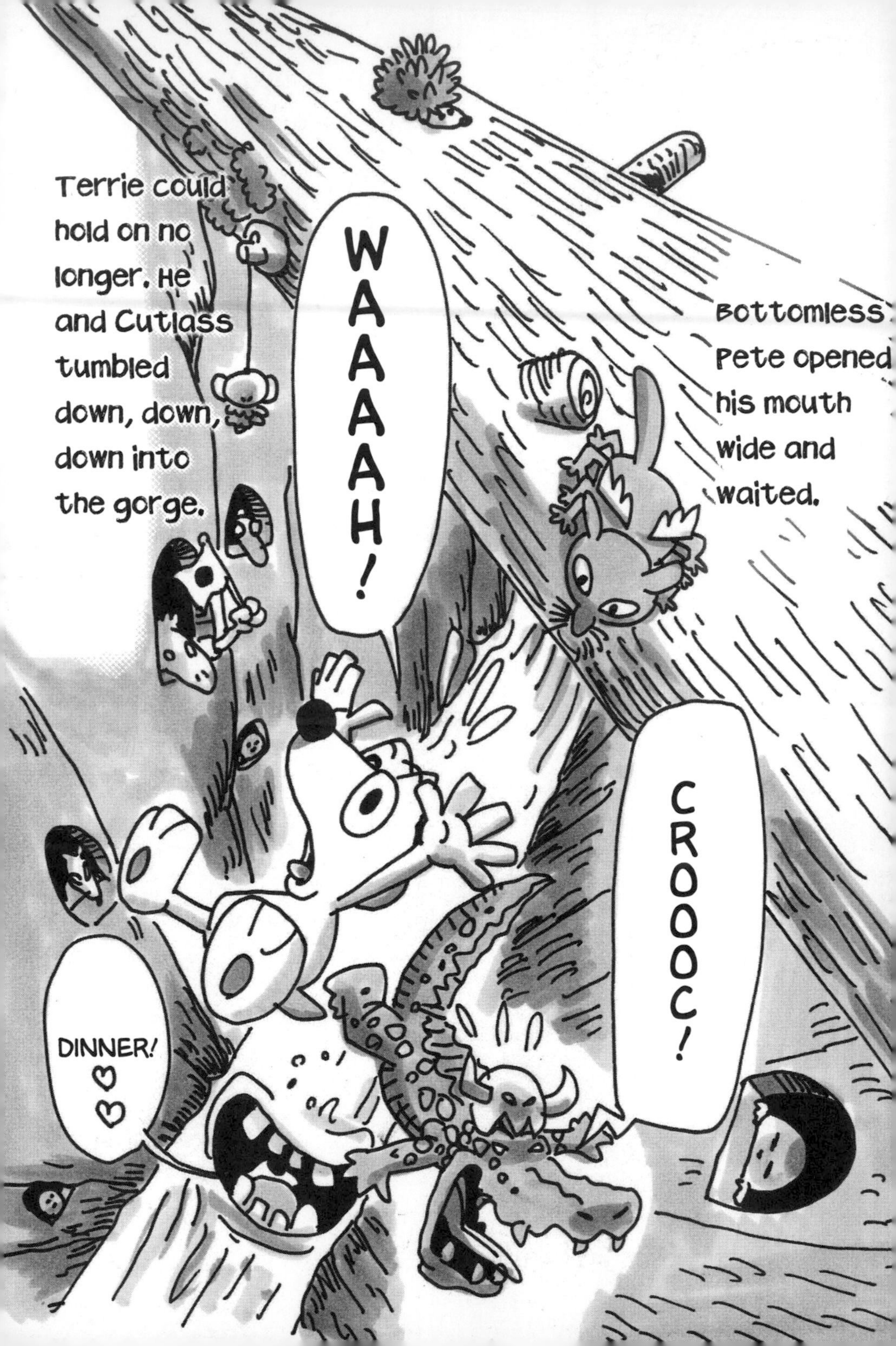
Bottomless Pete opened his mouth wide and waited.
Terrie could hold on no longer. He and Cutlass tumbled down, down, down into the gorge.
WAAAAAH!
CROOOOC!
DINNER! ♡ ♡

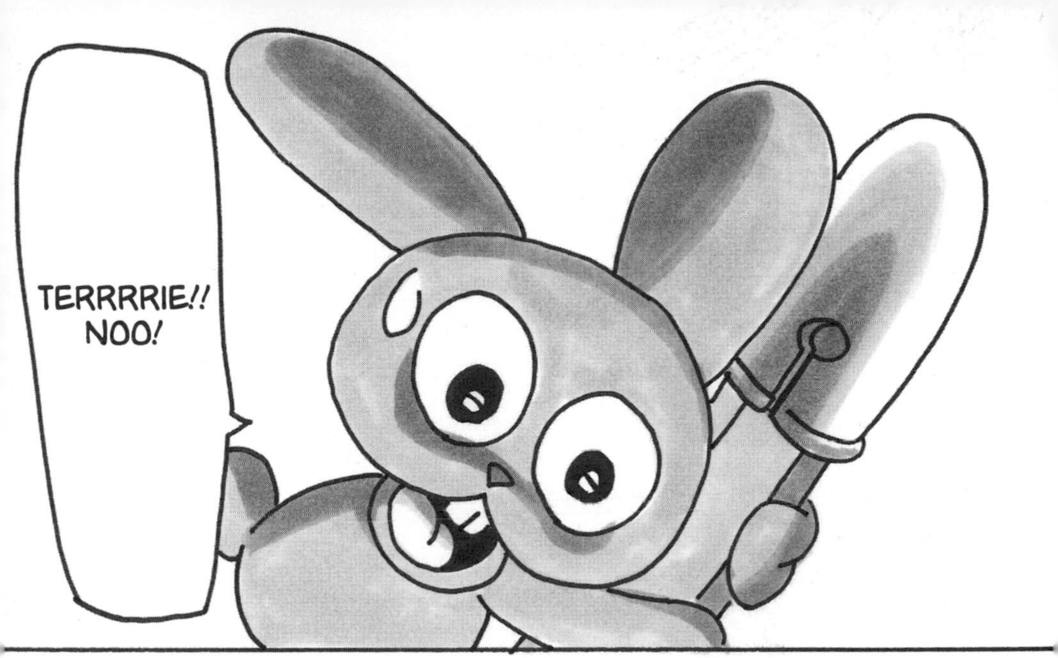
TERRRRIE!! NOO!

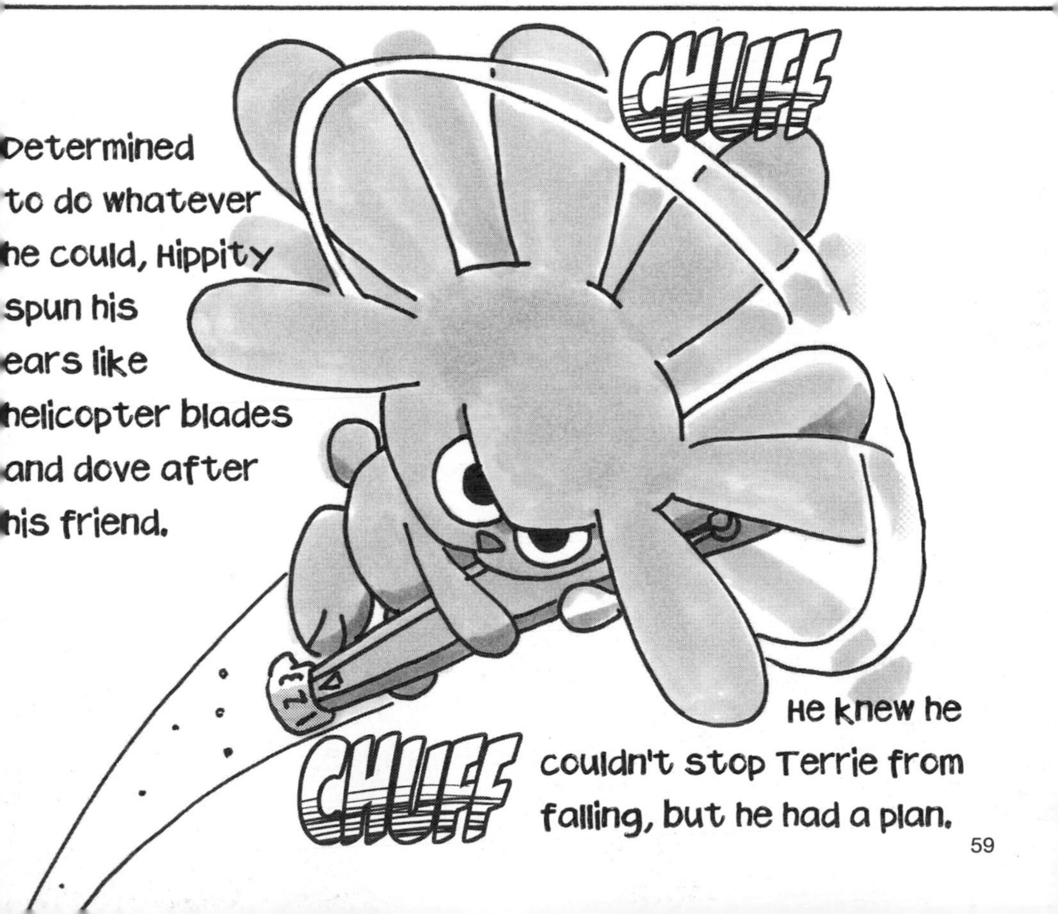
CHUFF
Determined to do whatever he could, Hippity spun his ears like helicopter blades and dove after his friend.
He knew he couldn't stop Terrie from falling, but he had a plan.
CHUFF

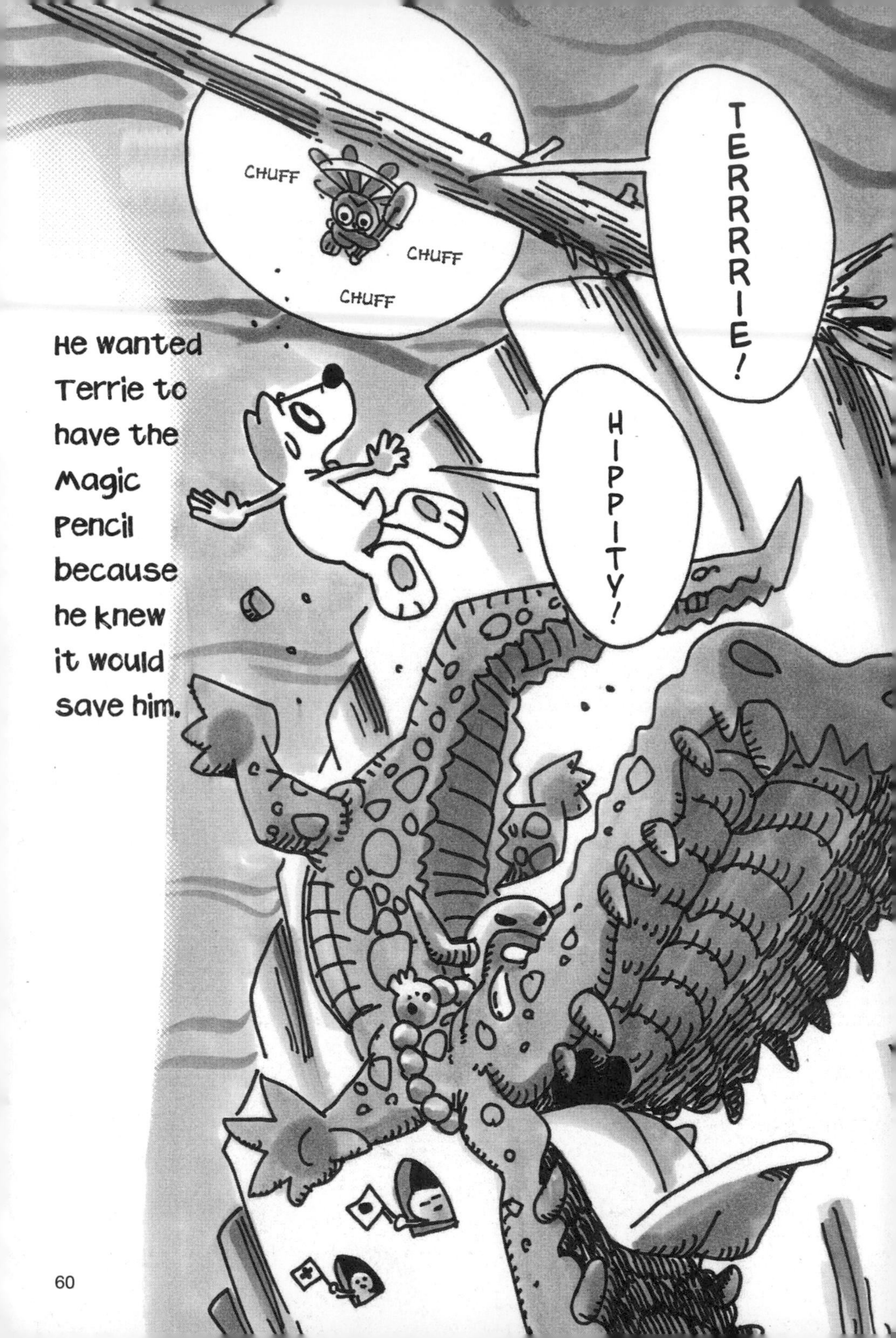
TERRRRIE!
HIPPITY!
CHUFF
CHUFF
CHUFF
He wanted Terrie to have the Magic Pencil because he knew it would save him.

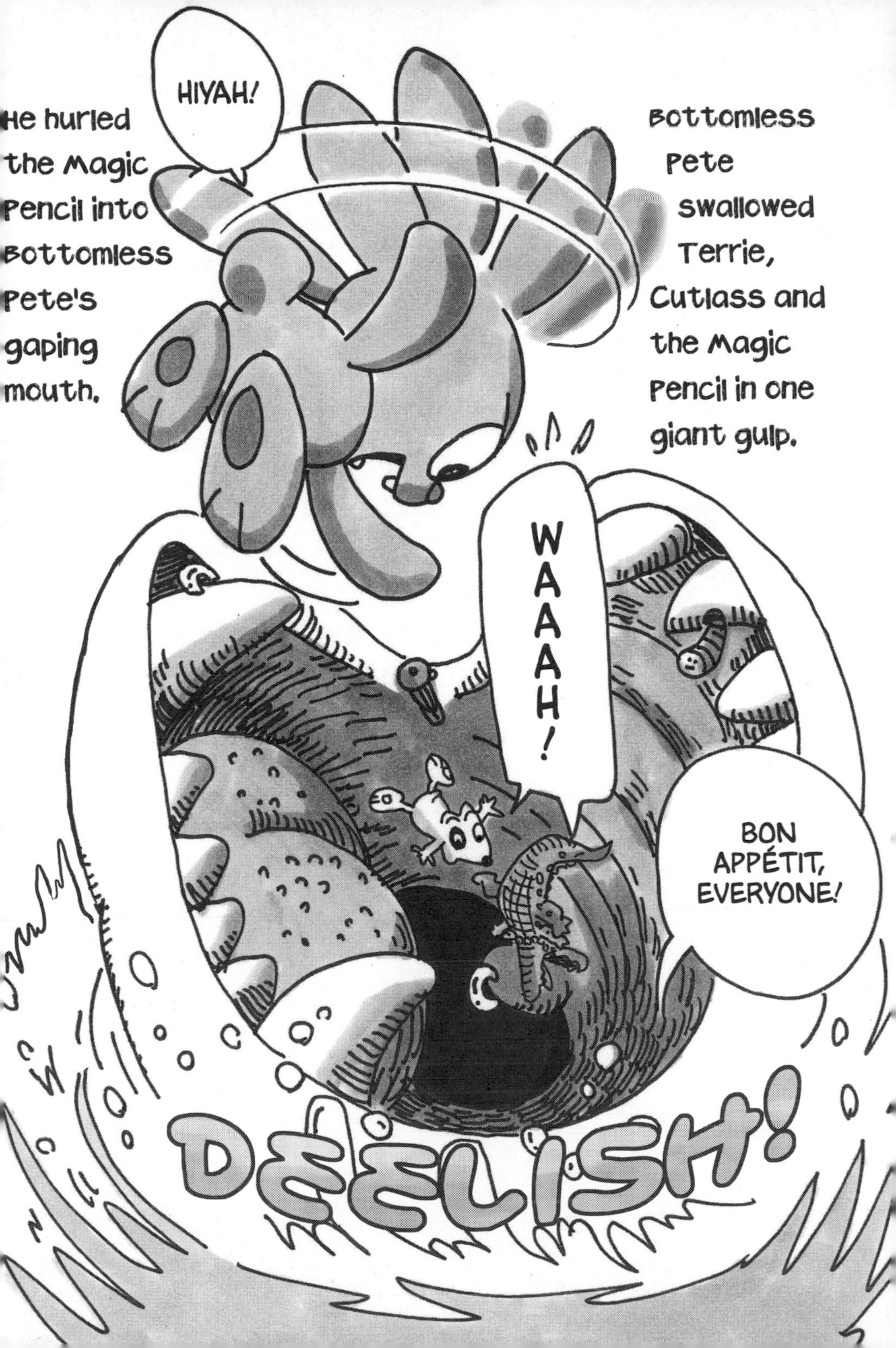
HIYAH!
He hurled the Magic Pencil into Bottomless Pete's gaping mouth.
Bottomless Pete swallowed Terrie, Cutlass and the Magic Pencil in one giant gulp.
WAAAAH!
BON APPÉTIT, EVERYONE!
DEELISH!

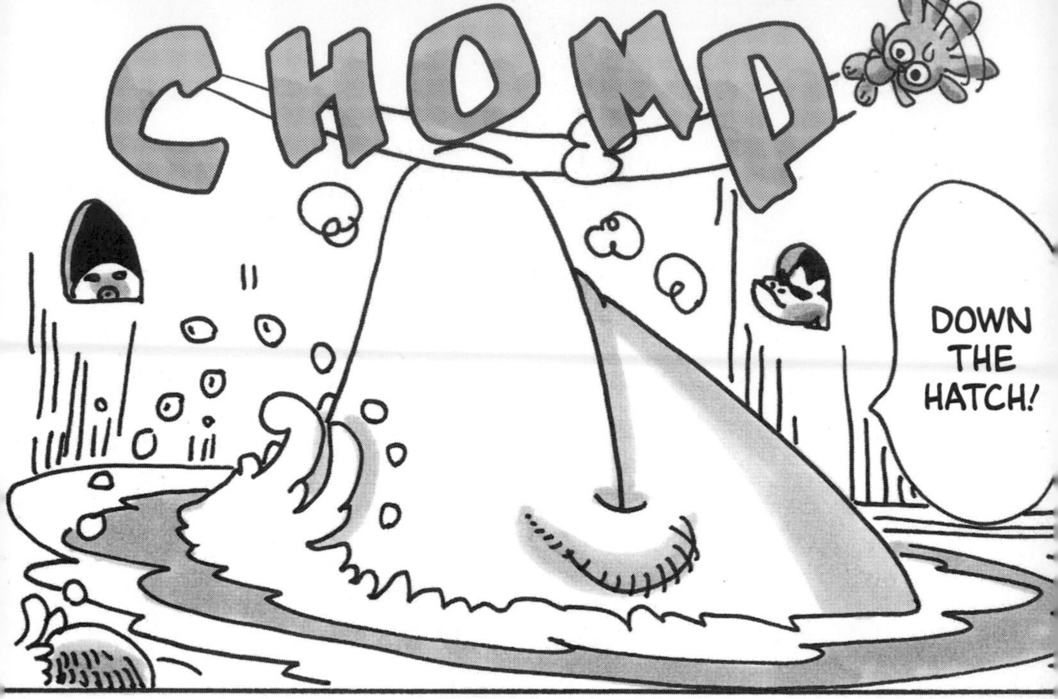
CHOMP
DOWN THE HATCH!

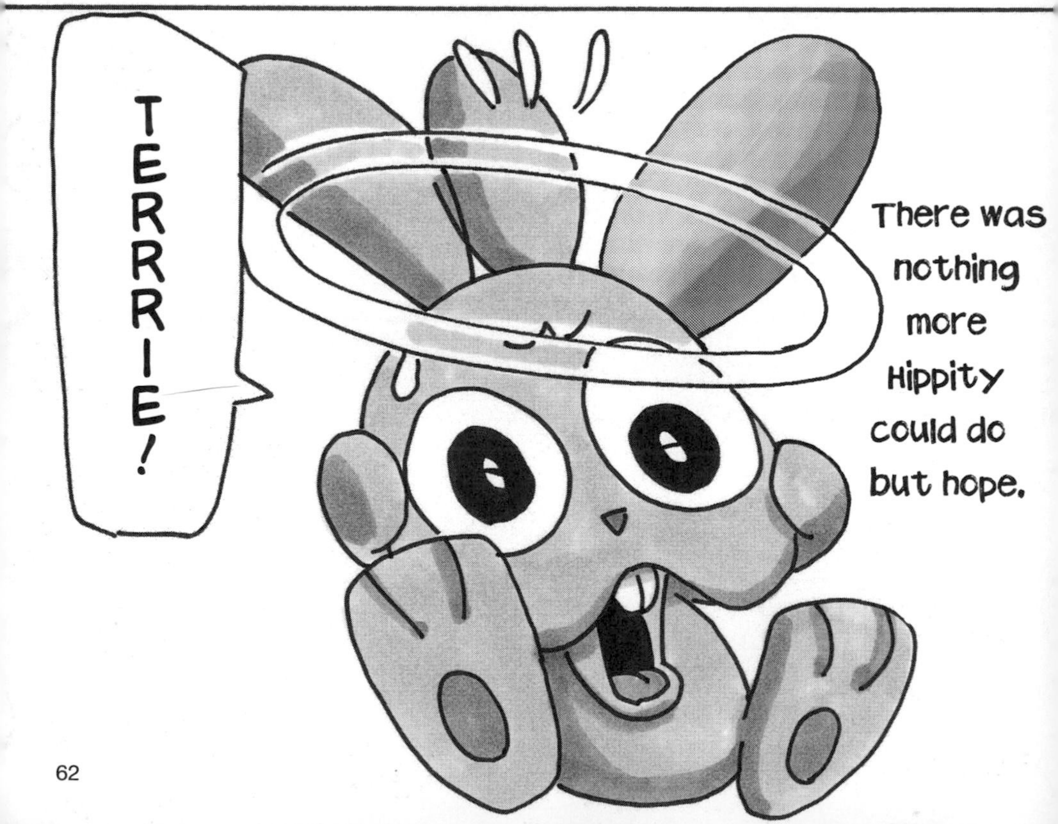
TERRRIE!
There was nothing more Hippity could do but hope.

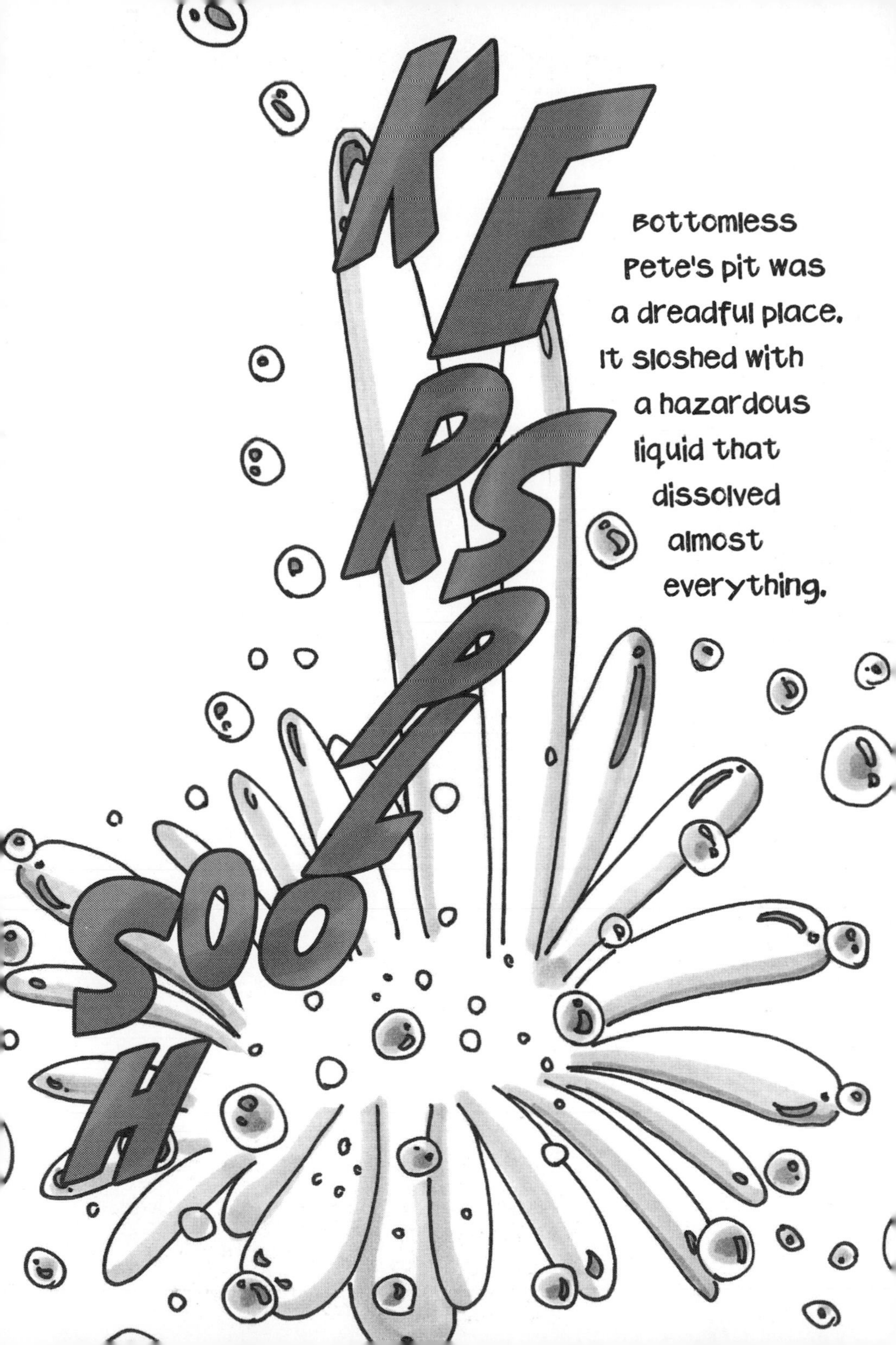
KERSPLOOSH
Bottomless Pete's pit was a dreadful place. It sloshed with a hazardous liquid that dissolved almost everything.

Terrie and Cutlass climbed onto an oil drum that floated nearby. With the Magic Pencil, Terrie drew a lamp to light the darkness. Then he held the pencil tight to keep it safe.

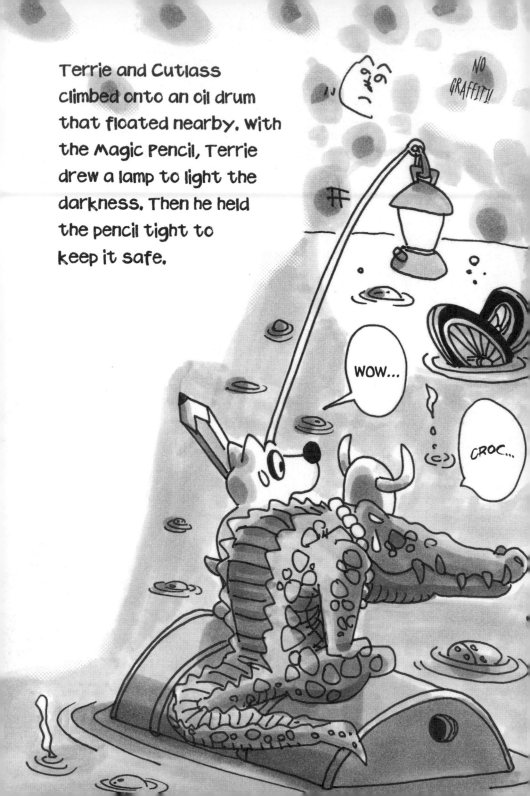

The liquid in Pete's stomach wasn't strong enough to dissolve everything.

Oil drums, bottles, cans, bicycles and refrigerators seemed to survive. They floated around in Pete's belly like vegetables in a great metal stew.

Terrie and Cutlass were certain they would be dissolved soon enough. They had to find a way out— and fast!

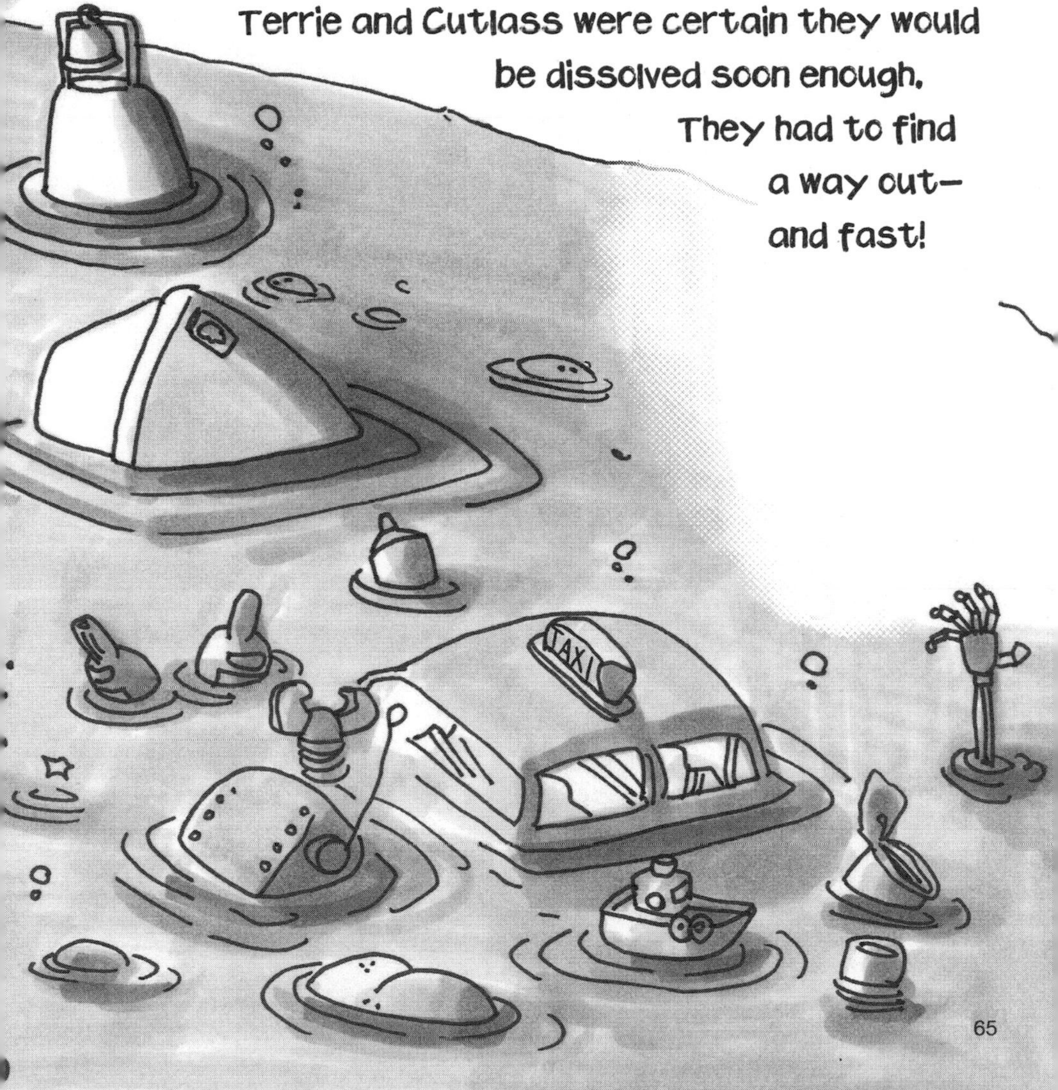
TAXI

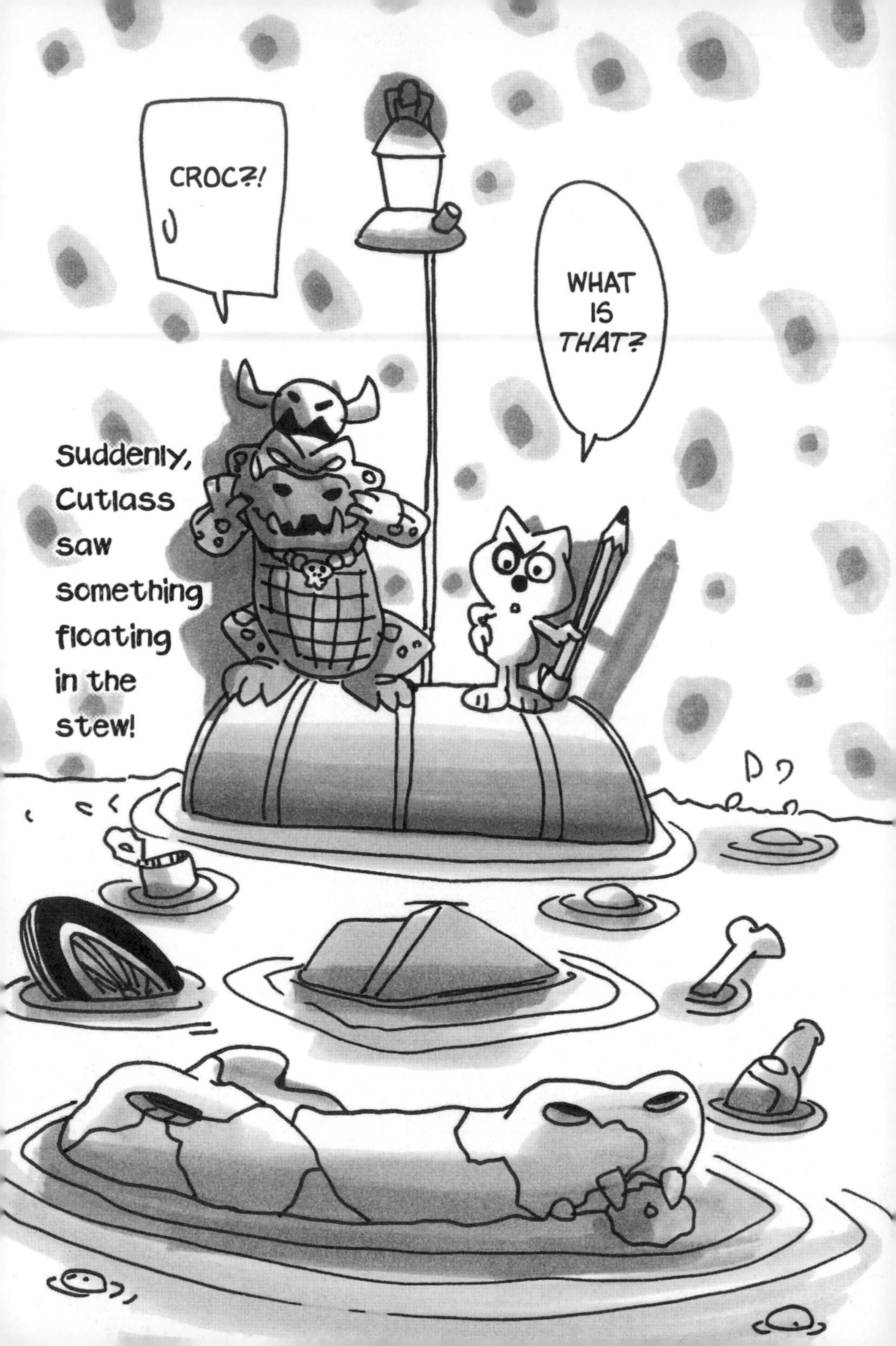
WHAT IS THAT?
CROC?!
Suddenly, Cutlass saw something floating in the stew!

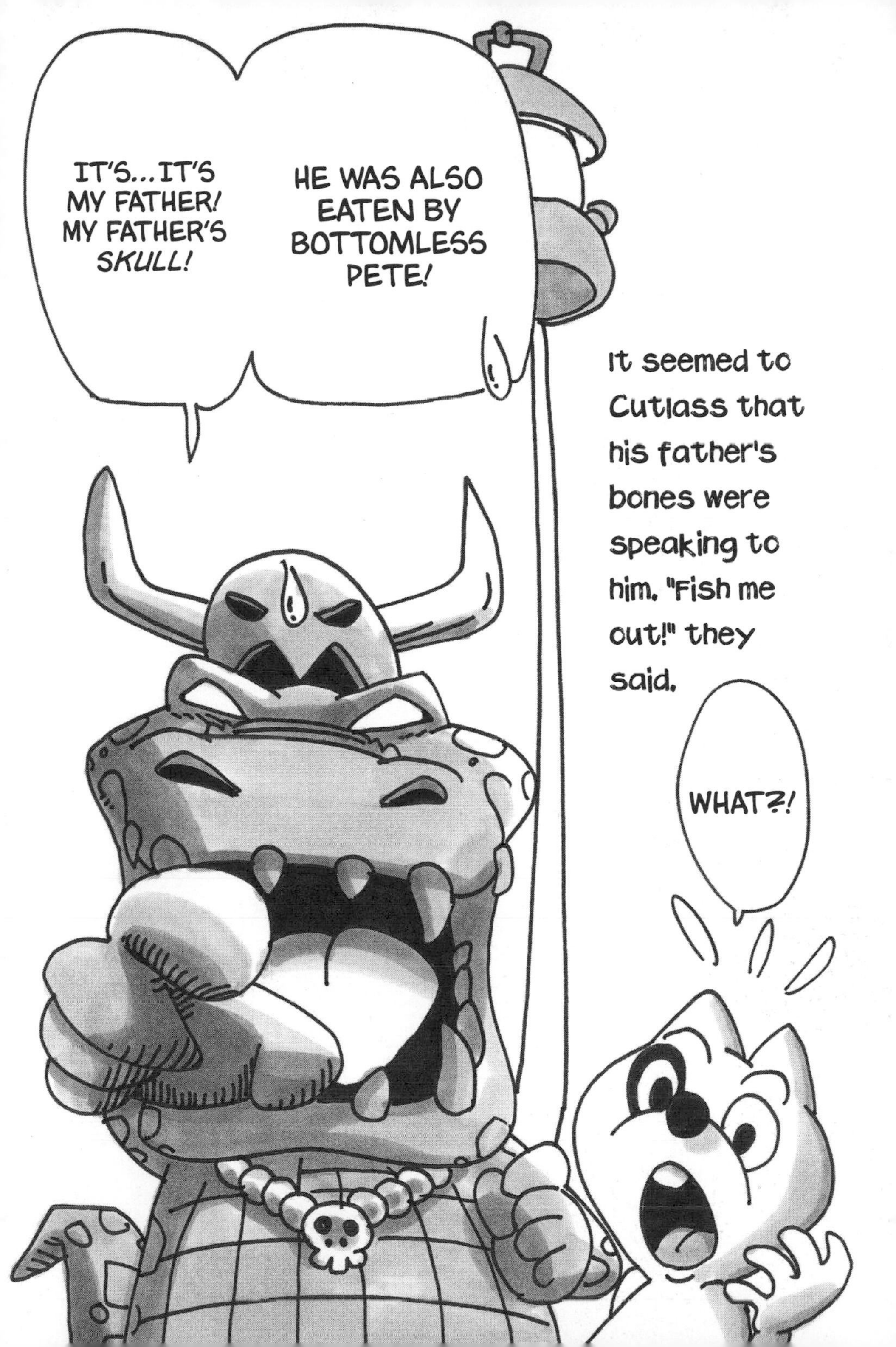
IT'S...IT'S MY FATHER! MY FATHER'S SKULL!
HE WAS ALSO EATEN BY BOTTOMLESS PETE!
WHAT?!

It seemed to Cutlass that his father's bones were speaking to him. "Fish me out!" they said.

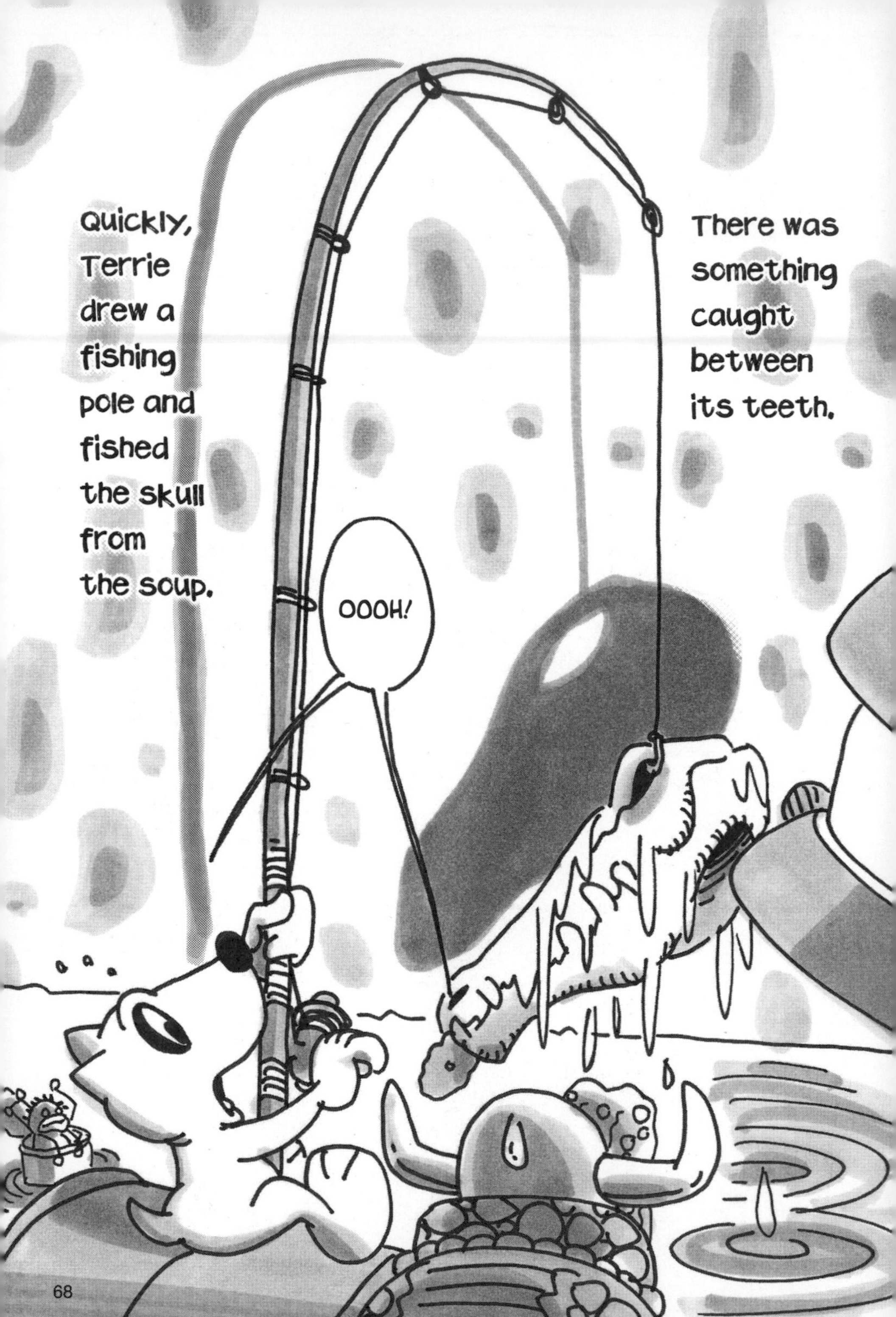
Quickly, Terrie drew a fishing pole and fished the skull from the soup.
OOOH!
There was something caught between its teeth.

It was the lid to a can that had not dissolved. When Terrie and Cutlass looked closer, they saw that the lid had something written on it.

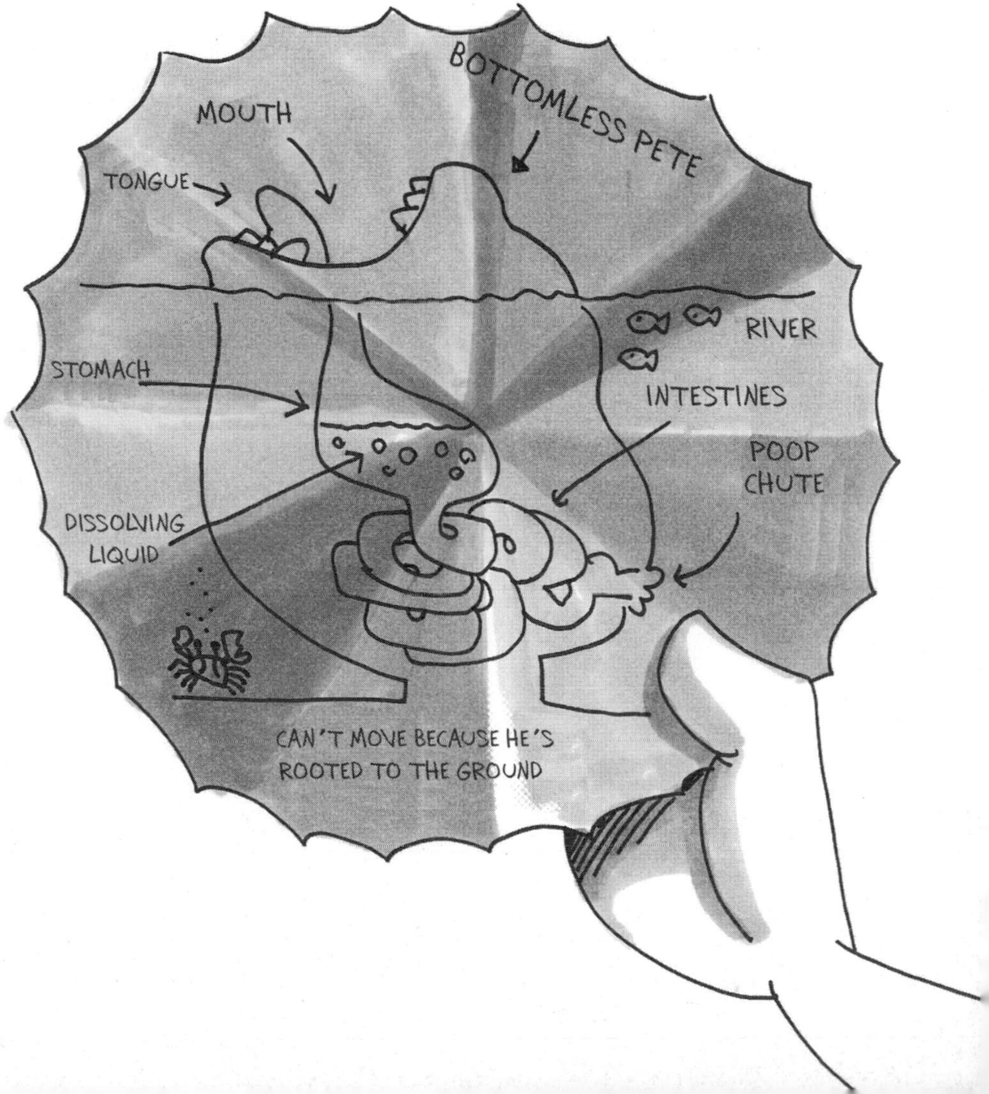
BOTTOMLESS PETE
MOUTH
TONGUE
RIVER
STOMACH
INTESTINES
POOP CHUTE
DISSOLVING LIQUID
CAN'T MOVE BECAUSE HE'S ROOTED TO THE GROUND

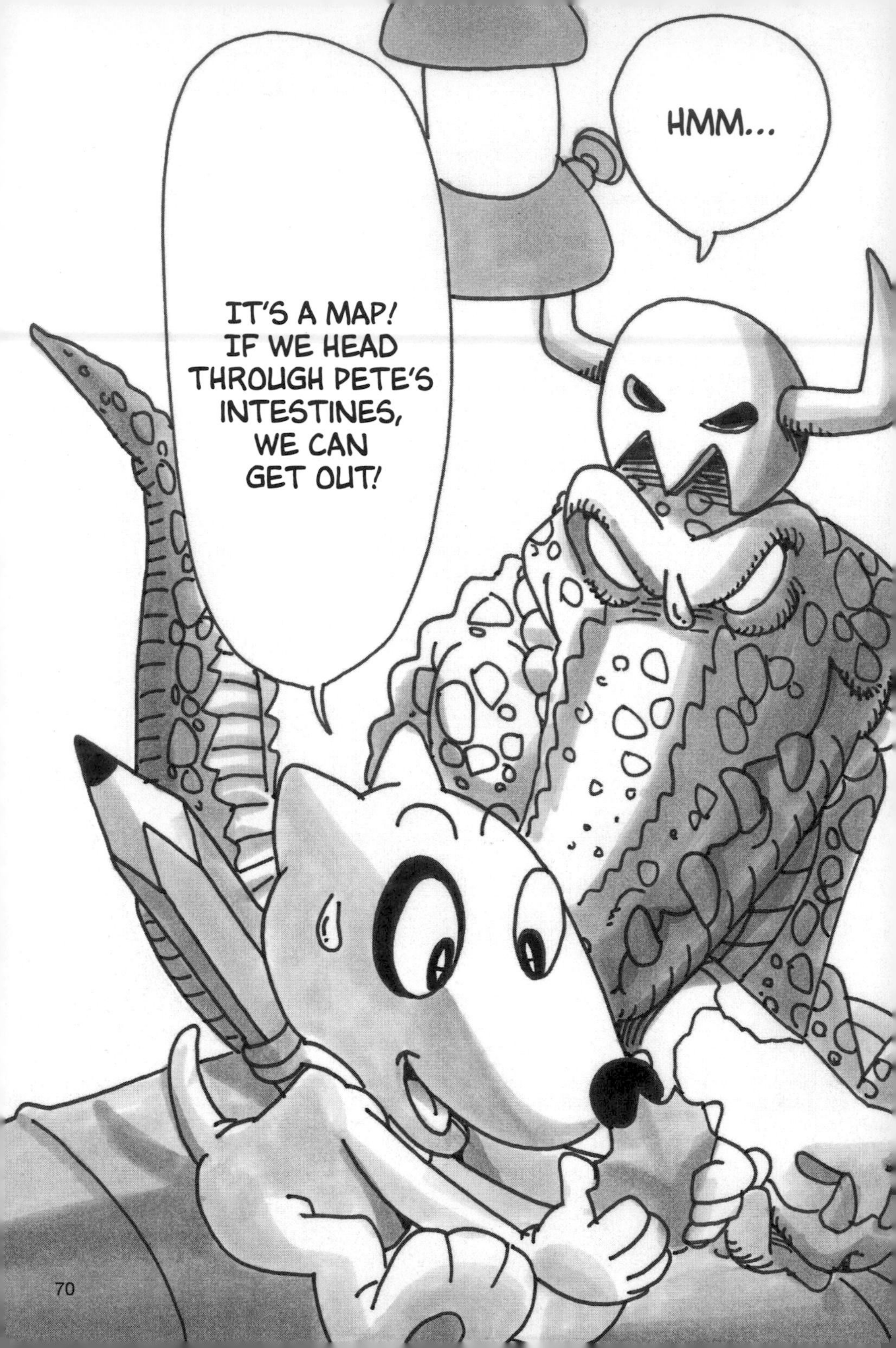
HMM...
IT'S A MAP! IF WE HEAD THROUGH PETE'S INTESTINES, WE CAN GET OUT!

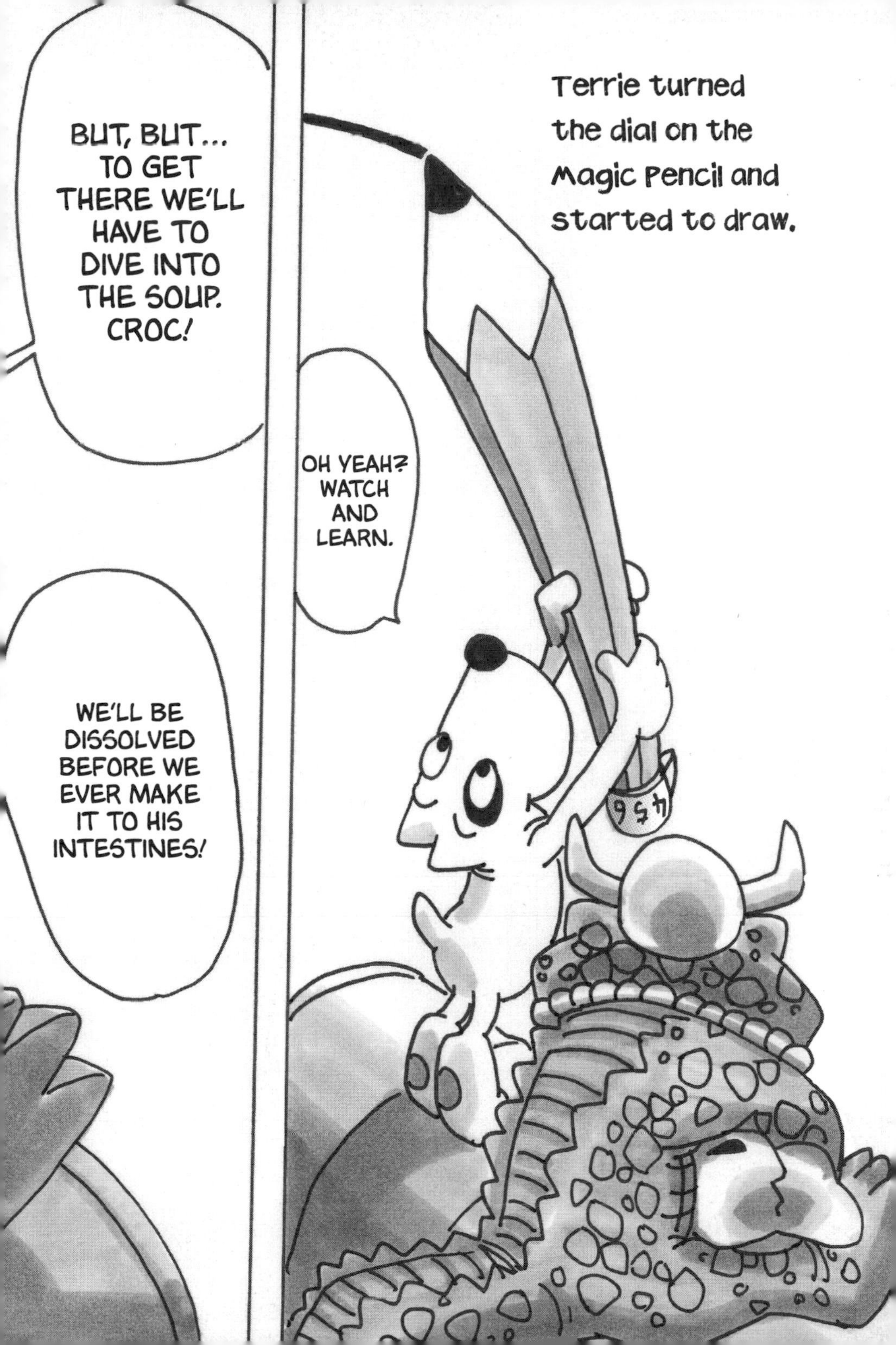
BUT, BUT... TO GET THERE WE'LL HAVE TO DIVE INTO THE SOUP. CROC!
WE'LL BE DISSOLVED BEFORE WE EVER MAKE IT TO HIS INTESTINES!
Terrie turned the dial on the Magic Pencil and started to draw.
OH YEAH? WATCH AND LEARN.

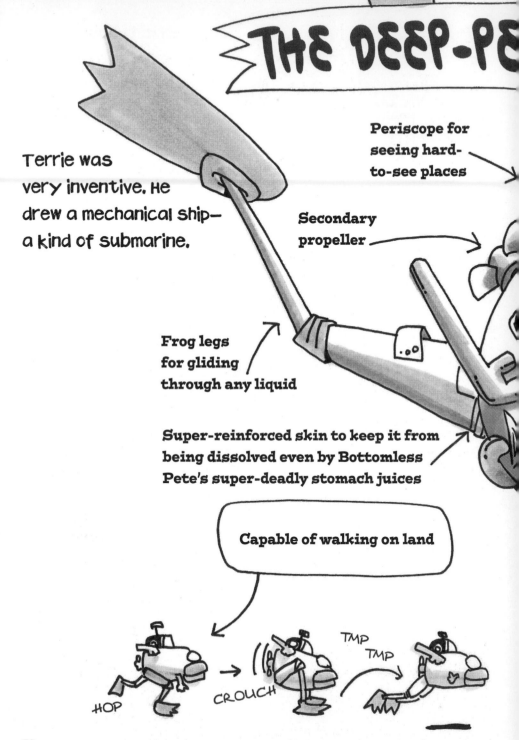

Terrie was very inventive. He drew a mechanical ship— a kind of submarine.

Periscope for seeing hard-to-see places

Secondary propeller

Frog legs for gliding through any liquid

Super-reinforced skin to keep it from being dissolved even by Bottomless Pete's super-deadly stomach juices

Capable of walking on land

HOP

CROUCH

TMP TMP

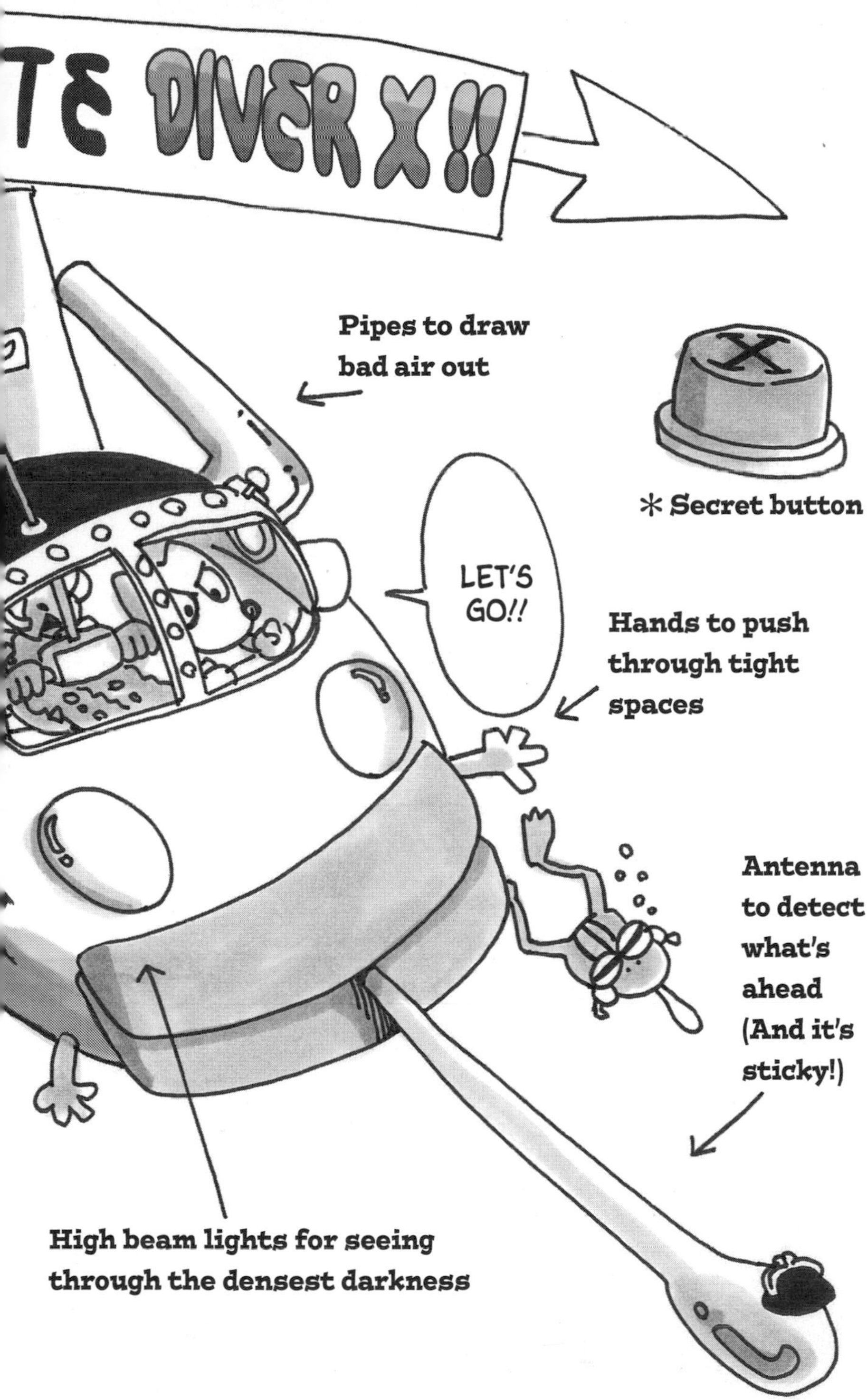

TE DIVER X!!
Pipes to draw bad air out
Secret button
LET'S GO!!
Hands to push through tight spaces
Antenna to detect what's ahead (And it's sticky!)
High beam lights for seeing through the densest darkness

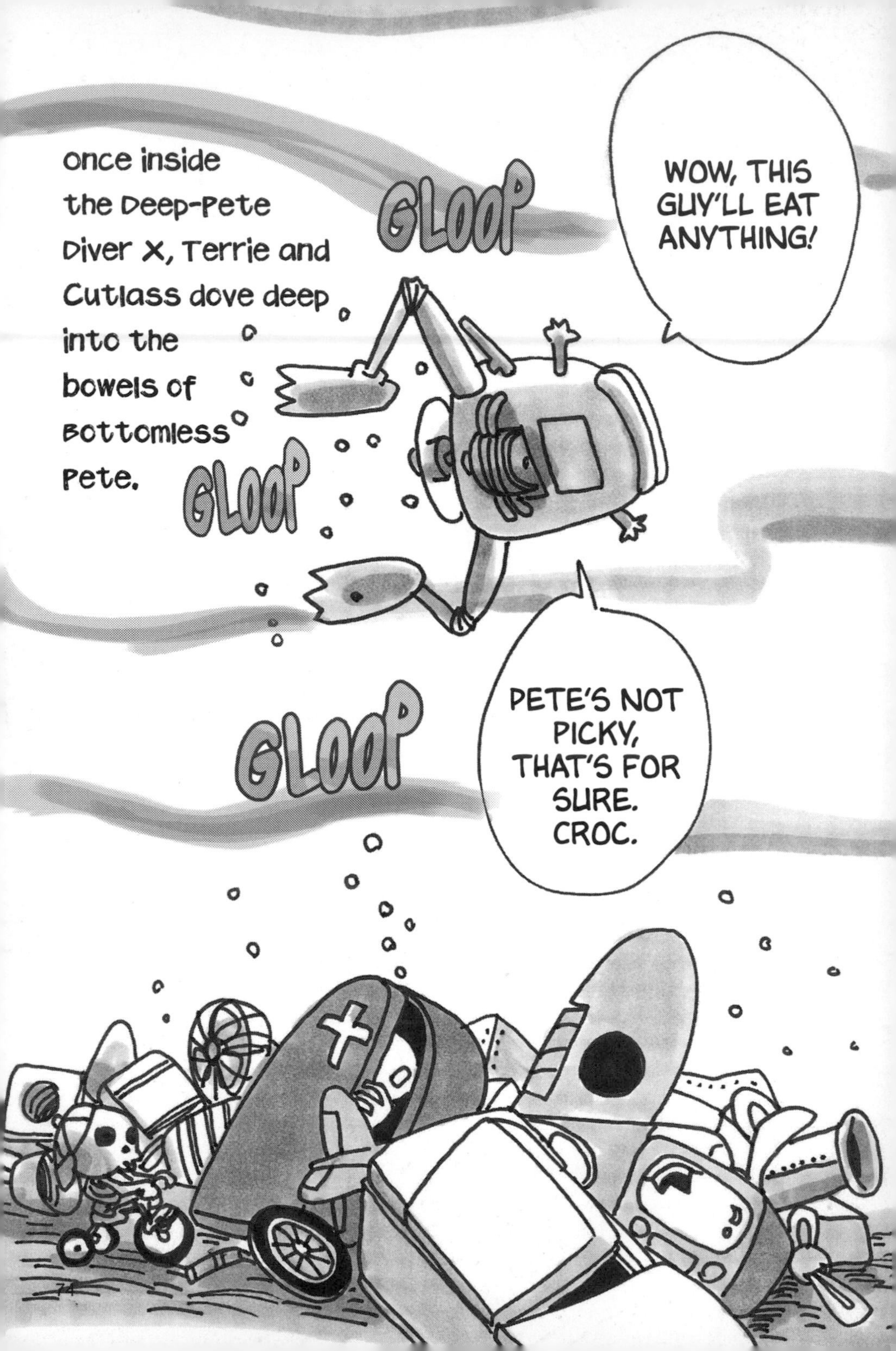
once inside the Deep-Pete Diver X, Terrie and Cutlass dove deep into the bowels of Bottomless Pete.
GLOOP
WOW, THIS GUY'LL EAT ANYTHING!
GLOOP
PETE'S NOT PICKY, THAT'S FOR SURE. CROC.
GLOOP

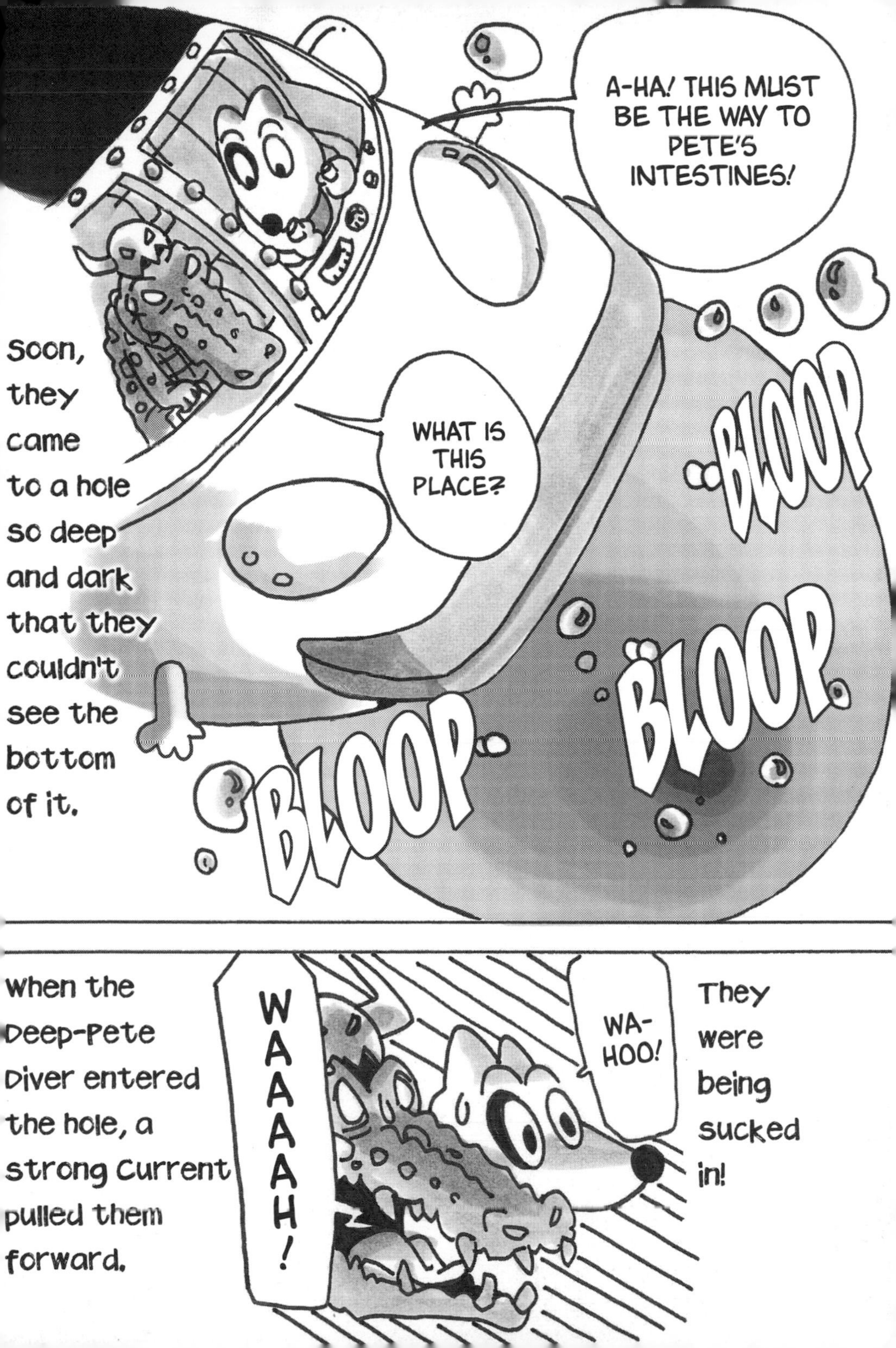
Soon, they came to a hole so deep and dark that they couldn't see the bottom of it.
WHAT IS THIS PLACE?
A-HA! THIS MUST BE THE WAY TO PETE'S INTESTINES!
BLOOP
BLOOP
BLOOP
When the Deep-Pete Diver entered the hole, a strong current pulled them forward.
WAAAAAH!
WA-HOO!
They were being sucked in!

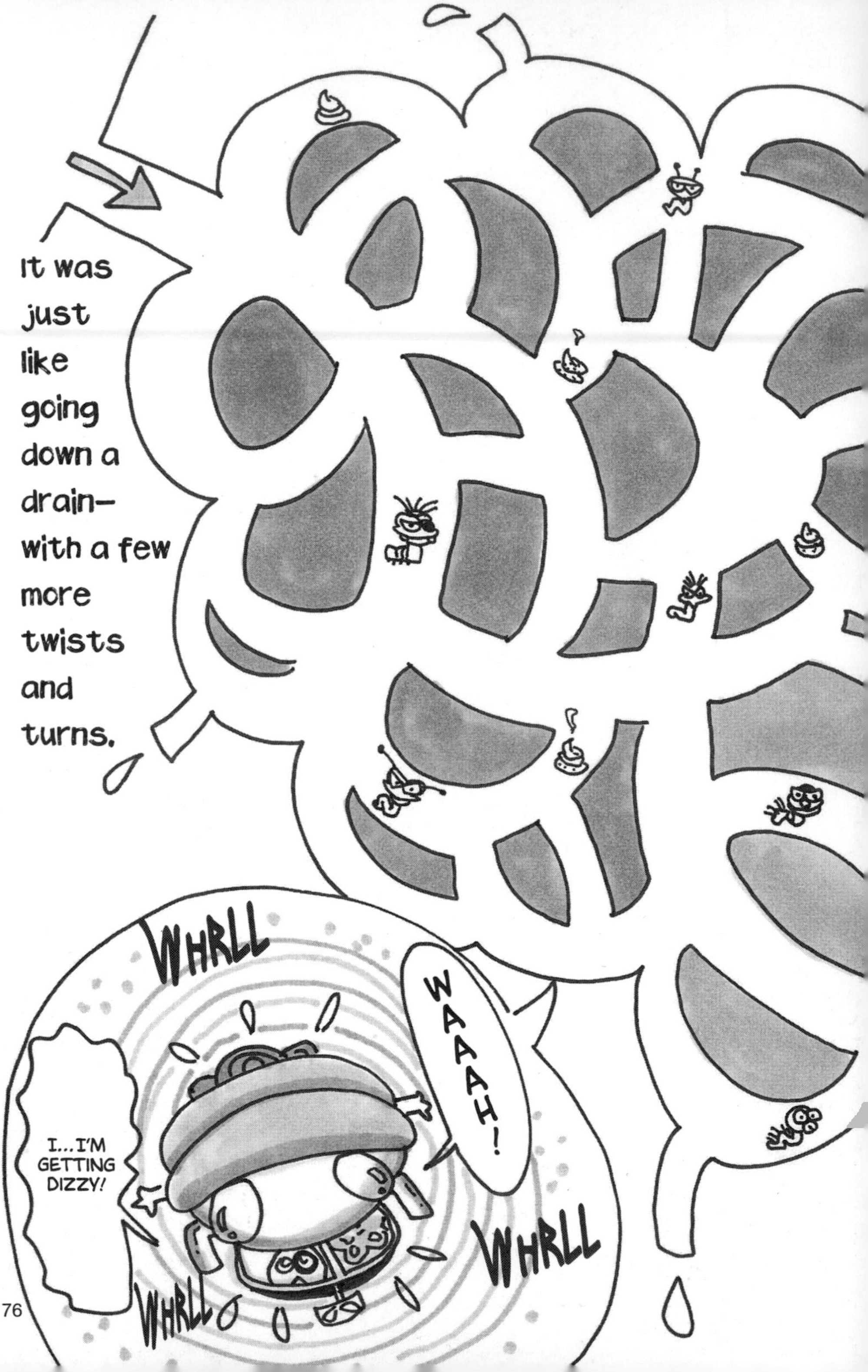
It was just like going down a drain—with a few more twists and turns.
WHRLL
WAAAAH!
I...I'M GETTING DIZZY!
WHRLL
WHRLL

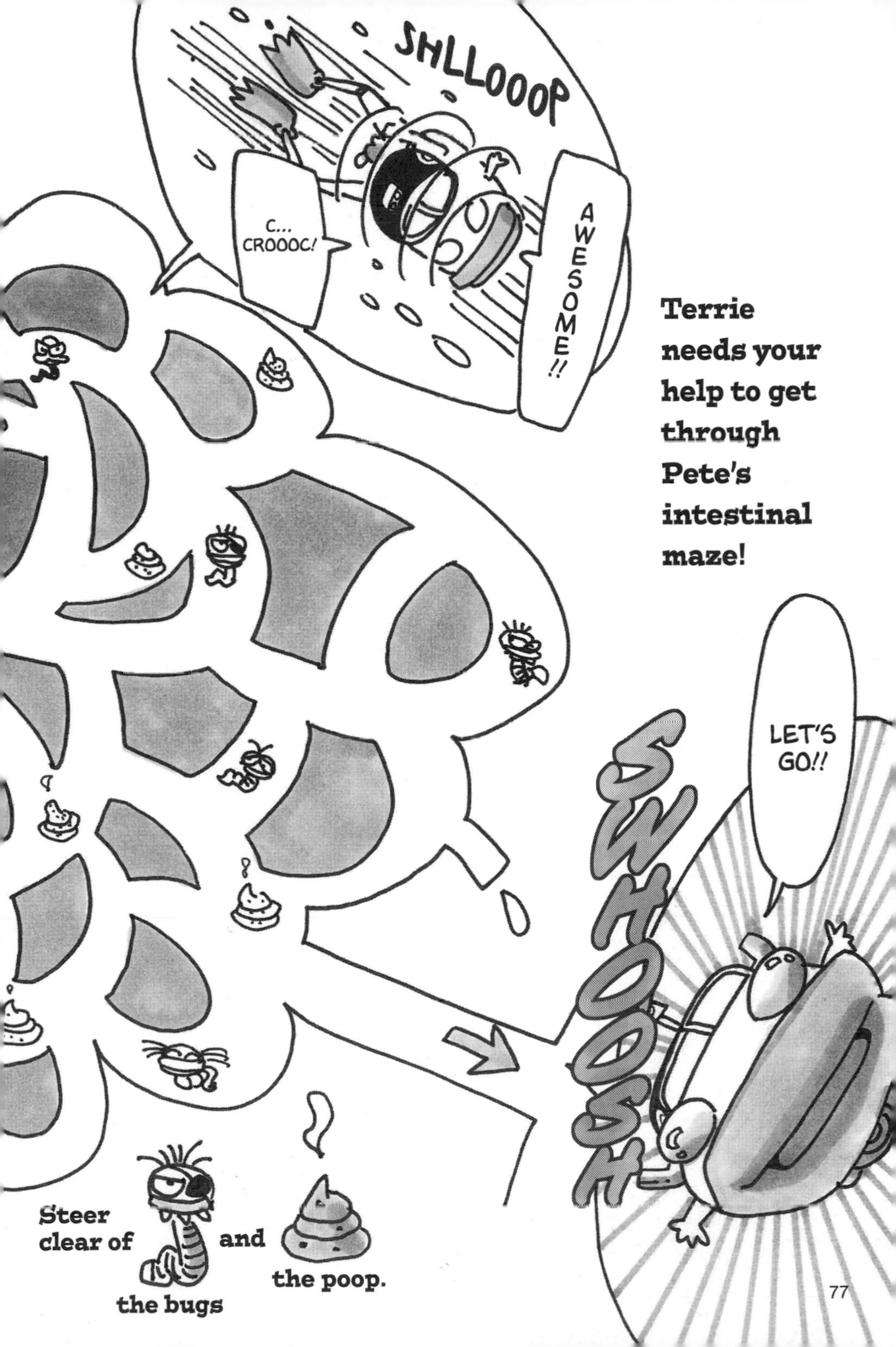
SHLLOOOP
AWESOME!!
C... CROOOC!
Terrie needs your help to get through Pete's intestinal maze!
LET'S GO!!
SWHOOSH
Steer clear of the bugs and the poop.

Pete's poop chute couldn't be far now! Or so Terrie and Cutlass thought. Unfortunately, Pete's pipes were packed with all the pieces he couldn't pass.

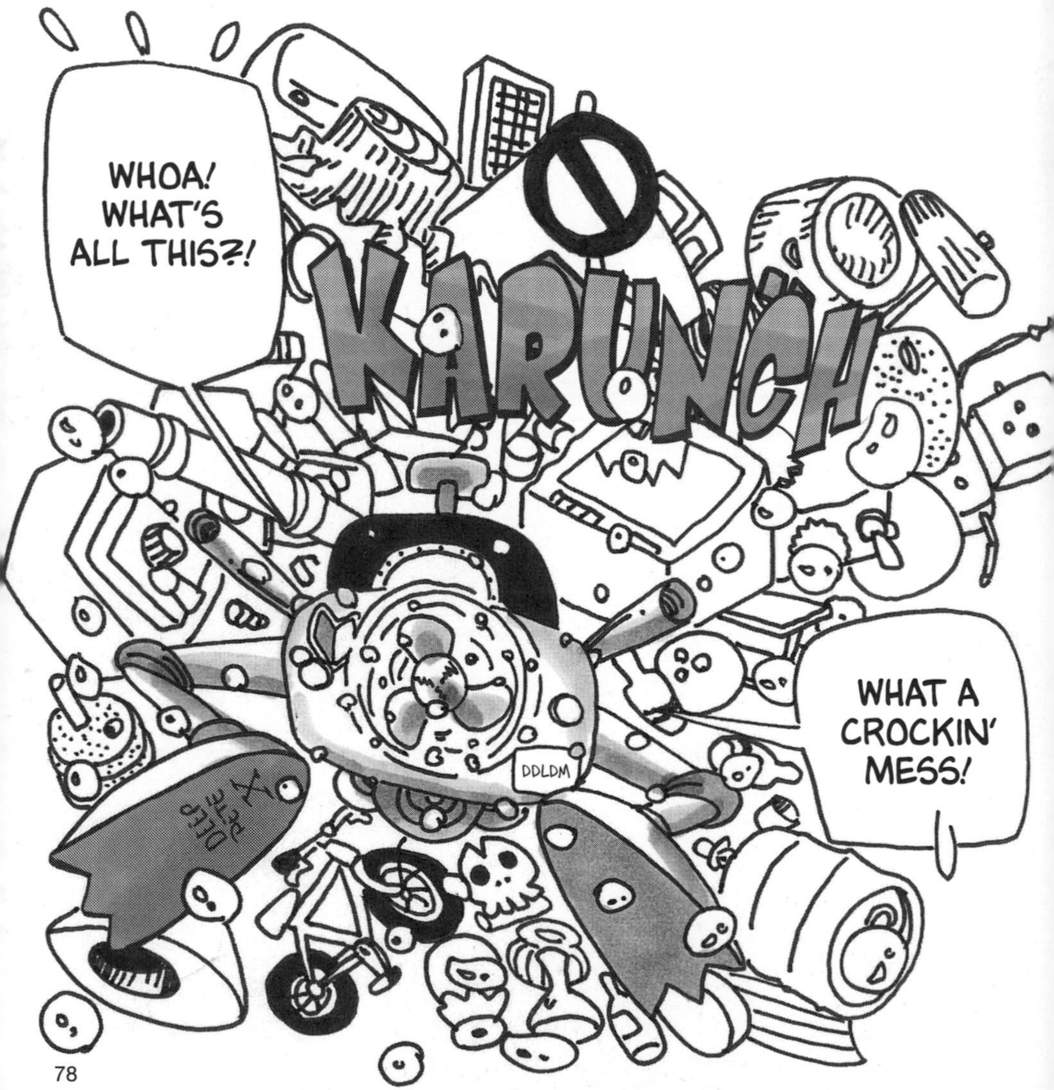
KARUNCH
WHOA! WHAT'S ALL THIS?!
DDLDM
WHAT A CROCKIN' MESS!

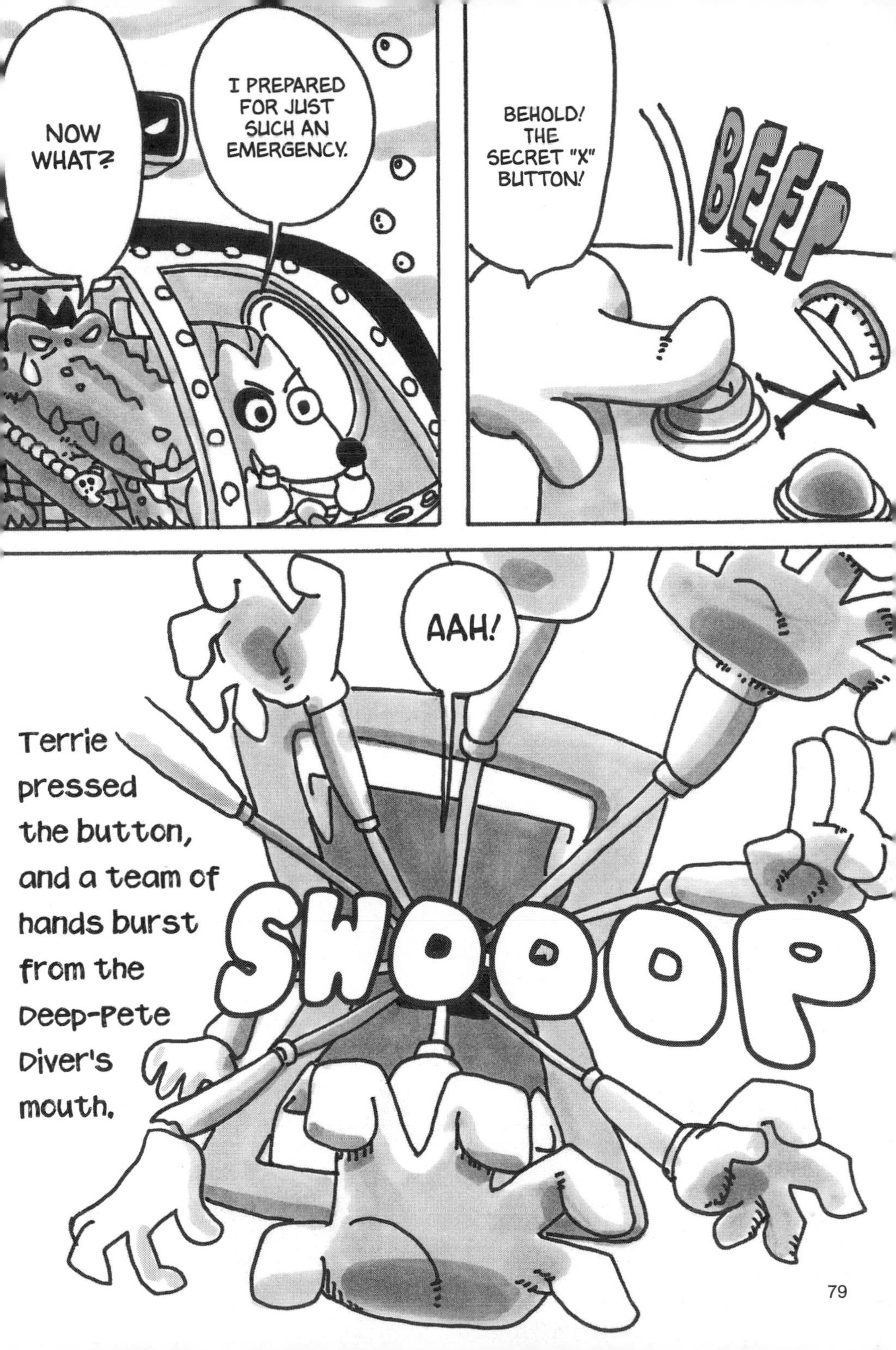
NOW WHAT?
I PREPARED FOR JUST SUCH AN EMERGENCY.
BEHOLD! THE SECRET "X" BUTTON!
BEEP
X
AAH!
Terrie pressed the button, and a team of hands burst from the Deep-Pete Diver's mouth.
SHOOOP

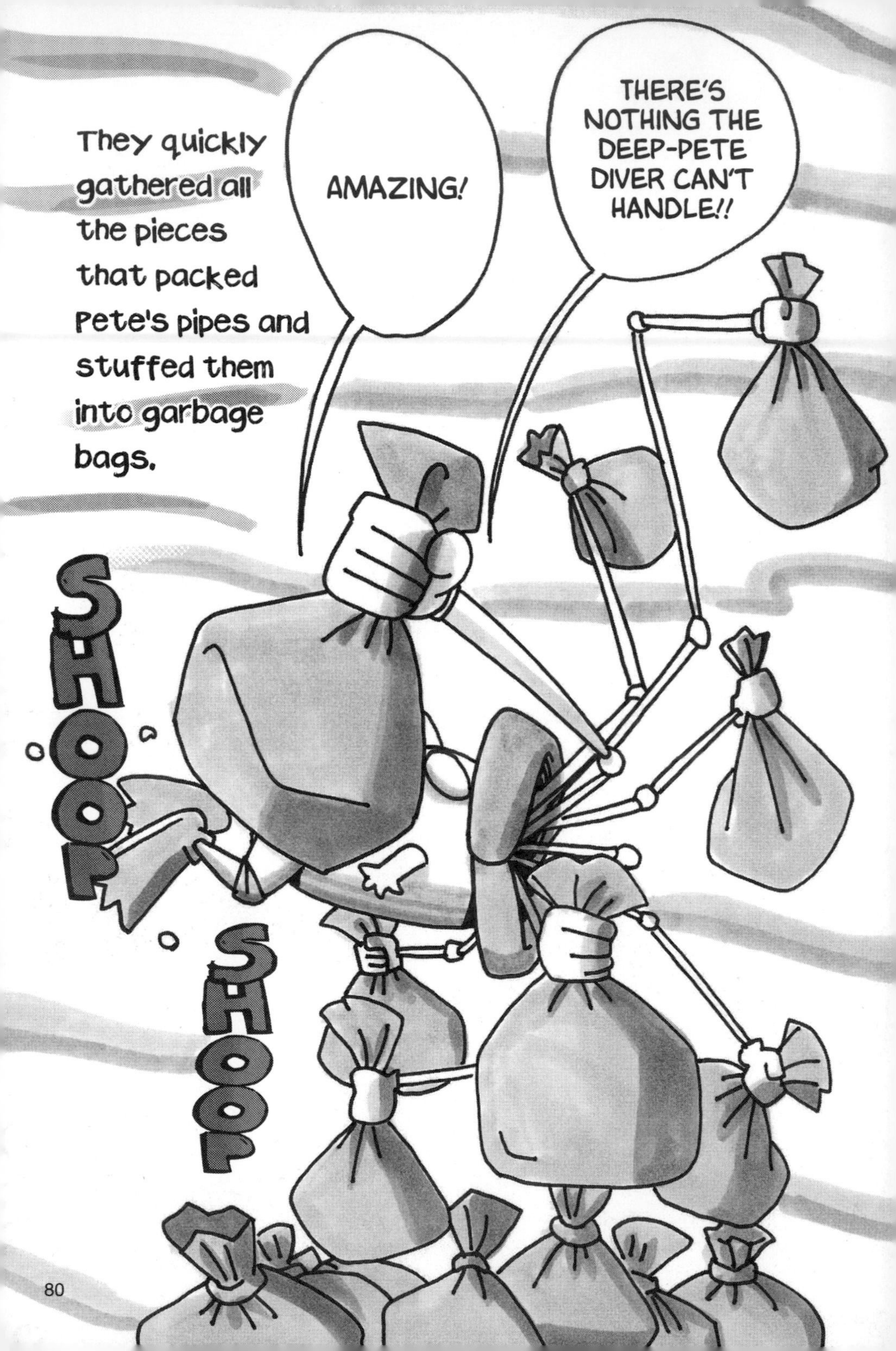
THERE'S NOTHING THE DEEP-PETE DIVER CAN'T HANDLE!!
AMAZING!
They quickly gathered all the pieces that packed Pete's pipes and stuffed them into garbage bags.
SHOOP
SHOOP

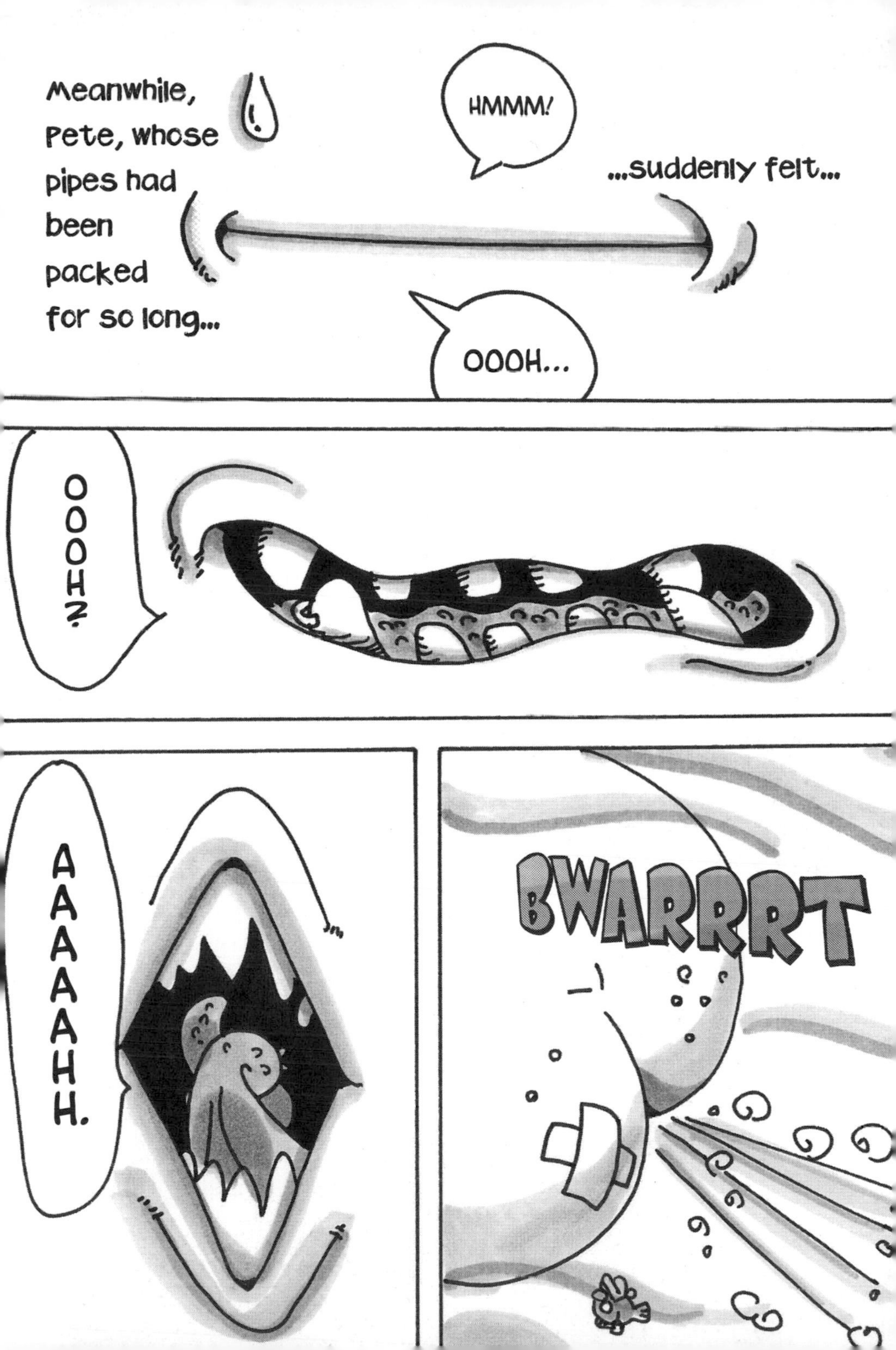
Meanwhile, Pete, whose pipes had been packed for so long...
HMMM!
...suddenly felt...
OOOH...
OOOH?
AAAAAHH.
BWARRRT

With a mighty poot, Pete pushed the Deep-Pete Diver out into the river at the bottom of the gorge. Garbage bags and all.

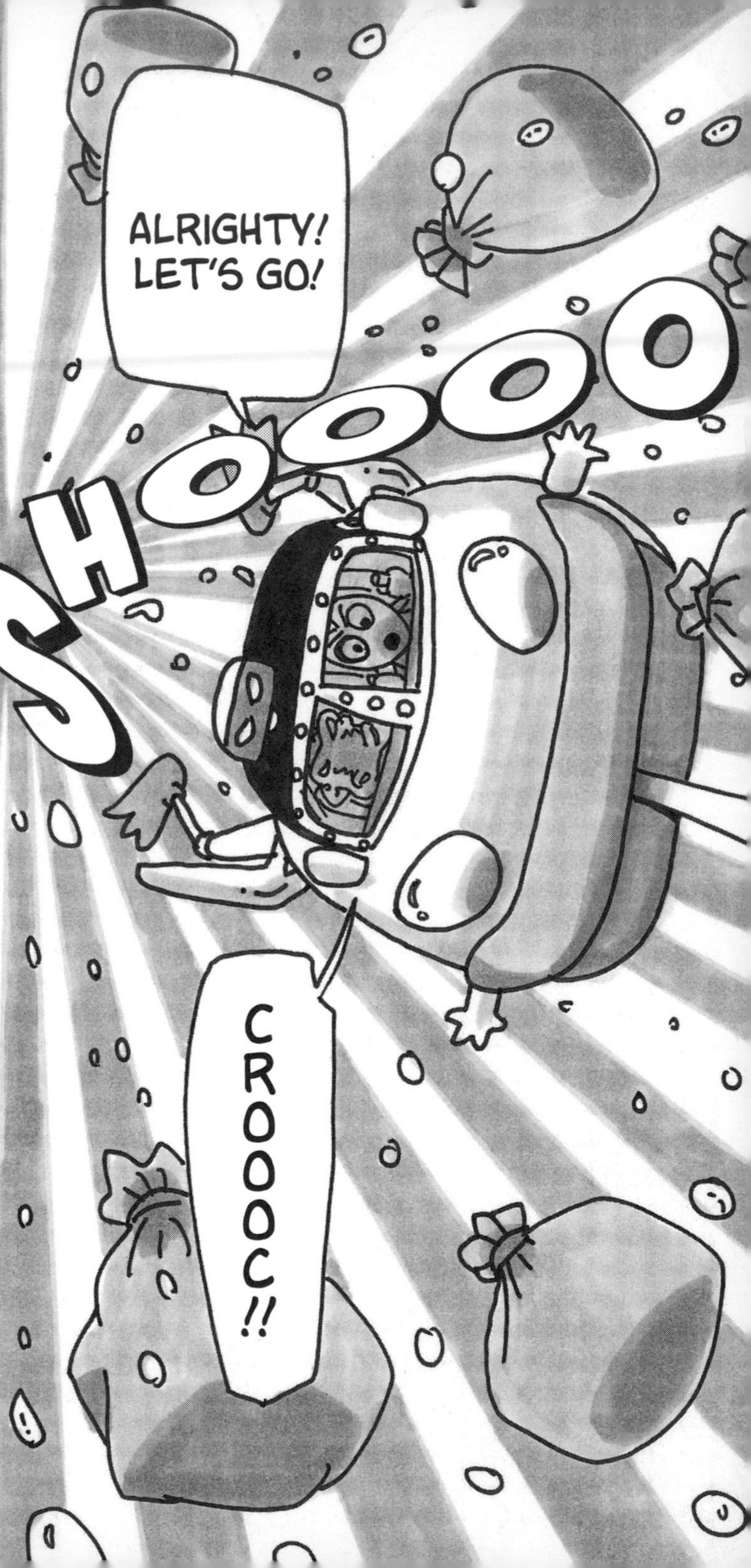
ALRIGHTY! LET'S GO!
SHOOOOO
CROOOOC!!

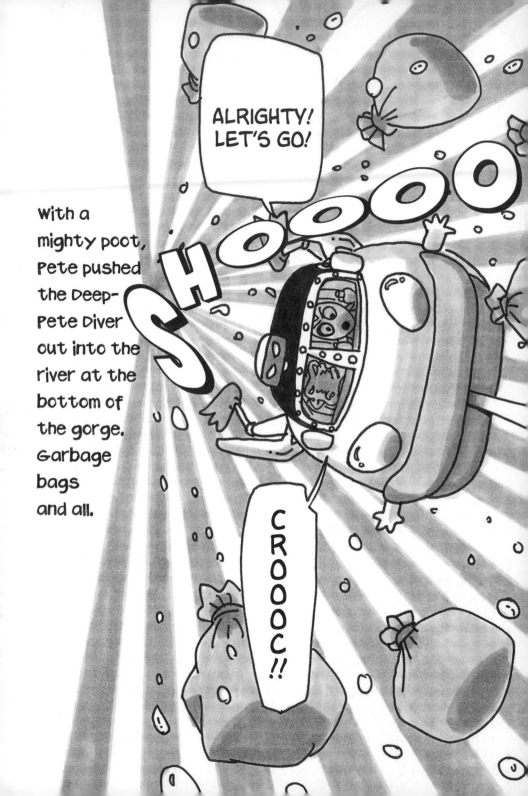

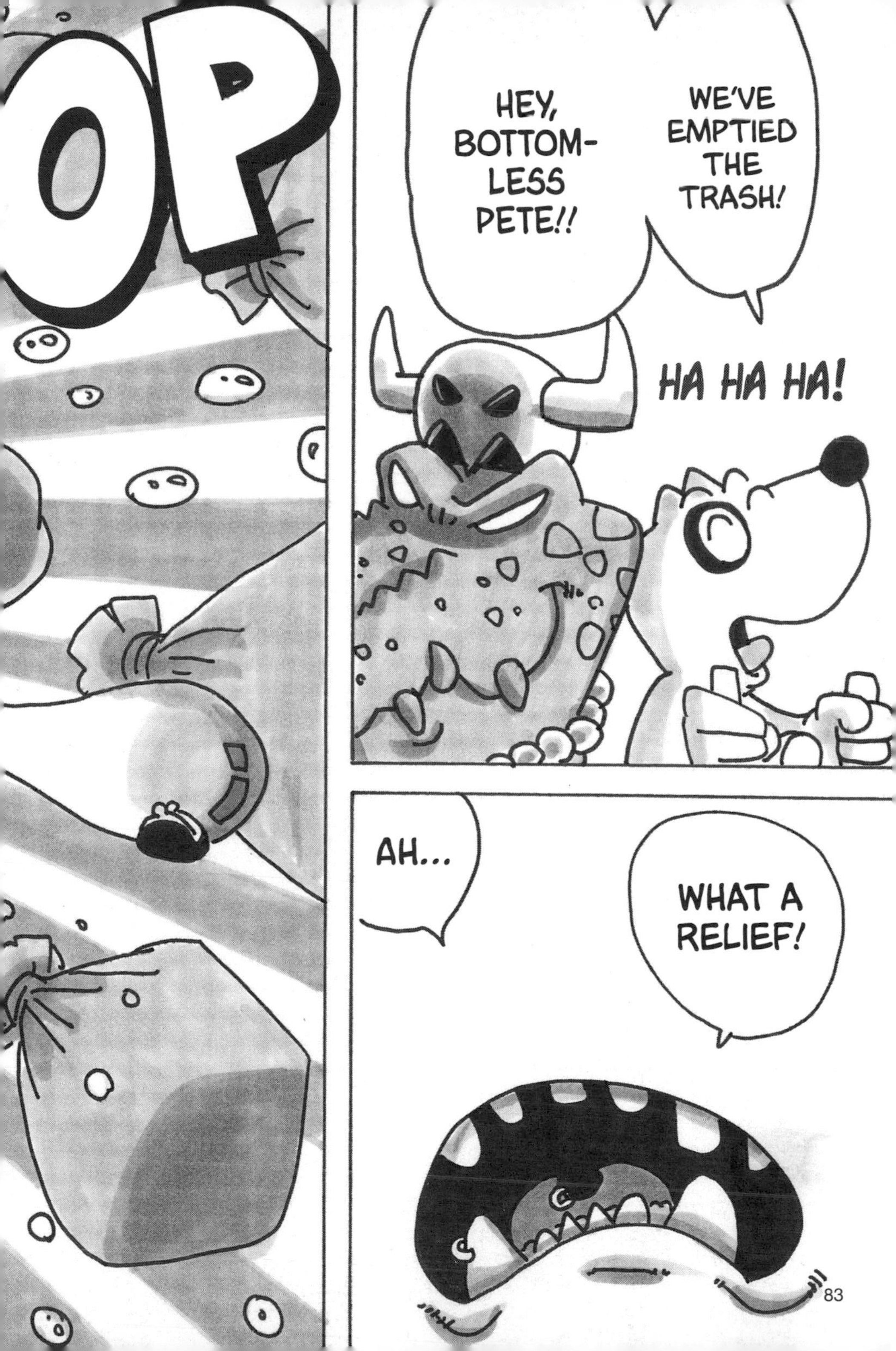
OP
HEY, BOTTOM-LESS PETE!!
WE'VE EMPTIED THE TRASH!
HA HA HA!
AH...
WHAT A RELIEF!

When they came to the surface, Cutlass gave Terrie his helmet as a token of thanks.

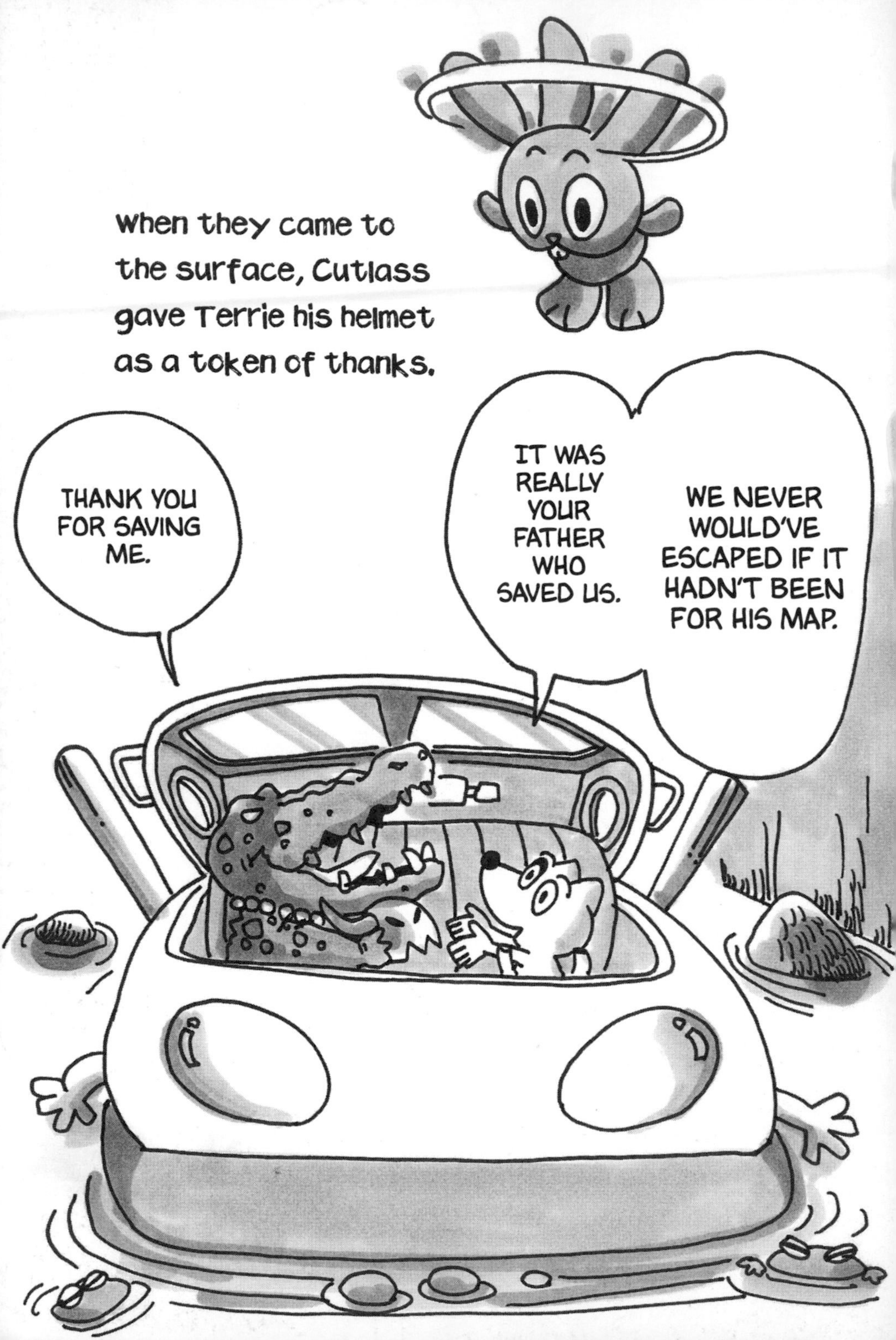
IT WAS REALLY YOUR FATHER WHO SAVED US.
WE NEVER WOULD'VE ESCAPED IF IT HADN'T BEEN FOR HIS MAP.
THANK YOU FOR SAVING ME.

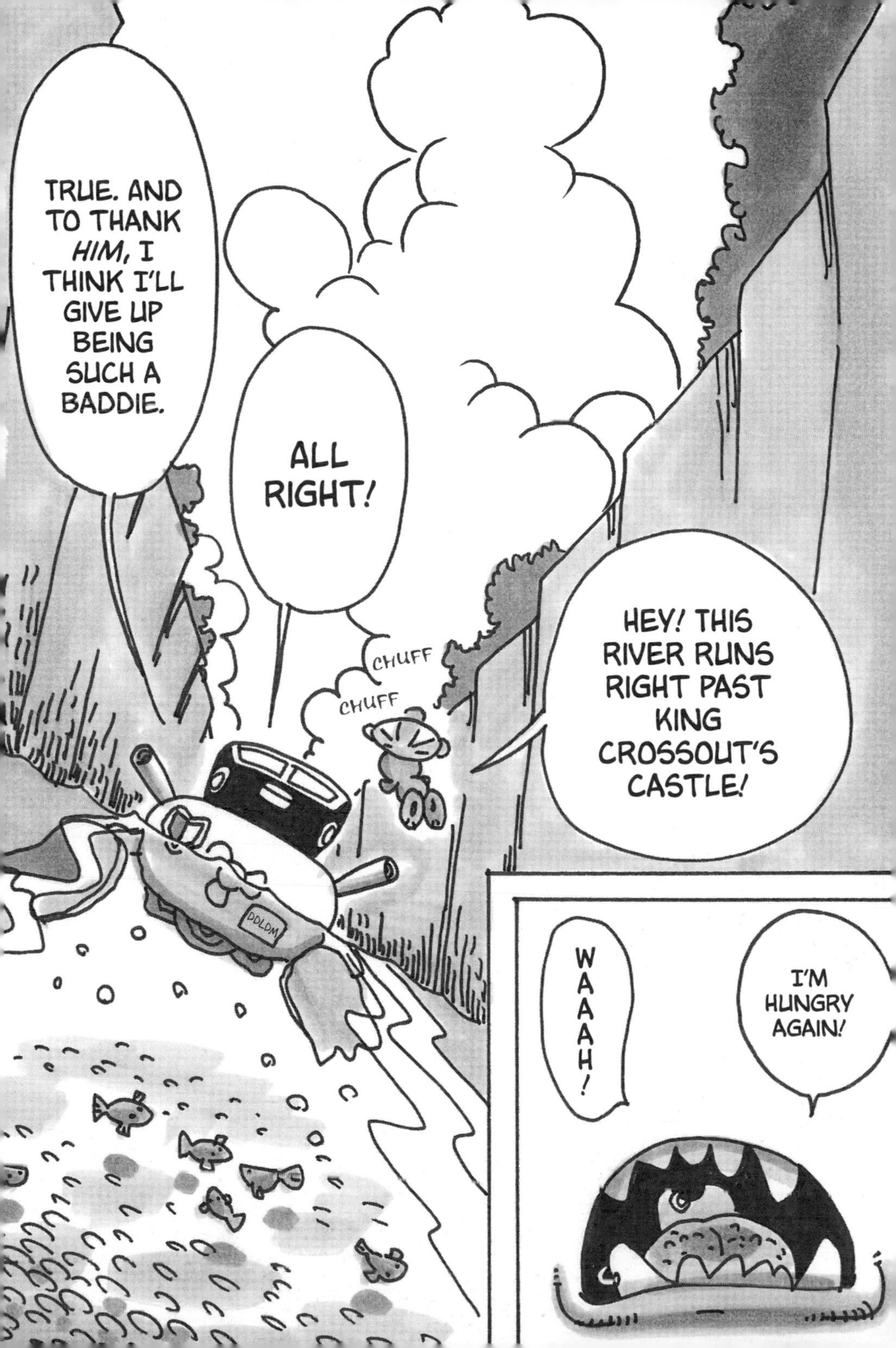
TRUE. AND TO THANK *HIM*, I THINK I'LL GIVE UP BEING SUCH A BADDIE.
ALL RIGHT!
CHUFF
CHUFF
HEY! THIS RIVER RUNS RIGHT PAST KING CROSSOUT'S CASTLE!
DDLDM
WAAAH!
I'M HUNGRY AGAIN!

Like any good spy, Tattle-Tail had seen and heard everything. Off he flew to deliver his report to the king. When he arrived at the castle, he found King Crossout enjoying the heat of his favorite electric blanket, which he plugged in even in the summertime.

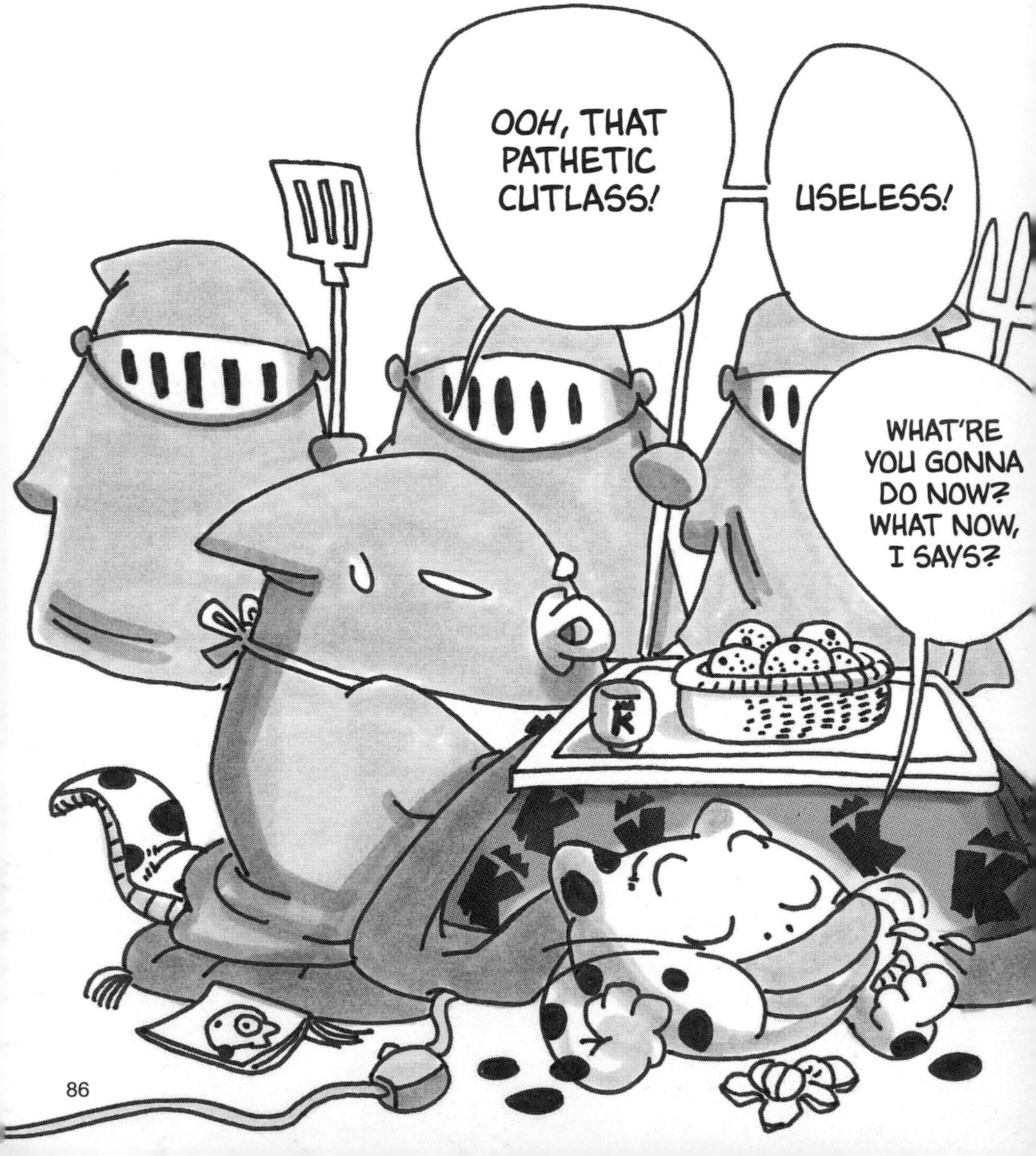

OOH, THAT PATHETIC CUTLASS!
USELESS!
WHAT'RE YOU GONNA DO NOW? WHAT NOW, I SAYS?

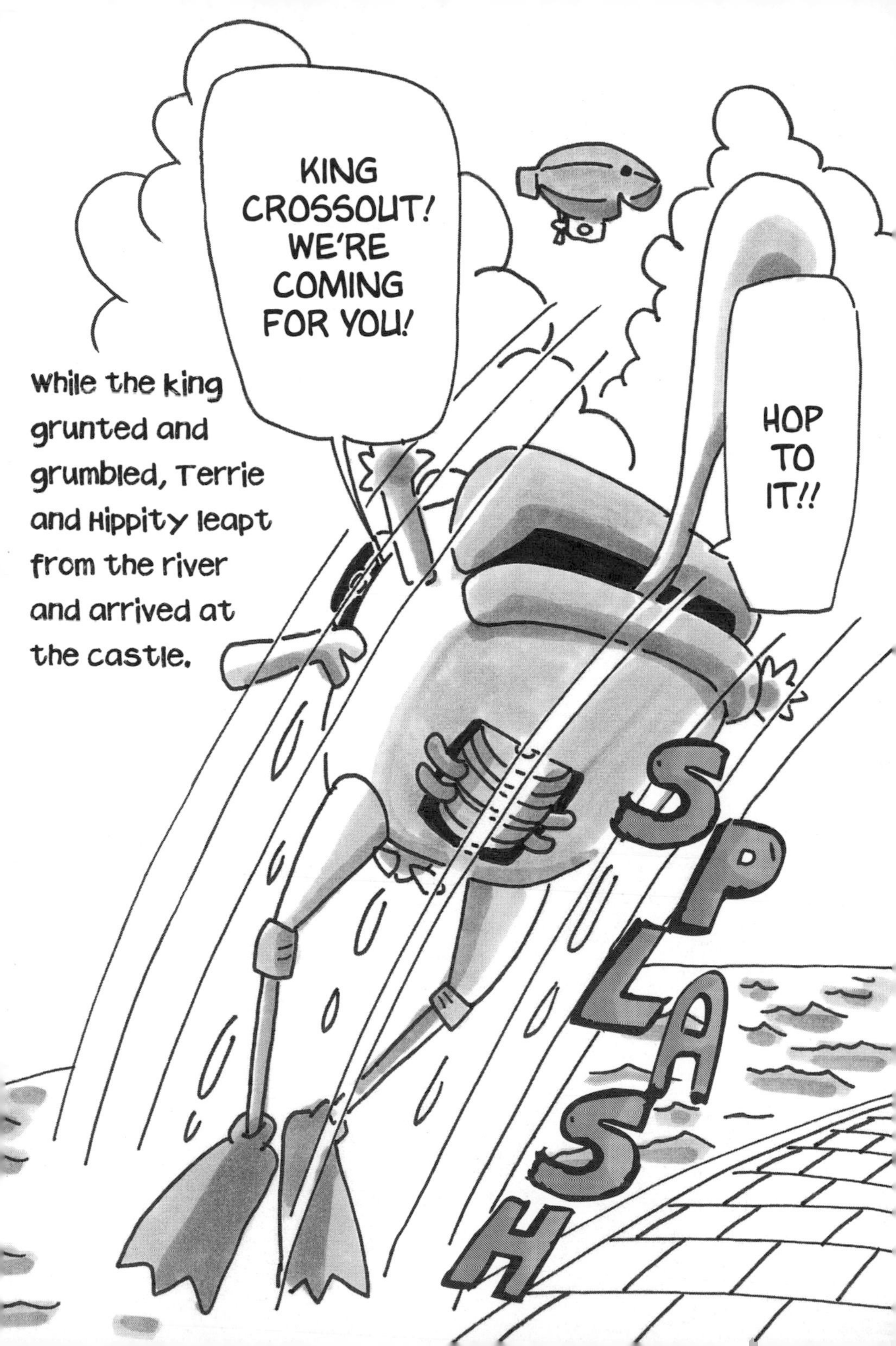
While the king grunted and grumbled, Terrie and Hippity leapt from the river and arrived at the castle.
KING CROSSOUT! WE'RE COMING FOR YOU!
HOP TO IT!!
SPLASH

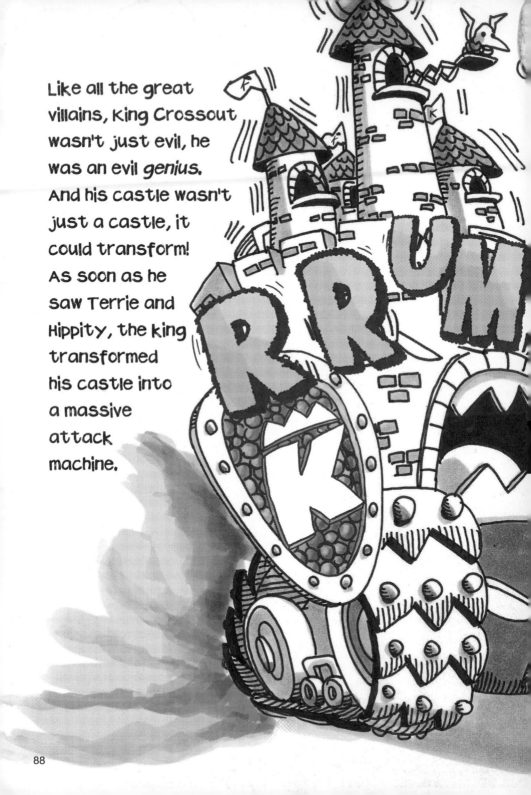

Like all the great villains, King Crossout wasn't just evil, he was an evil *genius.* And his castle wasn't just a castle, it could transform! As soon as he saw Terrie and Hippity, the king transformed his castle into a massive attack machine.

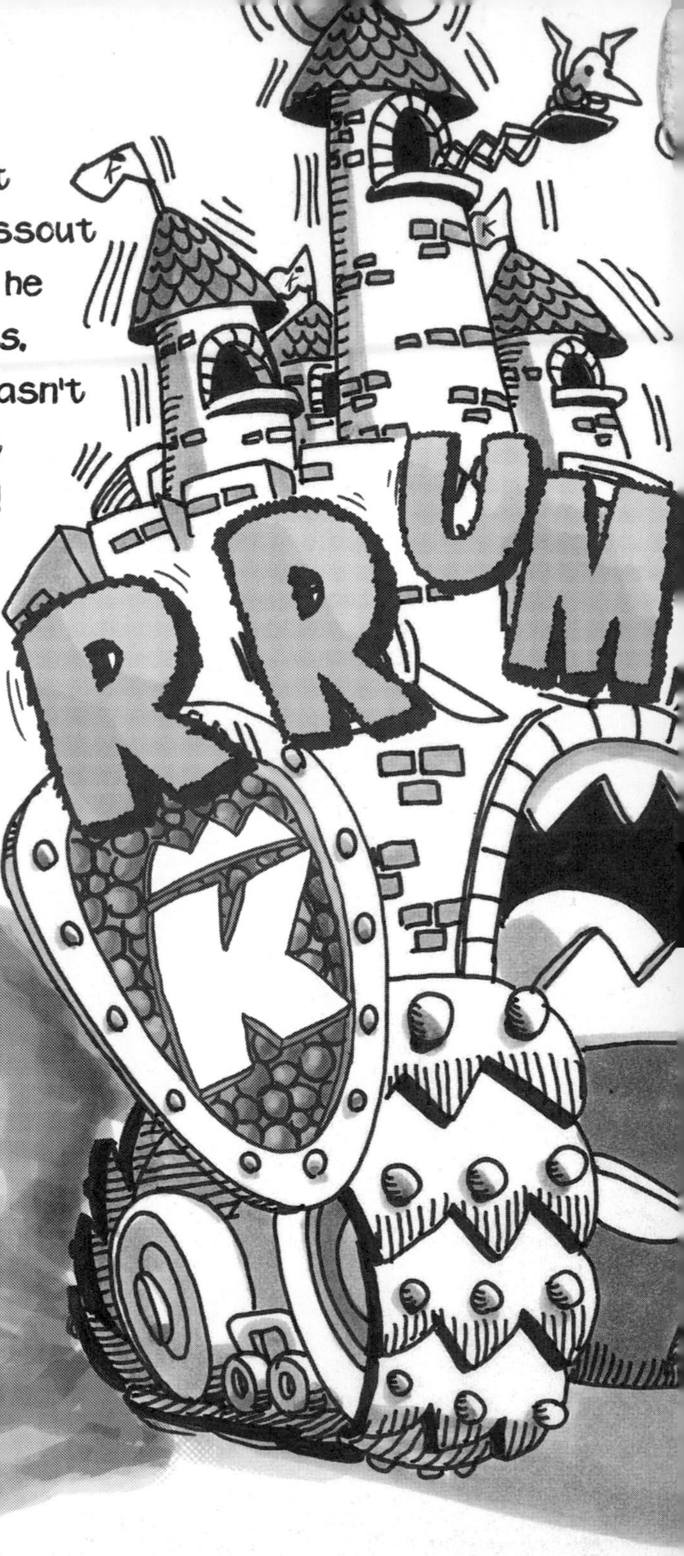
RRUM

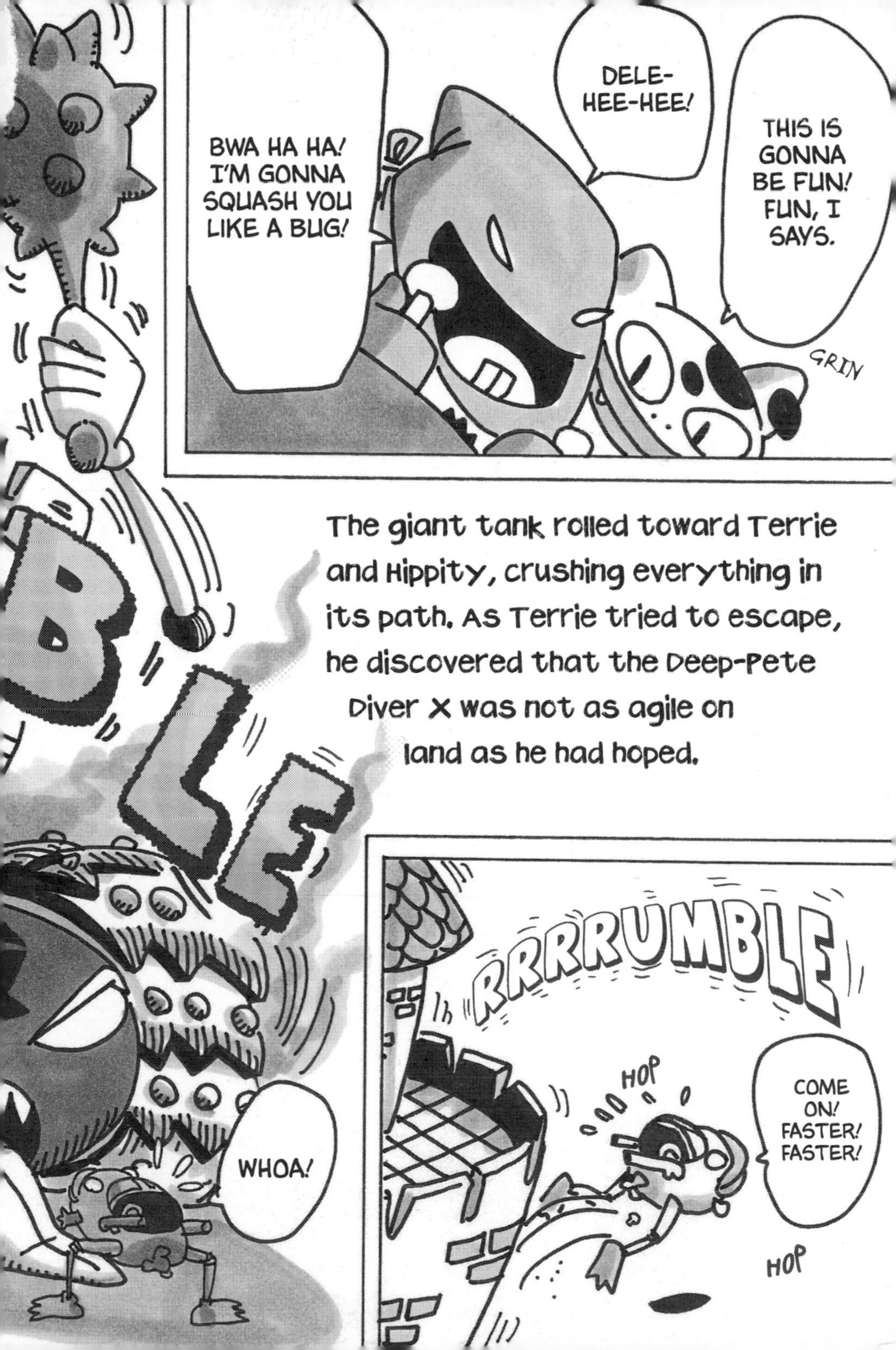
BWA HA HA! I'M GONNA SQUASH YOU LIKE A BUG!
DELE-HEE-HEE!
THIS IS GONNA BE FUN! FUN, I SAYS.
GRIN
The giant tank rolled toward Terrie and Hippity, crushing everything in its path. As Terrie tried to escape, he discovered that the Deep-Pete Diver X was not as agile on land as he had hoped.
RRRRUMBLE
HOP
COME ON! FASTER! FASTER!
HOP
BLE
WHOA!

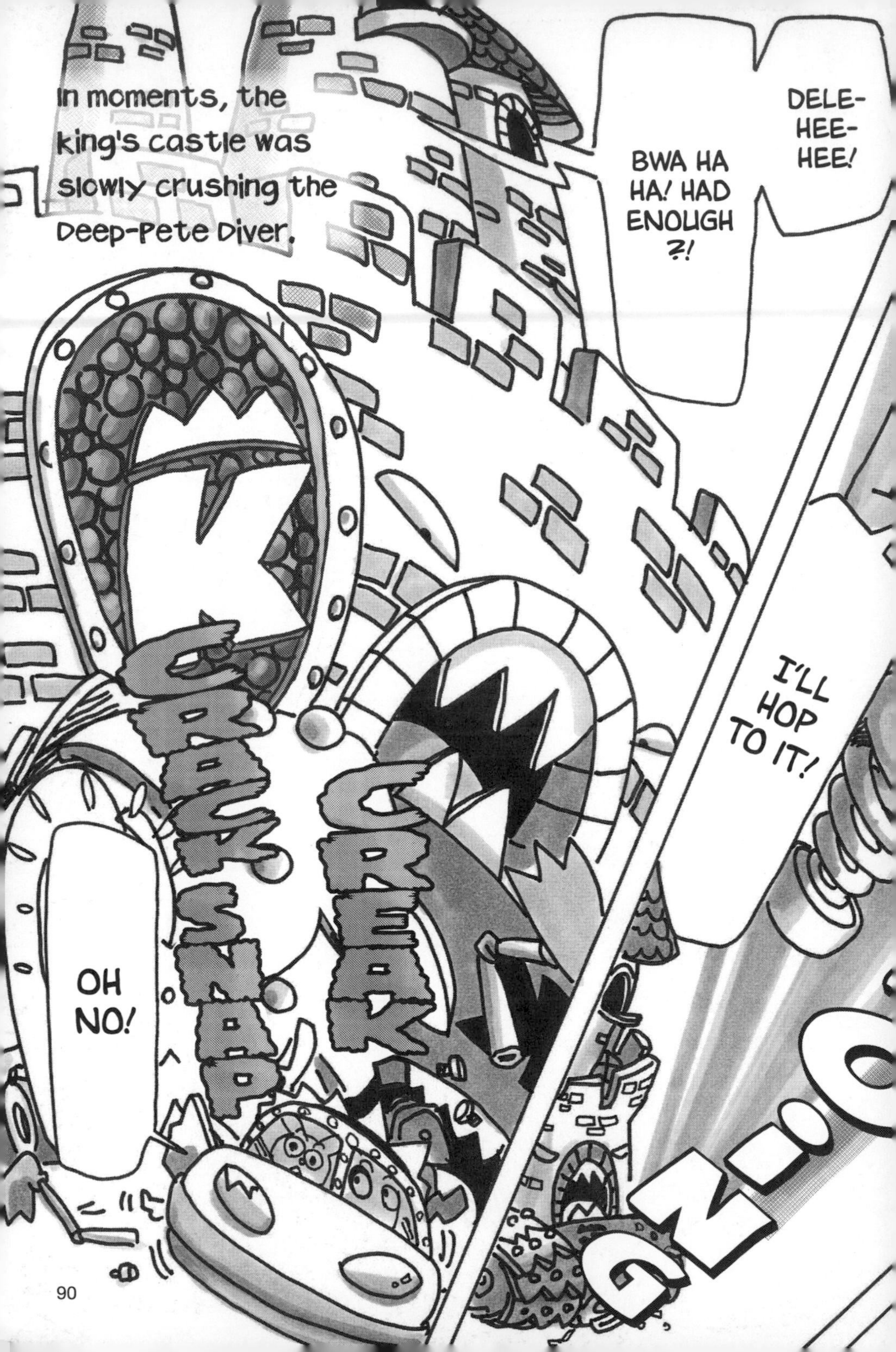
In moments, the king's castle was slowly crushing the Deep-Pete Diver.
DELE-HEE-HEE!
BWA HA HA! HAD ENOUGH ?!
CRACK
SNAP
CREAK
OH NO!
I'LL HOP TO IT!
GM...O

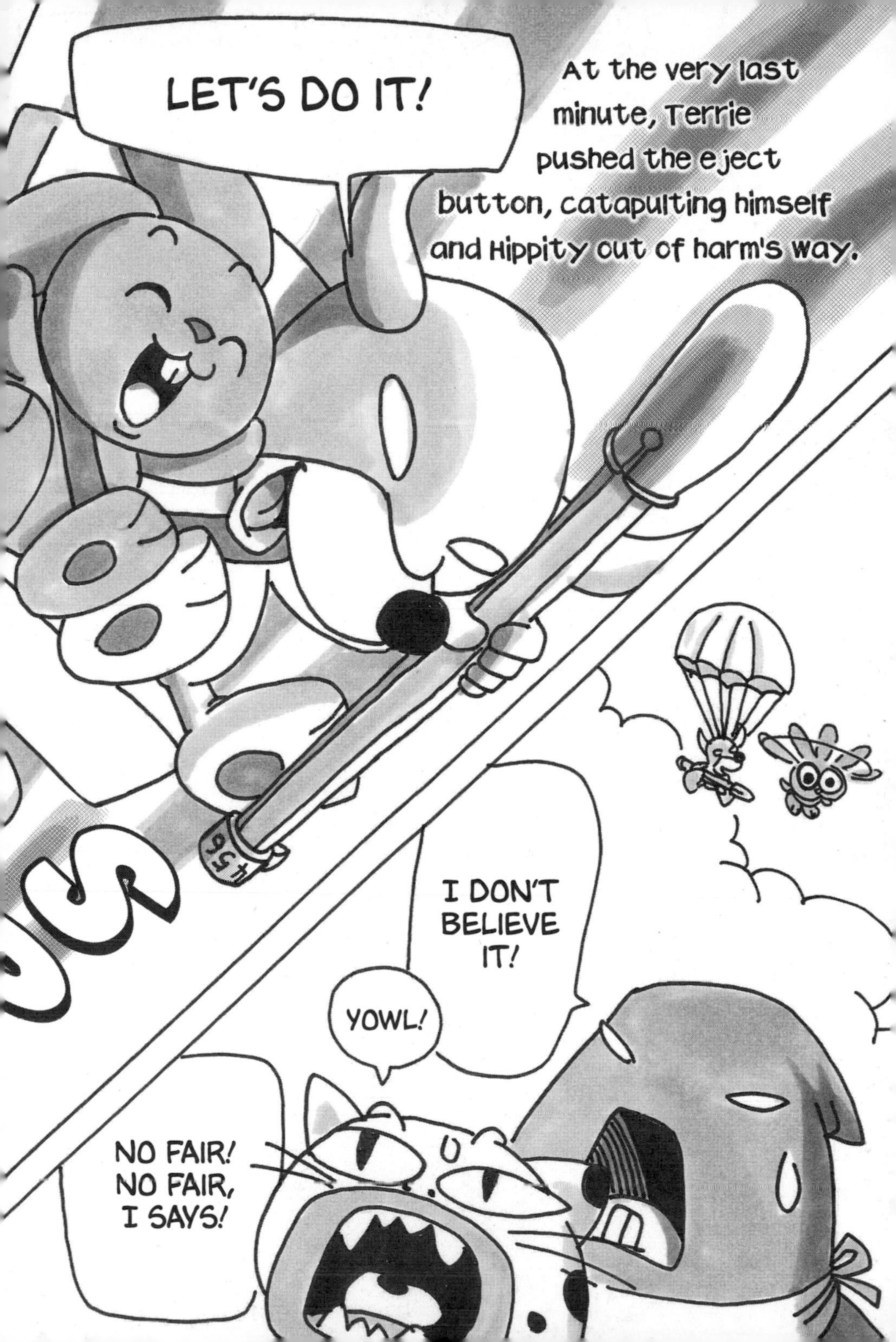
At the very last minute, Terrie pushed the eject button, catapulting himself and Hippity out of harm's way.
LET'S DO IT!
I DON'T BELIEVE IT!
YOWL!
NO FAIR! NO FAIR, I SAYS!

Once they landed safely, Terrie used the Magic Pencil to draw a bunch of bowling balls.

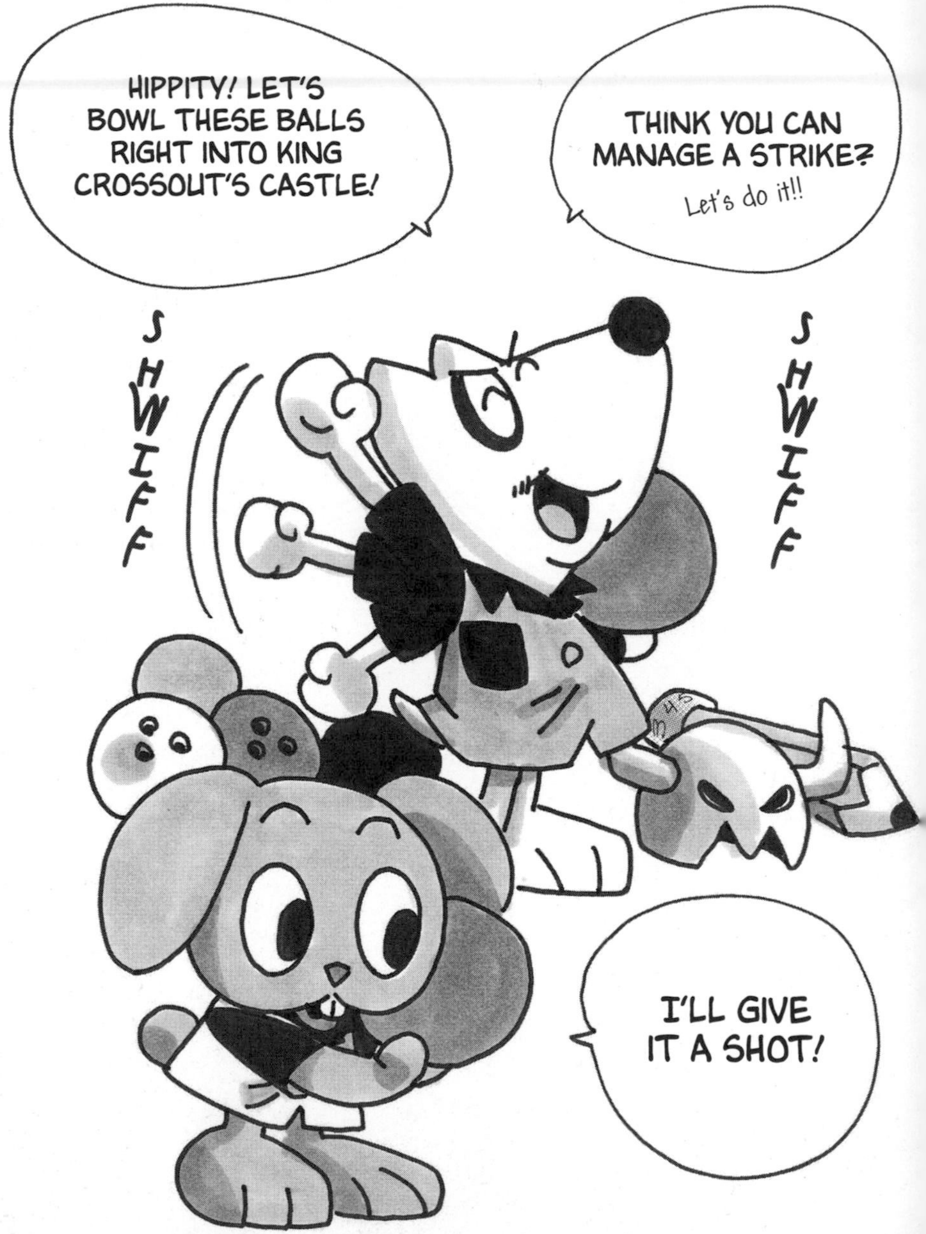
THINK YOU CAN MANAGE A STRIKE?
Let's do it!!
HIPPITY! LET'S BOWL THESE BALLS RIGHT INTO KING CROSSOUT'S CASTLE!
SHWIFF
SHWIFF
I'LL GIVE IT A SHOT!

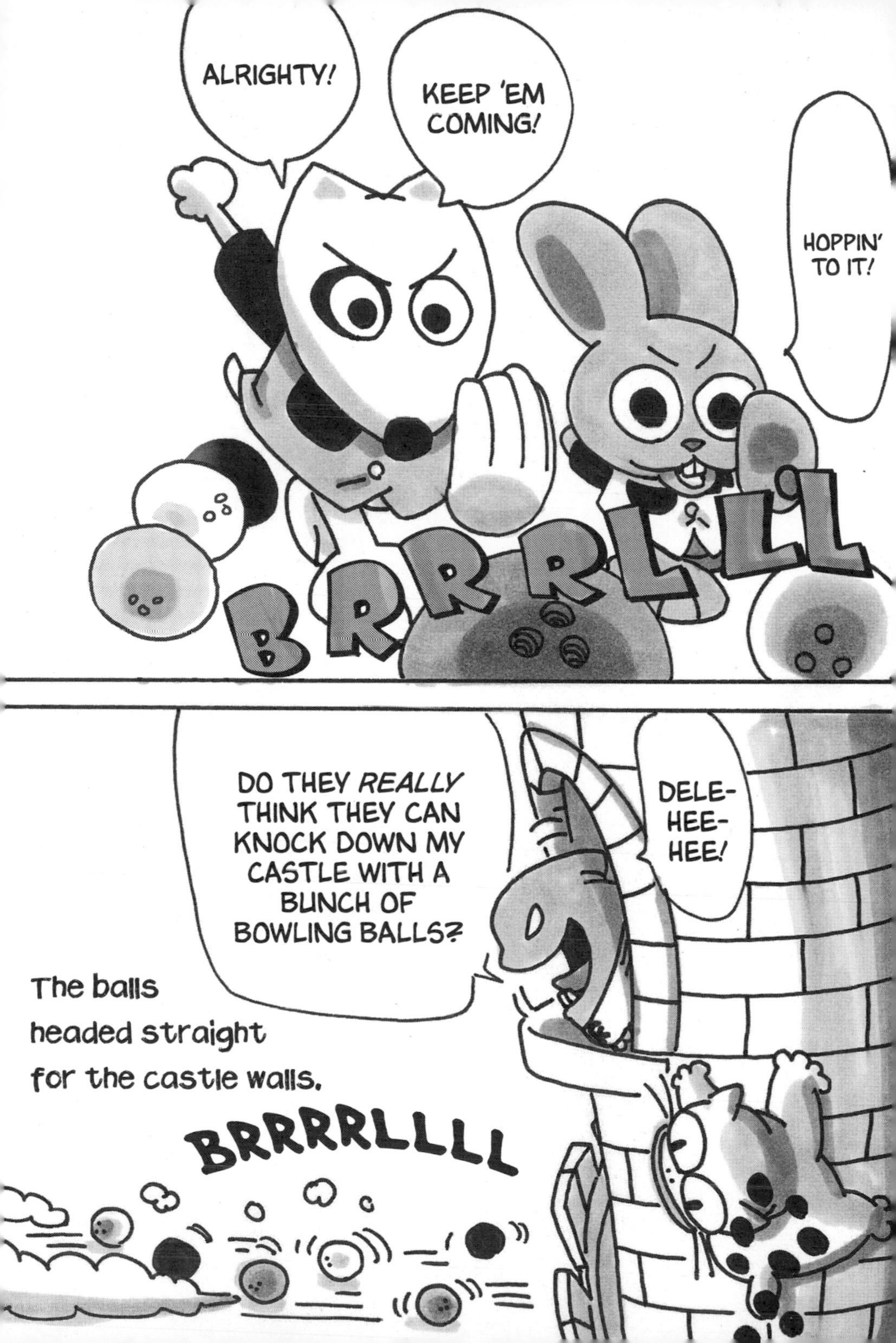
ALRIGHTY!
KEEP 'EM COMING!
HOPPIN' TO IT!
BRRRLLL
DO THEY *REALLY* THINK THEY CAN KNOCK DOWN MY CASTLE WITH A BUNCH OF BOWLING BALLS?
DELE-HEE-HEE!
The balls headed straight for the castle walls.
BRRRRLLLL

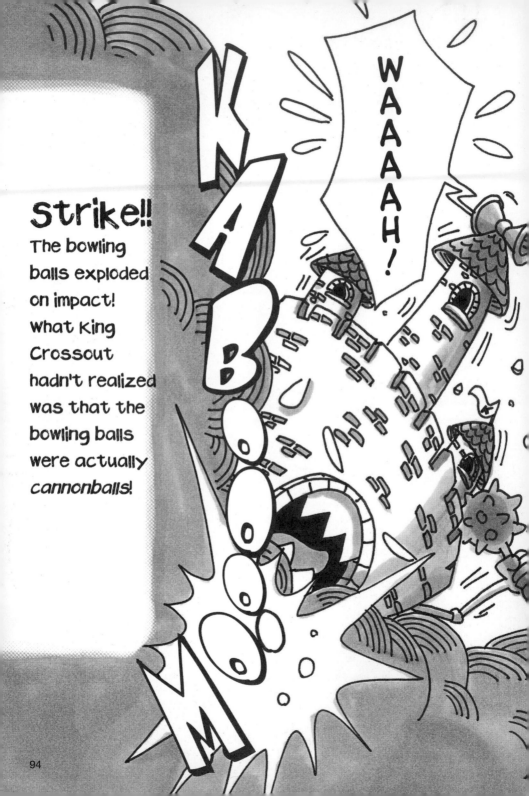

Strike!!

The bowling balls exploded on impact! What King Crossout hadn't realized was that the bowling balls were actually *cannonballs*!

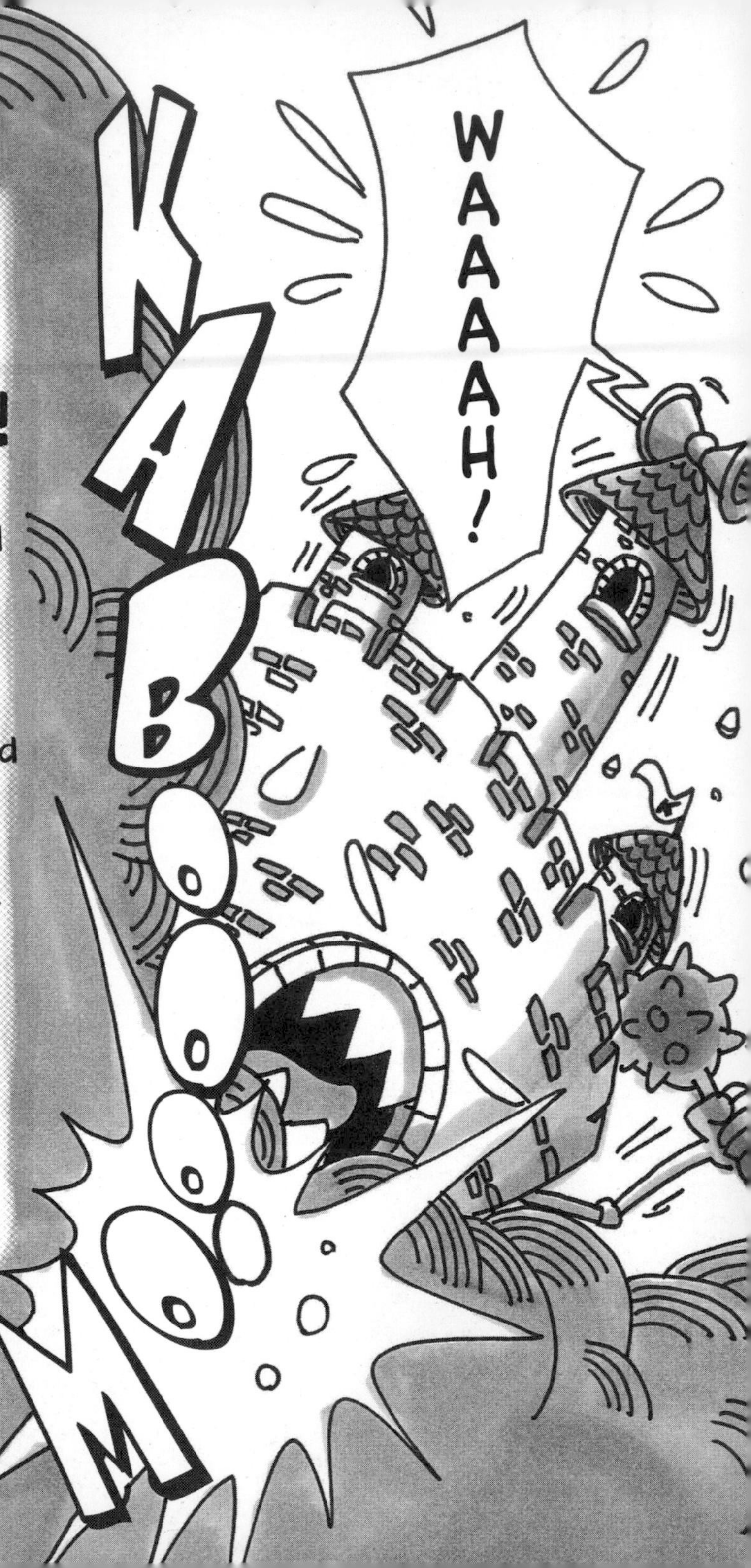
WAAAAH!
KABOOOOM

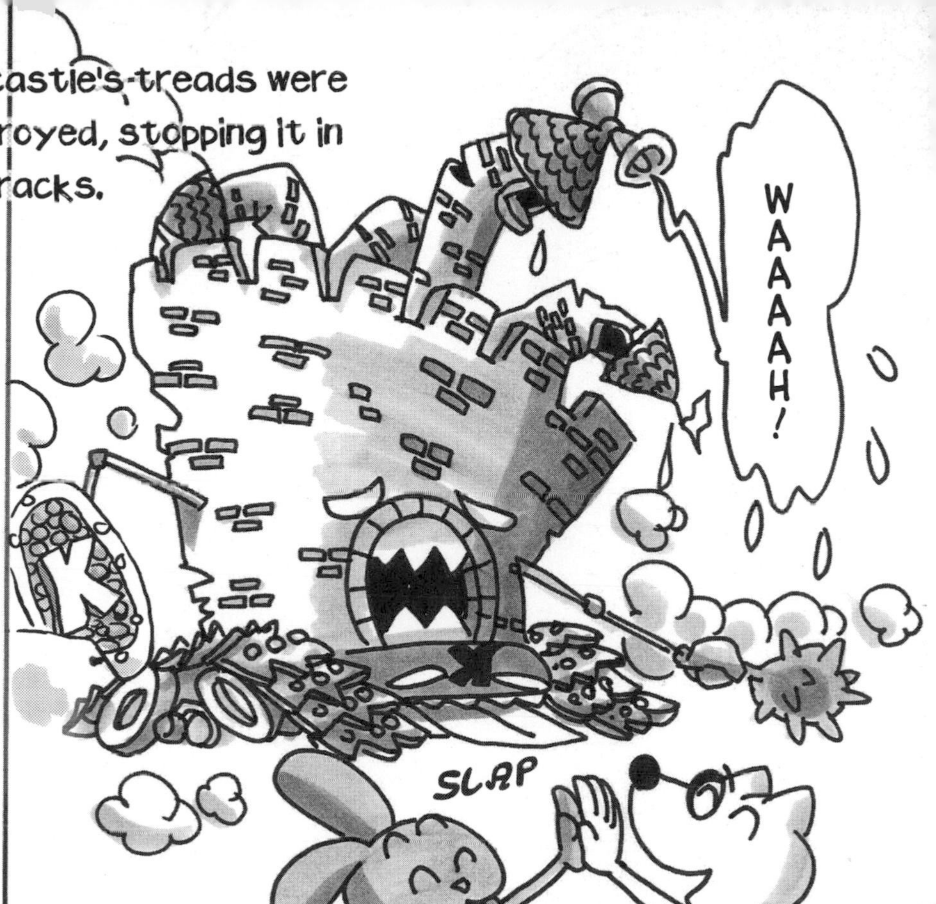
The castle's treads were destroyed, stopping it in its tracks.
WAAAAAH!
SLAP

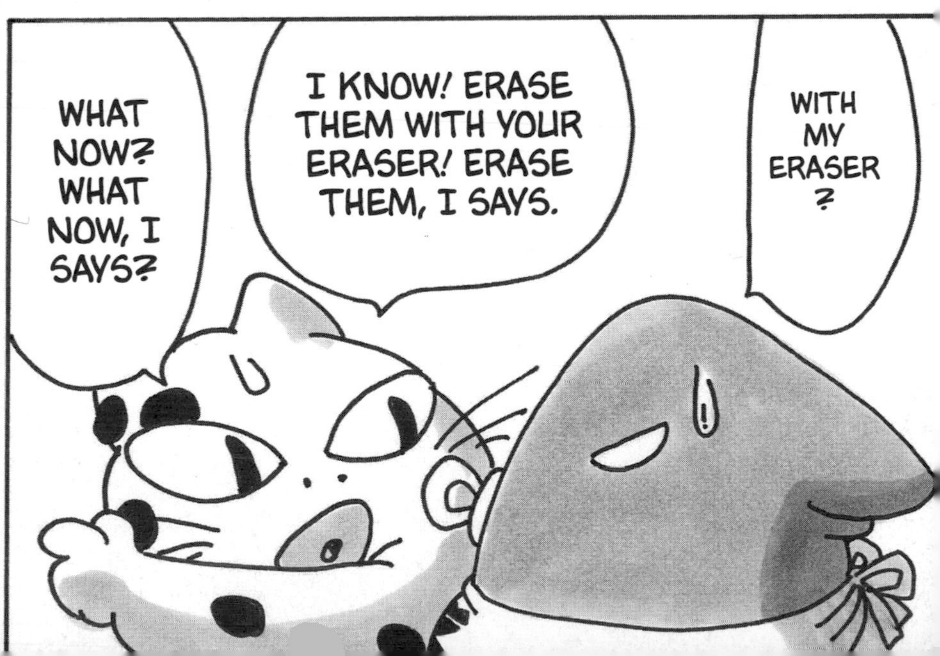
WHAT NOW? WHAT NOW, I SAYS?
I KNOW! ERASE THEM WITH YOUR ERASER! ERASE THEM, I SAYS.
WITH MY ERASER?

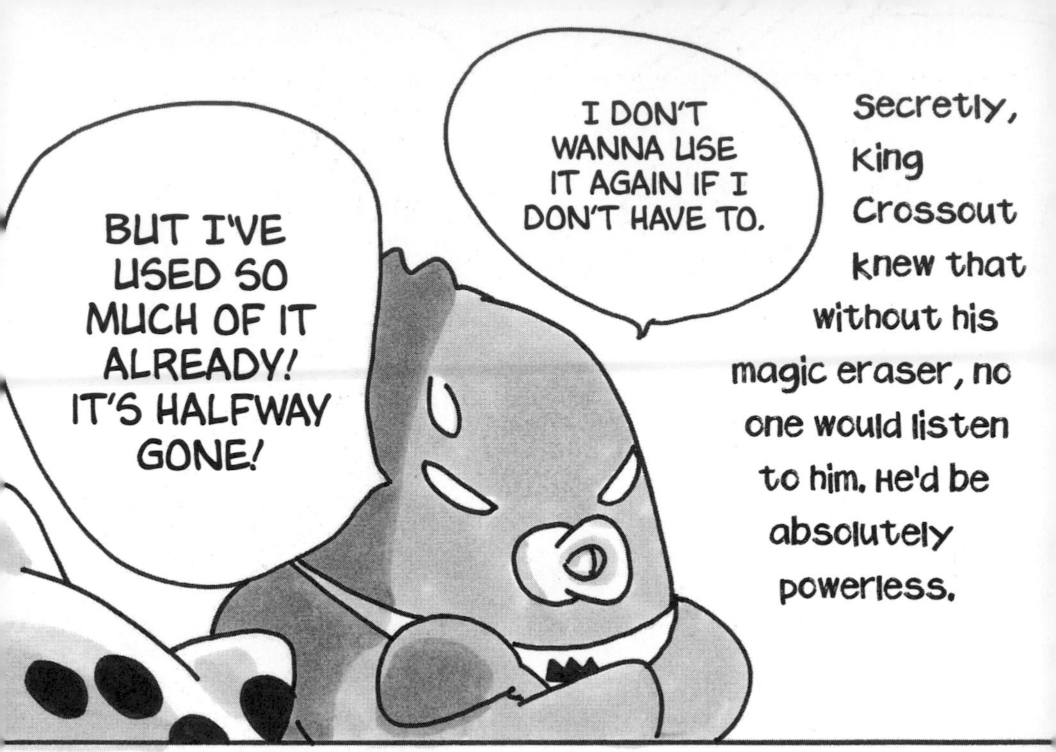
BUT I'VE USED SO MUCH OF IT ALREADY! IT'S HALFWAY GONE!
I DON'T WANNA USE IT AGAIN IF I DON'T HAVE TO.
Secretly, King Crossout knew that without his magic eraser, no one would listen to him. He'd be absolutely powerless.

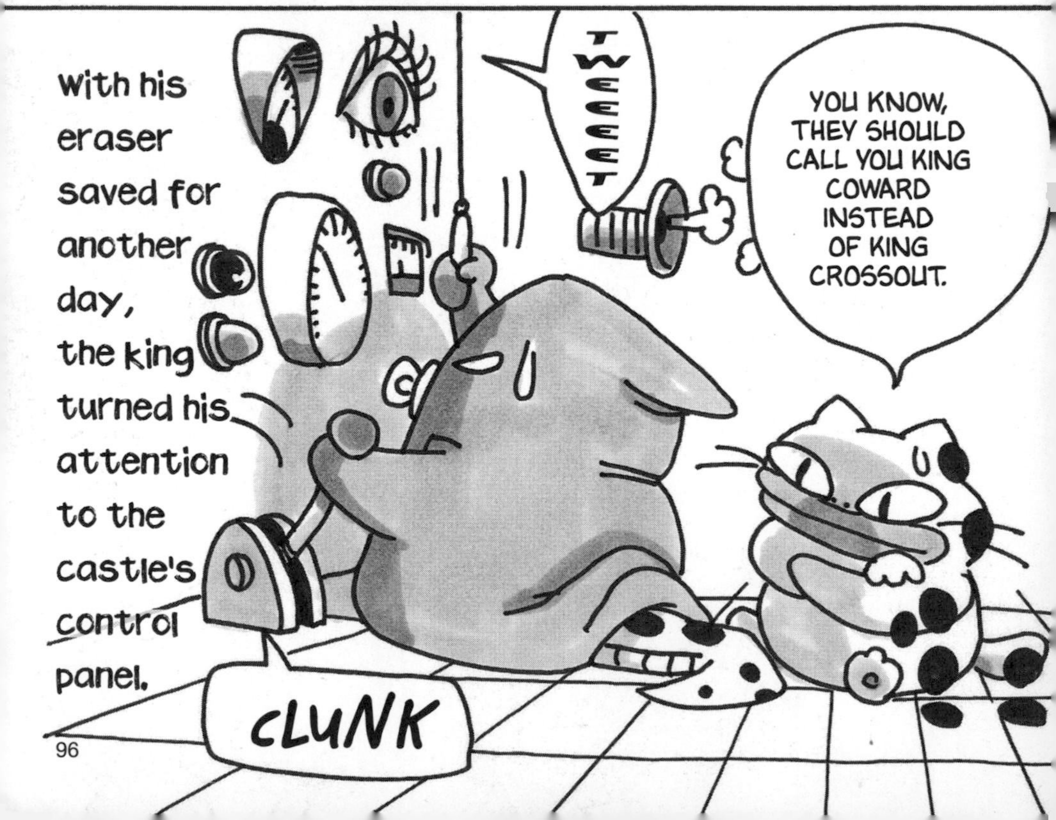
With his eraser saved for another day, the king turned his attention to the castle's control panel.
TWEEEET
YOU KNOW, THEY SHOULD CALL YOU KING COWARD INSTEAD OF KING CROSSOUT.
CLUNK

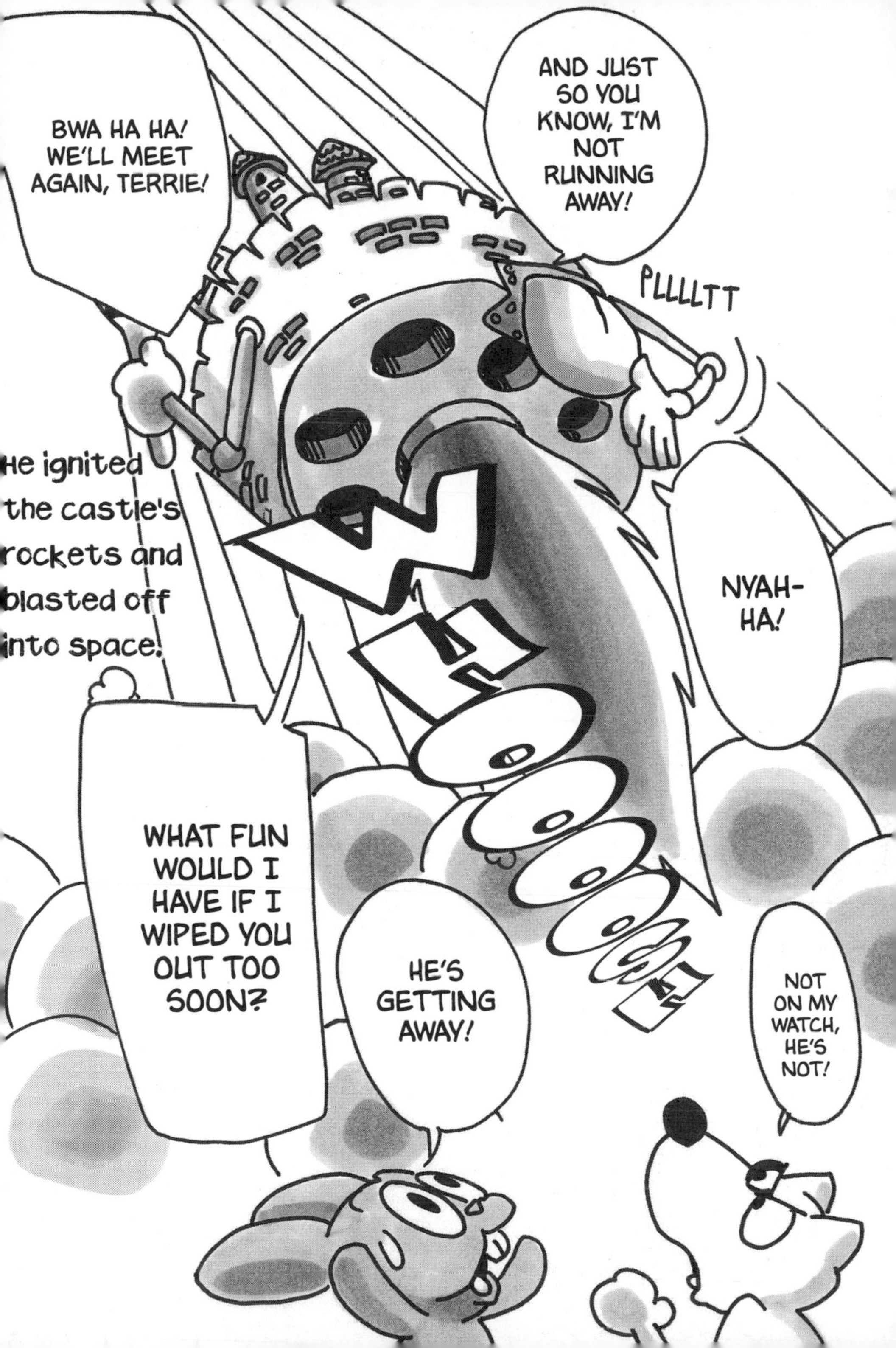
BWA HA HA! WE'LL MEET AGAIN, TERRIE!
AND JUST SO YOU KNOW, I'M NOT RUNNING AWAY!
PLLLLTT
He ignited the castle's rockets and blasted off into space!
NYAH-HA!
WHOOOOOOOOH
WHAT FUN WOULD I HAVE IF I WIPED YOU OUT TOO SOON?
HE'S GETTING AWAY!
NOT ON MY WATCH, HE'S NOT!

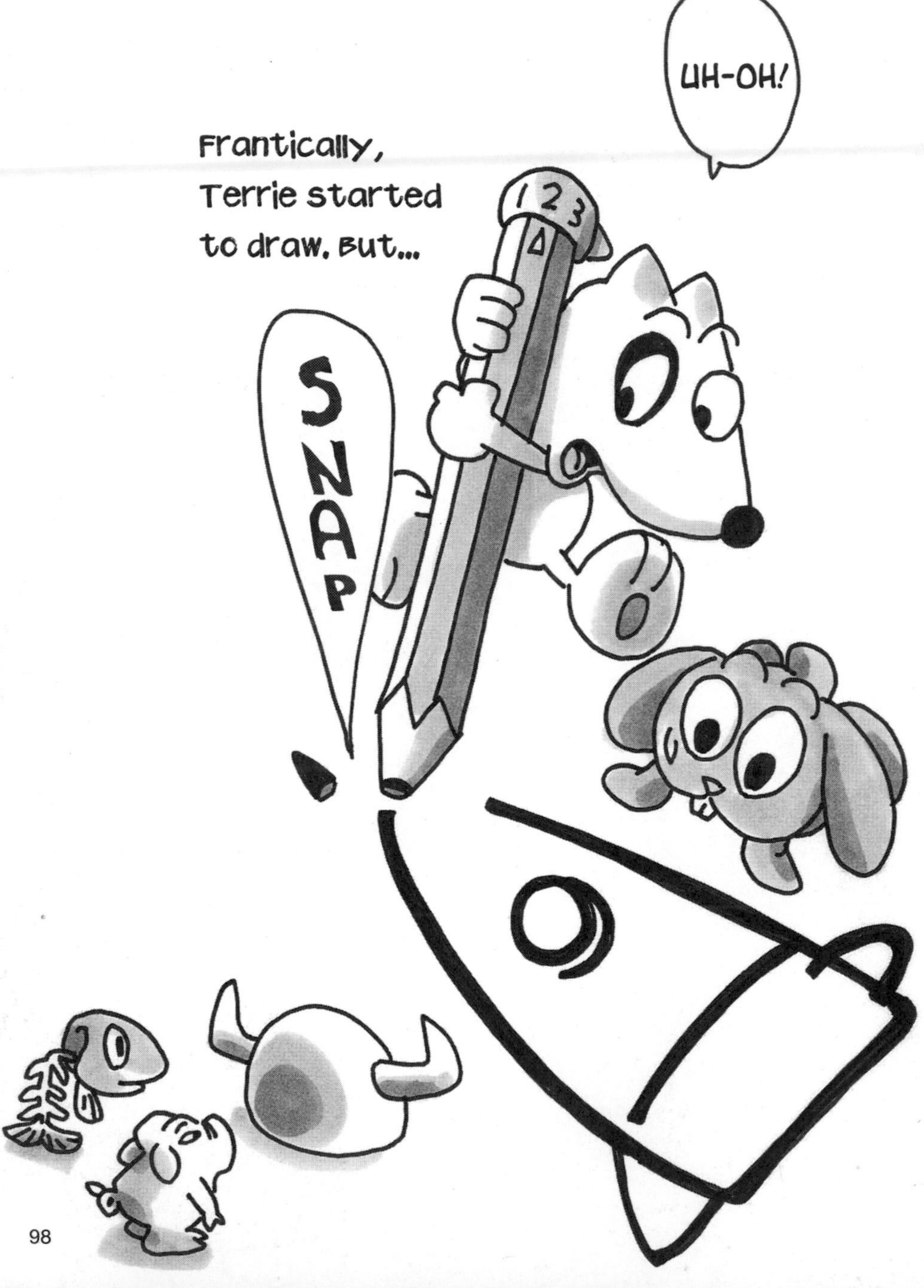
UH-OH!
Frantically, Terrie started to draw. But...
SNAP
123

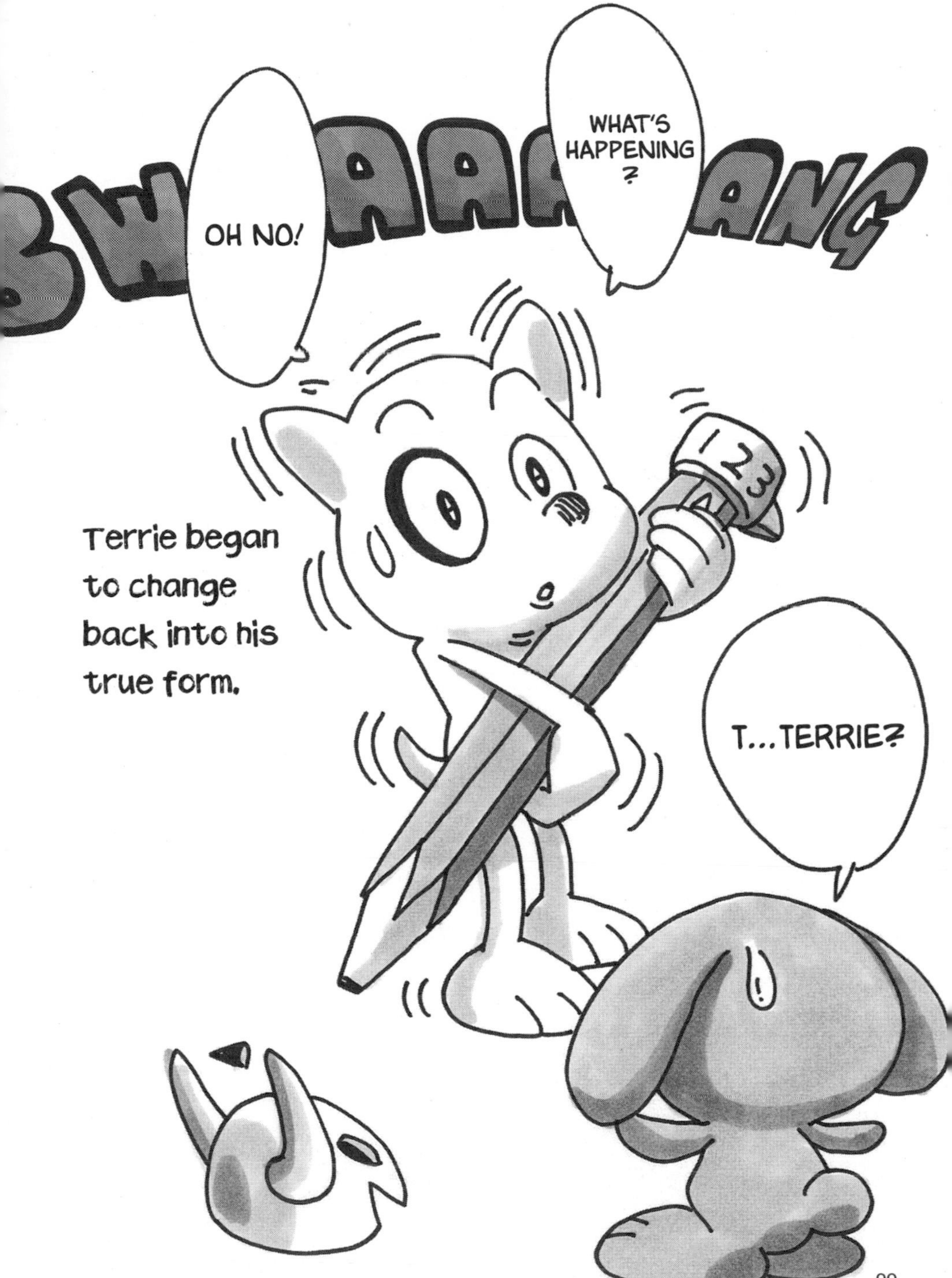
SWAAAAANG
WHAT'S HAPPENING?
OH NO!
Terrie began to change back into his true form.
T...TERRIE?

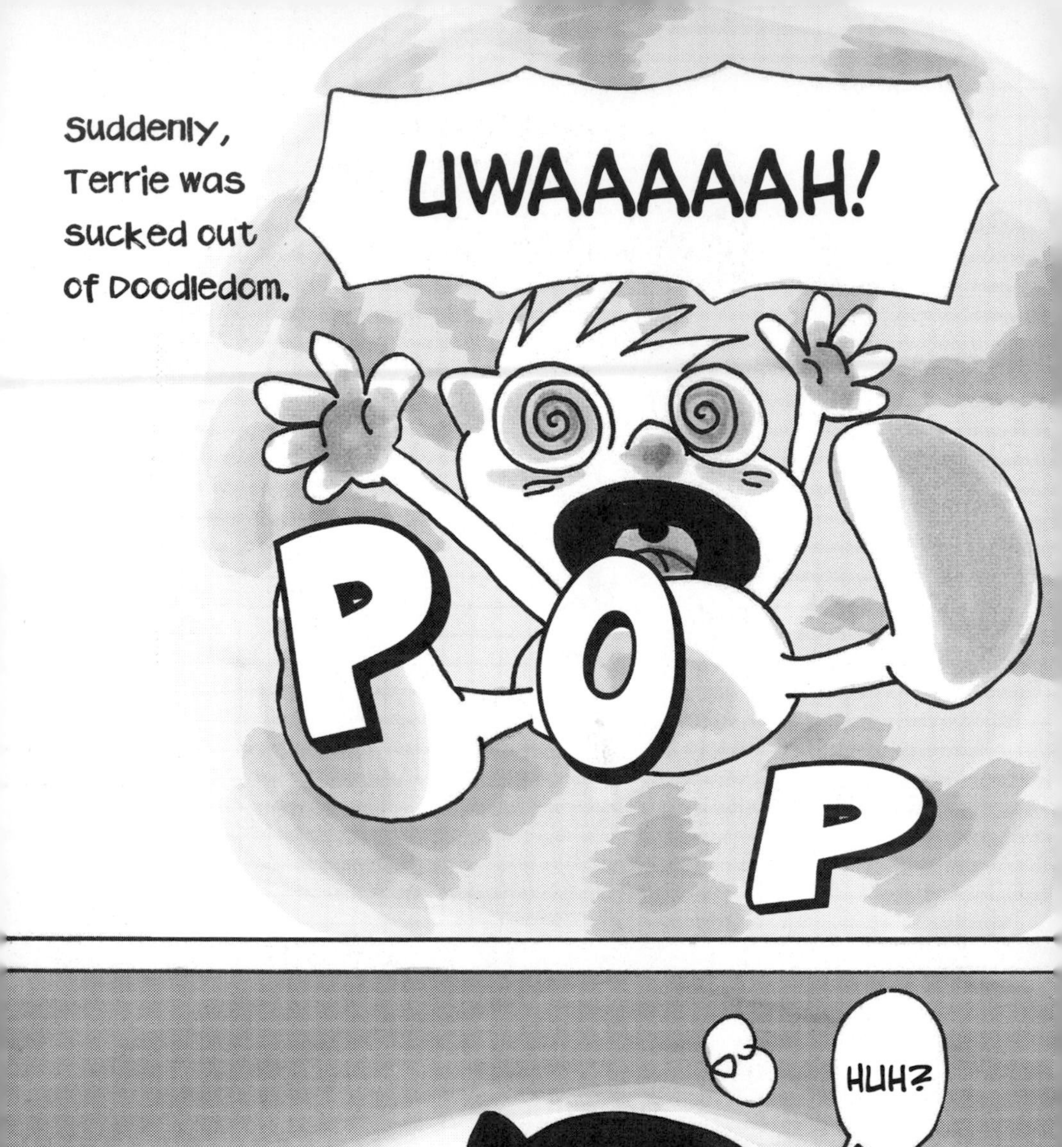
Suddenly, Terrie was sucked out of Doodledom.
UWAAAAAH!
POP
POP

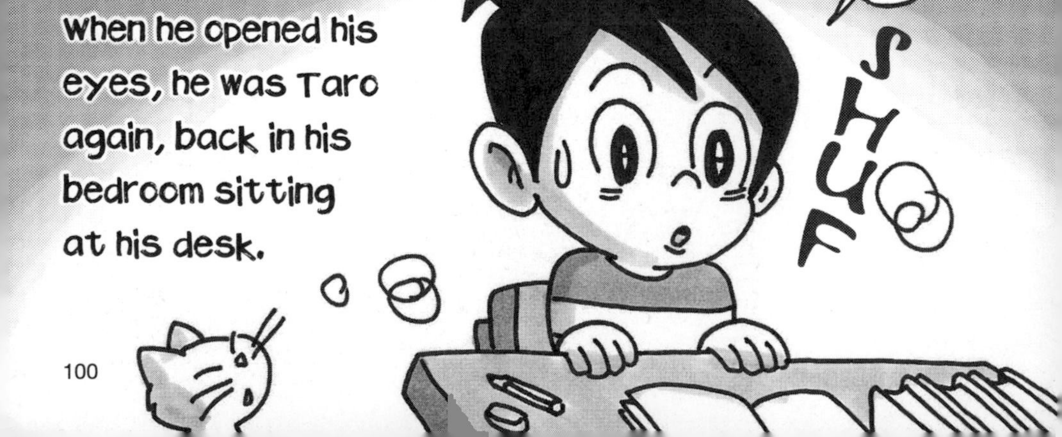
HUH?
When he opened his eyes, he was Taro again, back in his bedroom sitting at his desk.
SHUF

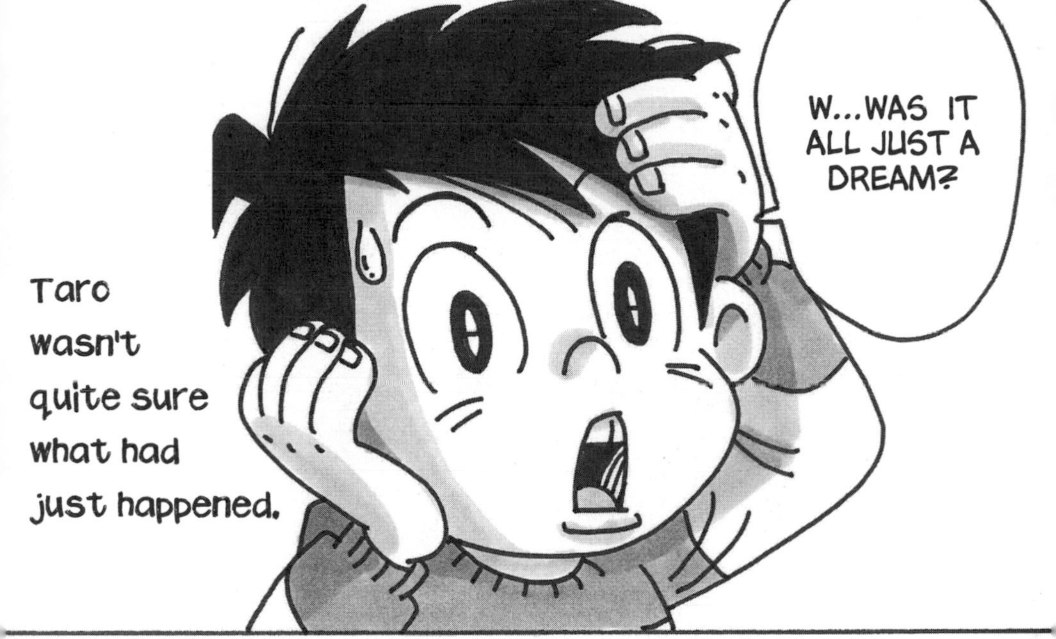
W...WAS IT ALL JUST A DREAM?
Taro wasn't quite sure what had just happened.

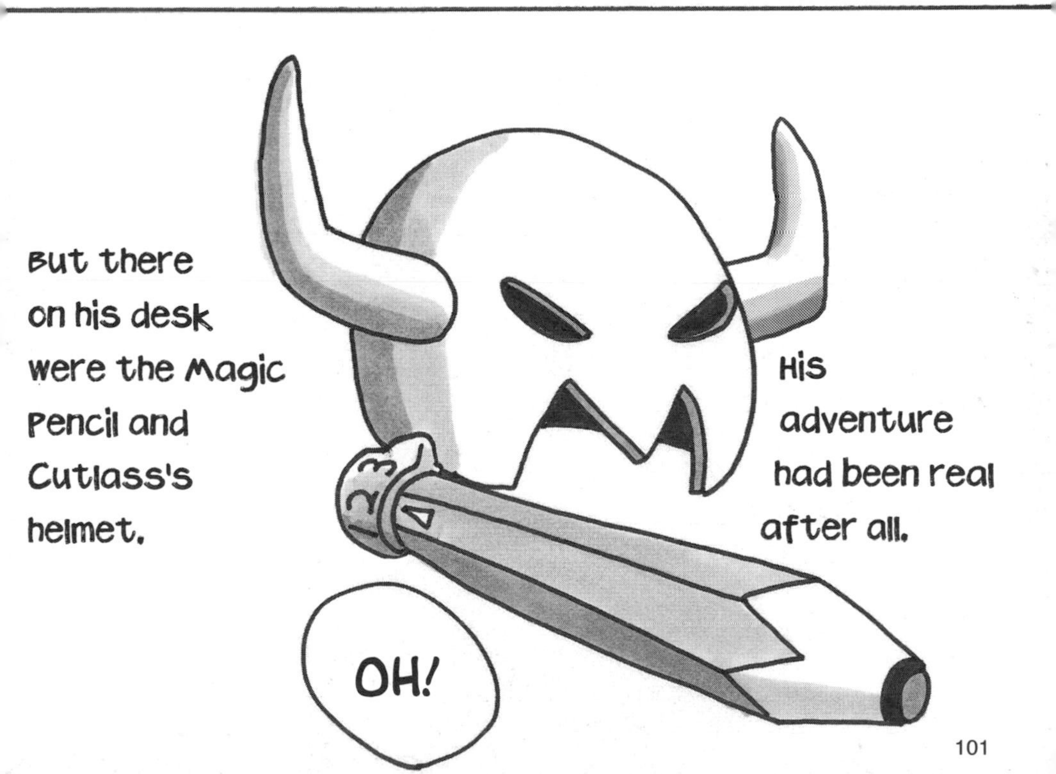
But there on his desk were the Magic Pencil and Cutlass's helmet.
His adventure had been real after all.
OH!

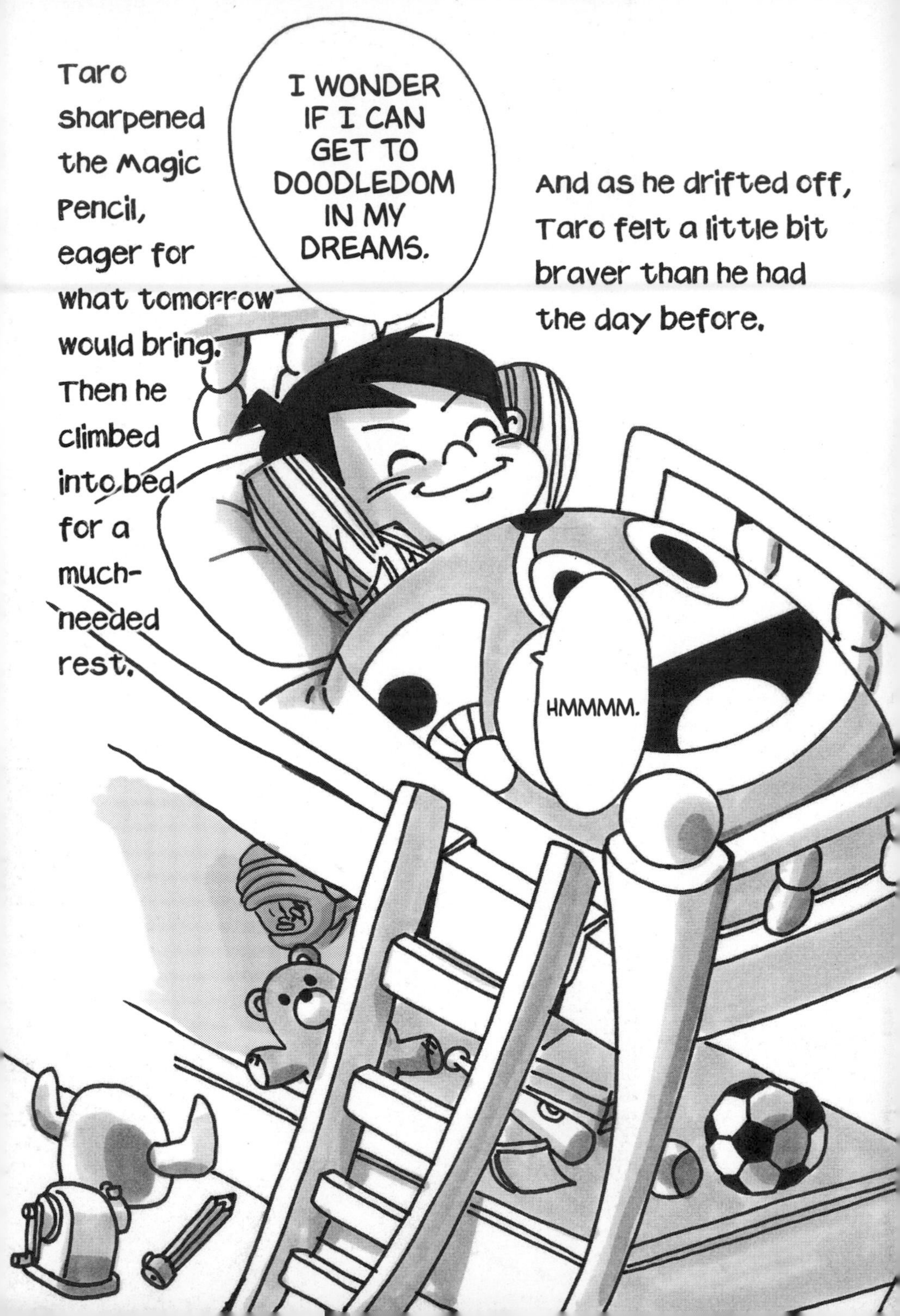
Taro sharpened the Magic Pencil, eager for what tomorrow would bring. Then he climbed into bed for a much-needed rest.
I WONDER IF I CAN GET TO DOODLEDOM IN MY DREAMS.
And as he drifted off, Taro felt a little bit braver than he had the day before.
HMMMM.

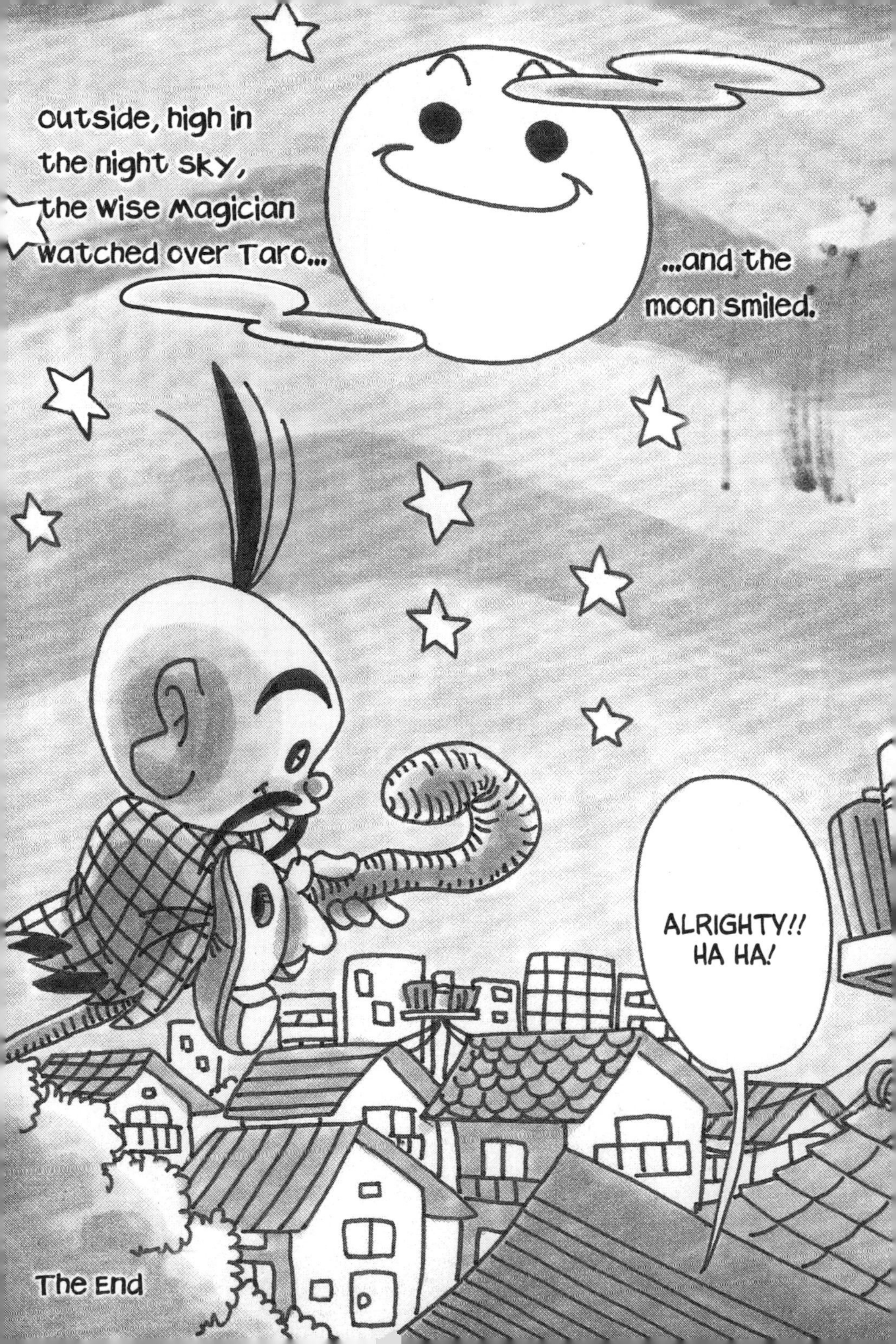
outside, high in the night sky, the wise Magician watched over Taro...
...and the moon smiled.
ALRIGHTY!! HA HA!
The End

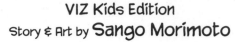

TARO AND THE MAGIC PENCIL

VIZ Kids Edition

Story & Art by Sango Morimoto

Translation/Katherine Schilling
Rewriting/Deric Hughes
Touch-up Art & Lettering/John Hunt
Graphics & Cover Design/Hidemi Sahara
Editor/Traci N. Todd

VP, Production/Alvin Lu
VP, Sales & Product Marketing/Gonzalo Ferreyra
VP, Creative/Linda Espinosa
Publisher/Hyoe Narita

Printed in China

Published by VIZ Media, LLC
P.O. Box 77010
San Francisco, CA 94107

10 9 8 7 6 5 4 3 2 1
First printing, November 2010

vizkids
www.vizkids.com

VIZ media
www.viz.com

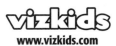

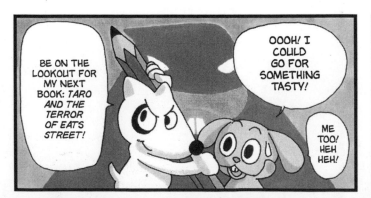

BE ON THE LOOKOUT FOR MY NEXT BOOK: *TARO AND THE TERROR OF EATS STREET!*
OOOH! I COULD GO FOR SOMETHING TASTY!
ME TOO! HEH HEH!

About the Author & Artist

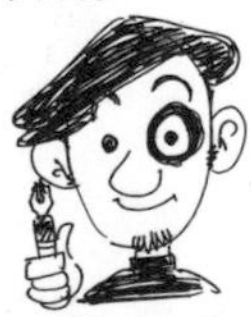

Sango Morimoto was born in 1955 in Tokyo. He is best known for *Friends of Harpo* and *Oshidori Chidori*, both published by Shueisha.